BY HALLE BUTLER

Banal Nightmare
The New Me
Jillian

Banal Nightmare

Banal Nightmare

A NOVEL

Halle Butler

Random House | New York

Banal Nightmare is a work of fiction. Names, characters, places, and incidents are the products of the author's imagination or are used fictitiously. Any resemblance to actual events, locales, or persons, living or dead, is entirely coincidental.

Copyright © 2024 by Halle Butler

All rights reserved.

Published in the United States by Random House, an imprint and division of Penguin Random House LLC, New York.

RANDOM HOUSE and the HOUSE colophon are registered trademarks of Penguin Random House LLC.

Library of Congress Cataloging-in-Publication Data
Names: Butler, Halle, author.
Title: Banal nightmare : a novel / Halle Butler.
Description: First Edition. | New York : Random House, 2024.
Identifiers: LCCN 2023044556 (print) | LCCN 2023044557 (ebook) |
ISBN 9780593730355 (hardcover) | ISBN 9780593730379 (ebook)
Subjects: LCGFT: Novels.
Classification: LCC PS3602.U8716 B36 2024 (print) |
LCC PS3602.U8716 (ebook) | DDC 813/.6—dc23/eng/20231005
LC record available at https://lccn.loc.gov/2023044556
LC ebook record available at https://lccn.loc.gov/2023044557

International edition ISBN 978-0-593-73383-7

Printed in the United States of America on acid-free paper

randomhousebooks.com

First Edition

Banal Nightmare

Sometime in the not too distant past...

One

Margaret Anne "Moddie" Yance had just returned to her native land in the Midwestern town of X, to mingle with the friends of her youth, to get back in touch with her roots, and to recover from a stressful decade of living in the city in a small apartment with a man she now believed to be a megalomaniac or perhaps a covert narcissist. She was trying not to think about it, trying to have a decent time in her new life, but invariably some bleak thought would draw her back and then the memories would start, vivid, cinematic, relentless, like a brainwashing clip reel for a cult with an unclear mission statement.

It was summertime. She was currently sitting in the backseat of a car on a dark, damp evening, looking out of the rolled-down window, consciously relaxing her muscles by group. The streetlights illuminated round sections of the green maple leaves that formed a canopy over the street. The air smelled good, like clean mulch with subtle undertones of motor oil. The trees, the smells, the sounds, the sights, the breezes, all activated a primal sensation in Moddie, a sensation she felt between her solar plexus and crotch, a feeling that was somewhat similar to unwelcome sexual arousal. She relaxed her shoulders. Her arms. Attempted to avoid slipping back into her dreary memories as the car drove through the night.

The breakup had been precipitated by Moddie, who impulsively had sex three times with her coworker Toby. He was a colleague, not a superior, but treated Moddie like his underling. He was a foolish man. Toby was muscular and short with a vein that stood out on his forehead, and Moddie liked to publicly humiliate him with casual mockery. She knew no one liked him, and in the break room everyone said that he was "verbally abusive." Moddie was in charge of sorting the mail and answering the phones, so she knew about his court-mandated anger management classes, which were on Thursdays.

After she and Toby had sex for the third and final time, Moddie sat on a park bench to read Walt Whitman. Nick had been out of town on some kind of artistic retreat, but he would be waiting for her when she got home. As she pretended to read the poems, Moddie realized that she had been effectively dead, without a single emotional or spiritual or intellectual stirring in her adult life, until this tyrannical little idiot, a man she had no respect for or interest in, had harangued her into touching his dick in the supply closet.

How cruel, yes, life could be.

The breeze stirred her bangs, and her heart. As a young person, she'd made a vow to live within the pulse of life and to avoid the death-in-life that the poets all said was worse than death itself. If she stayed with Nick, she would break that vow and continue to live this dead, boring life. She blamed a lot of her problems on Nick's vanity. Moddie admired Uncle Walt, the crazy gay tree fucker, but she did not admire herself, a boring woman with trivial, boring problems. She walked from the park bench back to her desk, past the bullet-chipped storefront windows, weaving between broken glass and empty patterned dime bags, back to her seat in the lobby of the sleek and highly regarded educational nonprofit for underserviced youth, where she filed grant applications and acted as a liaison between administration, teachers (or rather "educators"—she never understood why this needed to sound like a euphemism), and community, and where she had to work as a kind of hostage negotiator for her boss, Tracy, who wanted the children to go do things like cheer up the craps corner with yarn bombs, insisting this would give them what she called "cultural capital," another euphemism.

She got to her desk. And she sat and sat, dazed to the brim with richest nausea. Strong light came in through the floor-to-ceiling windows, dazzling her. If Toby had walked by, she might have projectile vomited on the center of her corporate-donated thirty-two-inch Retina display monitor.

She drove home. The nausea ripened into a dissociative state. She didn't know what would happen when she opened the door to their apartment. Her movements were automatic. She was numb. It was the strangest she'd ever felt. It was as if she were inside an orb, watching as the actions of some other thing flowed through her. It was a dream. She was innocent. Of course, she felt guilty about the odious cheating, but she did not feel like she was about to begin a process of confession and repentance. In fact, that was unthinkable, because she was not sorry.

Her hand turned the knob of the front door, pushed, and the door opened on Nick lying flaccidly on the couch, not doing anything except looking at his phone. His brain was rotten, and all of his opinions were inherited, none of them spontaneous, completely rotten. His suitcases were dumped all over the floor. He had reheated and eaten all of the leftover chili, the chili that had taken her three hours to prepare, the chili she was planning to have, and he had left everything in the sink for her to wash. She did all of the laundry, cooked all of the meals, took out the trash, cleaned, shopped, paid the bills, all of it, he did none of it, she did all of it, holy god for ten years all of it. And what was Moddie making room for with all of these chores? These things took hours, meaning Nick took hours from Moddie, and what did he do with these hours, what great life of the mind was she aiding by giving him all of these hours? Looking at him with this thought in her mind made the blood rise up in her ears and made her feel faint, again. He even spoke to her in baby talk. Moddie's lips were numb and it felt like she was hovering inches above the ground. She'd told him in the first year, please, anything but baby talk, but her handsome boy, he was always so very *hungwy*. Moddie had been standing over him as he lay on the couch texting for at least one minute, maybe two, each submerged in their own private narrative.

He was probably texting with that girl he'd met at an art fair who, according to him, had been "actually" quite encouraging of all the bad behavioral patterns and habits and attitudes of his that always dragged him deep down into a time-sucking catatonic depression that Moddie was left to deal with whether she wanted to or not, goddamn it, that bitch.

Nick looked up at Moddie and his lip involuntarily snarled like a mean old goopy Maltese. Moddie felt her spirit puke out in anger. The words came out like heavenly music, as if Christ himself had reached his hand down and put his fingers in her mouth and used her as a puppet to transmit his divine decree, that she break up with him that instant.

In the moment before she felt herself speak, her mind became clear and analytical like a man's. Aside from a few compulsory and awkward concessions, they hadn't fucked in years. They didn't have or want children, they didn't have or want any large shared items like a house. The one time Moddie brought up marriage, Nick raised his eyebrows and said, "I don't think so." He told her she would make a terrible mother but said nothing after she handed him his peanut butter sandwich and said, "Oh, I don't know, I think I'm doing an okay job." He'd taken to saying things like "All men are more likely to be attracted to women in their twenties, because they just have better bodies and more open minds" and "When men and women break up in middle age it's uniformly pathetic for the woman. Inevitably she goes on some humiliating journey of self-discovery, joins a gym, gets a fun and funky haircut and some dimwitted affirmational therapist, and all she can manage to snag is a beat-down old divorcé with a broken dick and some other woman's children. Maybe he takes her on a few sad little vacations to Barbados. Maybe she wears a hot-pink bikini with her big ass cheeks hanging out. Maybe she gets a tattoo on one of her cheeks that says 'YOLO.'" He started talking this way soon after Moddie turned thirty-one, insisting they were deep into middle age, fat, neutered, depressing, the walking dead, but Toby had said she had movie boobs, and Toby looked like a tiny Channing Tatum and he didn't have any children or enough money to go to Barbados, so it turned out Nick wasn't a genie who could see into the future, just a mean man, and realizing this did make a difference. She was no longer afraid of the endless gaping void of loneliness. She spoke the words that coursed through her—this just is not working.

Whatever tense cloud of energy that had been hovering in the room between them burst. Nick began to cry, and Moddie felt her whole heart and chest and self rush toward him, my poor sweet baby, I'm so, so sorry.

She moved into a shitty furnished sublet and spent most of her free time either violently sobbing or on the phone with Nick apologizing profusely for dumping him, and spent her days at the office avoiding Toby. She got no rest. Nick called her almost every night and kept her on the phone late, well past her bedtime, telling her how angry he was and telling her that he didn't understand how she could throw him away like that, like a piece of garbage, and sometimes he asked her what kind of a person could do something like that. What kind of person, Moddie? *A piece of garbage.* When she tried bringing up some of the things he'd done that had hurt her, he said he was going to jump in front of a train if he even thought about it for one second. After these phone calls, Moddie would sit in the corner and rock back and forth sobbing, wondering why she was such a cruel and hateful person who was sort of like a living poison, and why was she always saying and doing such mean horrible things like treating people like pieces of garbage. Sometimes she thought it might be safer for everyone if she were dead, even for her parents, who were surely getting tired of her daily, sobbing, hysterical phone calls.

They tried to reconcile like this for months. Nick said he didn't want to meet up in person unless they were going to get back together—it's too hard—then he said he couldn't sleep, couldn't eat, he felt dead, and so Moddie, still in love and deeply moved by his suffering, caved one night and said, "I want to come home."

This seemed to cheer Nick up for a moment.

But later, as soon as Moddie started to mention specific

plans, when and where to meet, whether or not Moddie should look for a permanent apartment or if she should delay with the aim of moving back in, Nick became alternatingly cocky and coy—oh, he'd never meant to imply he was ready to get back together, these things take time—and, after much pressing, he eventually did agree to meet up at their old apartment, where they had an unspeakable night, truly among the worst of Moddie's nights, during which he revealed he'd just begun a relationship with a twenty-four-year-old arts administrator and veritable shit-for-brains named Gracie.

Moddie knew all about Gracie, oh yes. One night, after a party where Gracie had clung to Nick's arm, saying, "I've always wondered about you, because when I checked our astrological charts we were a match, and I've always blah blah blah blah blah . . ." Nick gave a speech about how interesting Gracie was and Moddie, who at that moment had been particularly tanked, said something unkind about Gracie's physical appearance and then said she didn't think men were attracted to women who looked like that and Nick said, "Uuh, [disdainful patronizing chortle], I have no complaints with the way she looks."

"No, I said I thought *men*," said Moddie, and he threw her a shitty glance. "What's her last name?"

After a pause he said, "Schneider."

"Aaaaahhh, Herr *Schnei*-dah."

"Yeah, I believe that would be *Fräulein*," said Nick, who then winked despite himself, in a way that Moddie found deeply unattractive.

Moddie looked up Gracie and found her website, which included a substantial amount of self-portrait photography, which of course Moddie began to critique until Nick started muttering, "You're such a fucking prude you're so stuck up you're jealous that people find her sexually attractive there's nothing wrong with someone wanting to have a website where they can express themselves through photographs and self-portraits it's a good website the photography is good it has good qualities it shows sensitivity you're such a fucking prude you've always been a prude and a killjoy and a drag and a mentally unstable asshole you're just mean not interesting or funny or smart or cool and I've thought you were a closet queer for years."

The things about being a closet queer and a prude hurt, of course, but did not hurt as much as the notion that he—that anyone—could possibly interact with this work and fool themselves into thinking that it had any artistic merit.

"You probably respond to her work," said Moddie, "because it is one hundred percent nonthreatening to your own work, in terms of its quality, and is therefore completely unthreatening to your masculinity. I'll give it to her, if she's doing this on purpose, she's a fucking genius. If she's going out of her way to make work that makes her seem like an insipid moron who a man might be able to teach a few things, she's [chef's kiss]. *Brahvah, mein Herr,* as her people might say."

Moddie drained her beer at the precise moment Nick picked up and threw her sketchbook across the kitchen. It hit the wall and landed on its open pages, pathetic and rumpled, resembling garbage. Moddie looked at Nick, who said nothing more. They stayed eye-locked until Moddie started talking in a quiet, measured tone, "I'm going to hurt you so fucking much one day you won't be able to breathe right for months. This version of me, right here, this one now, I'm the fucking Manchurian candidate. I've now sworn an oath with god and country to destroy you. Someday something's going to set me off and I'm going to come back and finish what you started here tonight and you won't even know what hit you and you won't ever be the same for the rest of your life."

Nick rolled his eyes and shook his head slowly in disgust. "You haven't even seen *The Manchurian Candidate*. You never have any idea what the fuck you're talking about."

After learning that Nick and Gracie were together, and after a few more harrowing conversations with Nick, the memories of which clicked in and out of her awareness like a stupid semaphore, Moddie spent two months in a fugue state, going into the office like a zombie, falling asleep as soon as she got home, and then one day she called her best friend, Nina, who lived in X, to explain, again, that she couldn't take another moment of her stupid fucking life. "Not another fucking minute, or I'm going to coldcock myself with a hammer."

Nina said, "Fuck it, just move here instead," and told her how cheap apartments were. They were startlingly cheap. "Maybe you could freelance."

Moddie did some quick math and quit her job the next morning. Her resignation letter was obsequious, written from the perspective of a humble and grateful character, and Tracy made her stand by the desk in the large executive suite while she read it over and frowned. Moddie could hear some of the kids running around and shouting and laughing in the hallway. She thought about the potentially necessary interplay between freedom and failure, and the next week she cashed out her retirement savings, found an ostentatiously cheap place in X, and absconded. And now she sat, with a sour gut and wet palms, in the backseat of her friend Pam's car, on the way to a party with a mix of old high school acquaintances and university employees and their spouses, listening to Pam and her boyfriend, Craig, have a civil adult couple's discussion in the front seat. Pam was another of Moddie's close childhood friends—another bosom companion.

"Yes, but this is exactly what I was telling her. Precisely," said Craig.

Moddie's stomach twisted.

"I just think you need to have clearer boundaries," said Pam. "She's your student, so you shouldn't involve yourself in her personal life. I don't think it's wise or safe."

"Or cool," said Moddie from the backseat, tapping her foot, thinking about breaking the glass on the backseat window, diving out of it, and running in a straight line to the cave-like apartment where she now lived alone.

"Well, I have to be gentle with her about it. I'm a human being after all. We're both human beings." Craig tapped the steering wheel a few times.

"It's not appropriate, Craig." Pam spoke with authoritative directness and condescension that, even though Moddie certainly agreed with Pam, from what she could tell, did make Pam seem like a killjoy and a bitch. Moddie pressed her hand firmly over her mouth and squeezed. She did her best to avoid reminders of the painful past, because if she became too acutely reminded of certain thoughts and feelings, sometimes her behavior became erratic, like a car swerving to avoid a dog.

"Hey, do you guys remember that song 'Cotton Eye Joe'?" Moddie asked loudly. "That was one of my favorite songs in second grade. I had the radio station dedicate it to the boy I liked."

"That's racist," said Craig in a way that seemed more like a critique of finding things racist.

"I think it was Swedish," said Moddie.

"Even worse," said Craig.

"Sure," said Moddie. "All of our music is Swedish."

She hadn't called the radio station to dedicate "Cotton Eye Joe" to Kyle, she'd called to have the station dedicate the song to her from Kyle, but no one needed to know this hidden part of her memory, her shameful, selfish lie, because the winner creates the history, winner takes all, and who was Kyle to Pam and Craig? He was nothing, dirt, filth, nothing. Probably dead. Moddie smiled and almost laughed.

"Left," said Pam. "Le-f-t," she said again as if it had many syllables. She didn't seem to be having a very nice time. Pam often read as terse and dissatisfied, but it was just her way, her icy exterior. Sometimes people even thought Moddie was a bitch, but it wasn't true, it wasn't true!

They pulled up to Bethany's house, which was garish and large. Moddie placed the architectural style as Greek Revival Revival, and she wondered if Bethany—that bastion of teen liberalism—had ended up marrying a Republican.

"Am I close enough to the curb?" Craig twisted his body around in little jerks, like he was trying to see something.

"I really don't know, but I'm sure you're fine, it's hardly a *high-traffic area*," said Pam. Her long fingers rested against her temple and she was glaring at the large plastic mailbox, right at the little red schwing of a flag that indicated outgoing mail, which seemed strange, and perhaps forcefully mature.

"Ohh-*kay*," said Craig.

Bethany's home began with what one might call a "foy-ay," which funneled itself into a small birthing-canal-like hallway, which then opened up into a room with twenty-foot ceilings. All of the walls were white. A big mound of shoes lay on the left side of the foyer.

In the center of the large main room—Moddie thought they should call this "the joy room"—Bethany held court, draped in a large, thin pashmina, looking stately and glamorous like the sculpture of Balzac in the Rodin gardens. Bethany had recently published a twelve-hundred-word opinion article on the *New York Times* website, and now she was a real star or something according to everyone's mom.

Moddie looked blandly at the propane fireplace, the mostly empty bookshelves, the hardcover copy of Gloria Steinem's memoir, the sideboard, and the orchid in its geodesic cage. As Moddie surveyed the scene, she overheard Bethany and her admirers discussing an acquaintance of theirs, a recent divorcée who had just moved to New York.

"No, I love Amelia," said Bethany with a wave of her arm, "she's incredibly intelligent, but I just worry about her—please, for the love of god, no more losers, no more strivers, no more men with something to prove about themselves or their intelligence or whatever it is she seems to be so drawn to." She laughed.

"Still, it must be a little magical," said a short, thin woman sitting on the arm of the couch, smiling up at Bethany. "I can't imagine what it would be like to be looking for love in New York City," even though there had been literally thousands of books, movies, songs, articles, and TV shows dedicated to the topic, so this woman must have been some kind of a fucking idiot.

The woman on Bethany's left said, "Men are garbage," and then the one on her right laughed, looked around, and suggested they all "become lesbians."

Moddie left the joy room for a beer.

Drink in hand and ready to mingle, Moddie scanned the room for friendly faces. Nina had yet to arrive and she couldn't find Pam. She spotted a woman she believed to be named Chrissy, a friend of Pam's who she had met at a party in college. She approached Chrissy, with what she thought was open body language, and stood next to her and the woman she was talking to.

"We're really trying with Adler. He's not behind, but we're reading to him every night and encouraging him to try to pick out his favorite words, spelling and everything." Chrissy partially closed her eyes and shook her head in a minute, vibrating way. "It's a challenge."

"Ooh, my god. We're not quite there yet with Jonah," said Samantha, who Moddie did not know. "But, childhood literacy is so important."

Chrissy sighed again and said, "I know."

Moddie held up a finger, thinking that, even though this seemed to be a personal and specific kind of conversation, she should be bold in her advances into the land of friendship, and said, "I read something somewhere that said the best influence on kids, in terms of literacy and a lifelong interest in reading, is *full bookshelves*."

Moddie did not know any parents younger than sixty.

They both turned and looked at her with blank expressions. Samantha's eyes did a brief body scan, perhaps checking Moddie for signs of authority, motherhood.

"I'm Moddie, by the way. I think we met like twelve years ago."

Chrissy cocked her head to the side slightly and said, "Yeah, I'm not really sure what good it would do a three-year-old to have a bunch of adult novels lying around."

"Oh, you know, just how you unconsciously mimic your parents' behavior and attitudes," said Moddie, "so, if your kids see you taking pleasure in reading, they might be more inclined to do the same."

"Sure," said Chrissy in a *go fuck yourself* tone. "Although, that might be a little classist or something." Then she laughed, turned, and said, "Anyway . . ."

Moddie had always thought of herself as a great mingler, but over the past year or so she had been learning she didn't always have the clearest view of herself. She stopped herself from saying that it might be classist to say that that was classist.

Chrissy and Samantha kept talking, and after what seemed an appropriate beat, Moddie backed away slowly.

Nina texted that she would be there in 20, sorry!!! waiting on Tony for ride :(((((((((

Moddie put her phone back in her pocket and walked toward the counter to eat from the large pile of cheese and examine the magnets and photos on the massive steel refrigerator. One of the pictures was of the pussy-hat march on Washington, which Moddie thought looked like *Christ's Entry into Brussels*. This amused her, and for a moment she felt happy.

She refreshed her drink and went to pee in the half bath by the garage. She tried to hold on to the feeling of pleasant amusement, while also consciously stopping herself from letting this feeling unfold completely, because if it did unfold completely, it might lead her to imagine talking to Nick about this party—he would understand all of her criticisms, and likely congratulate her keen observational skills—and then it might make her feel regret, and then in an effort to counterbalance this regret, she might remember how Nick, whenever she tried to spend time with people she hadn't met directly through him, would savage these new acquaintances, usually focusing on psychosexual dynamics he thought they might have with their siblings, and these were thoughts and feelings she would rather not deal with here in this party, where she was trying to make new friends. She thought this kind of emotional sheep-dogging was one of her strengths, and considered herself an expert at not directly interacting with difficult emotions and memories.

Bethany's wedding photos were hung eye-level to the toilet, for the benefit of her guests. Moddie hadn't been invited to the wedding, which was fine, of course. Some of the photos were sepia and the men were wearing vests and armbands, which seemed decidedly steampunk. A little dog that looked like the dog from PBS who used to dress up as canonical literary characters was the ring bearer. Wishbone. Everyone was smiling into the camera, for the glory and honor of the wedding day.

Time passed. Moddie had another drink. She texted with Nina again, who said she would be there soon soon soon. Moddie breathed in through her nose, and out through her mouth, and then did what she believed to be a yellow chakra meditation. I relinquish control in order to gain control. She breathed into her stomach. It filled with bright yellow light, which she released on the exhale, and then the light surrounded her, in a way that indicated encouragement and stability. I don't actually care what happens to me. Images of freedom and relaxation danced in her mind, and she felt a slight slip, the beginning of an emotional free fall without end. This compelled her to find a corner she could laugh into privately.

After she wiped her tears and gathered her senses (Nina texted, "the hour is nigh omw"), she found herself in a circle of women—Pam, a woman named Kimberly, and Samantha—all performing the ceremonial repeating of facts and opinions. Moddie felt loose and unaware of her troubles, as if observing the night from a state of curious detachment.

Without warning, Kimberly turned to Moddie and said, "What brings you to town?"

"Oh, well, you know," said Moddie.

"No, I don't," said Kimberly, and then she laughed in a trilling, aristocratic way.

"Moddie grew up here," said Pam. "She was living in Chicago."

"Just back for a little something or other?" asked Kim in an upbeat tone. "Thought it was time to give the big city a rest?"

"Yes," said Moddie. "Yes, certainly. In Chicago, I made a series of increasingly questionable choices that led me to an enervating wasteland of superficial friendships with people I did not respect, some of whom I outright hated, and now I'm giving it all a nice big rest."

"Wow, okay."

After an awkward beat, Samantha began to recount what seemed to be an entire day's worth of facts from NPR.

Moddie had, despite herself, heard most of these programs. She was torn on the subject of NPR. On the one hand, she felt disdain for the center-leaning smugness of the programming and felt certain that the arch tweeness of NPR, the oohing and aaaahhing over synth sounds meant to evoke a sense of wonder, the British accents describing civilian bombings meant to evoke a sense of seriousness, had something to do with the coddling infantilization of her generation, who, though well into their thirties, seemed to need constant affirmation and authoritative direction to make it through the week (though, what did she know, perhaps every generation was the same). And on the other hand, she felt a strong nostalgia for the sounds of NPR, which reminded her of her childhood and of her parents—whose love she never doubted—cooking dinner in the structured safety of the evening.

She was chewing on these feelings, turning them over and over, until she felt herself say, in response to something, "Ah, yes, I heard that, too," and everyone turned to look at her. "It was interesting," she said, forgetting herself, "mostly because of how tedious it was." She relaxed a little more and said the tedium was "almost thrilling" and "bordering on erotic."

"I mean, what's more tedious than listening to an *SNL* cast member describe their audition? I feel like there are these annual requirements—like three times a year, you have to have someone come on and say, like, 'My god, we were so young, we didn't know what we were doing, and wow, I couldn't even believe it. *Me,* a TV star!' And they're always talking in this low, slowed-down, depressed-yet-humble voice. Like yeah yeah, we get it, comedians are sad and very serious people, tears of a clown, Jim Carrey, an intellectual, a painter, blah blah blah. I mean, I don't know, of all the things you could ask someone who is supposedly incredibly talented and smart, you want to ask them about how they got their job? *Je*-sus." Moddie shook her head and let out air. She stopped short of saying *Who gives a shit* but the phrase reverberated off of her, crystal clear.

"Yes, no? Agree, disagree?" she added, rubbing her hands together. Who gives a shit? Who gives a shit? Everything was fine, it was only a conversation. There was a moment of calm during which Pam breathed in and looked at Moddie sympathetically, as if Moddie had been incoherently ranting about the CIA, but that wouldn't come until later.

Patience, prudence, peace, and comfort, thought Moddie, grounding herself in her cardinals.

"Oh, I don't know," said Kimberly. "I actually think it's interesting when Terry adds career and business details to her interviews. My brother's girlfriend works in the industry in Los Angeles. I think it's thrilling to hear the practical side of how things are made. But maybe you're successful in the creative field, so this is all stuff you already know."

"No, I don't do that," said Moddie. "That's not really my, you know."

"Oh, come on, don't be modest," said Pam. "Moddie is very creative."

It was difficult not to hear this comment as hostile, a knife through Moddie's long-suffering heart, a bald reminder of her many failures.

"Oh, are you some big fancy artist?" asked Kimberly, with impunity.

"I'm unemployed," said Moddie.

"Well, if you're between positions, I know some recruiters," said Kimberly. "It seems like it would be awfully boring to move here without a job. Not that it's not boring—or, maybe just totally exhausting—working at the university. I mean, I wouldn't necessarily recommend it for you."

"Tell me about it," said Samantha.

Everyone laughed, except Moddie, and then they started talking about university politics. The molestation scandal was on everyone's mind. Many things were changing, structurally. Out with the old, in with the new.

"I'm trying to come up with a way to discuss the molestations in class on the first day, just so all of the students know that all of the professors and all of the administrators are really, seriously thinking and talking about this all the time—

and that we want them to know that it's safe for them to come to us and share their own personal molestation stories. They don't have to, but they can—and we want them to know that, even if they aren't feeling the strength from within to tell us their stories, we're going to be watching them for signs, and we will be reaching out to form a supportive bridge with them if we think they might have been assaulted or molested in any way, and then we can report them, or direct them to the appropriate mental health help center. We want this to be really student focused. The trick is to figure out a way to do this that is open and gentle, but that also protects the university," said Samantha. "From letting this happen again," she added quickly. "We're really trying to separate sex from the classroom, and in a global inter-student way, we're really trying to get the rape numbers down, so we're trying to start each fall with a rape and molestation questionnaire, which the teachers can disseminate in the first week, to track efficacy."

Kimberly nodded.

"Yeah," said Pam, and then she talked about maximizing opportunities for change.

After a while, Moddie finished her drink and said, "Yeah. Yeah, actually I was thinking about filing a class action lawsuit against Facebook. That could be my job."

She started rubbing her eyes like a sleepy child. She couldn't stop. She pressed harder and she saw brown, green, triangles, circles, red, shifting, beckoning.

"Oh, well, in that case you should talk to Martha's husband, Eric. All the boys are in the basement," said Kimberly.

"There are a bunch of men in the basement?" said Moddie.

"Of course."

Moddie tended to do well with men, she thought. Well, not always. No, not always.

She descended the carpeted stairs into the finished basement, which was filled with husbands and boyfriends. Craig was in the corner, holding a beer, his other hand jammed into his front pants pocket. He had blond stubble that made his face look out of focus. His khakis were too tight and displayed the vague outline of his penis. He rolled his eyes and nodded and tapped his finger several times on his beer bottle, in the typical fashion of an agitated man, then laughed. He was talking to a guy in a T-shirt with a picture of a bulked-out Mickey Mouse doing a dead lift on it.

Moddie approached a group at random.

"We love the Discover, but nobody takes it. The Amex is great for fast purchases, if you just want to get something big and not think about it, but it's honestly just not the ideal card, despite its reputation. I mean, you think Amex and . . ." the man made a face like *Come on, right, what the fuck?*

"Diane and I are really liking the credit union, which we were really surprised about. It used to be you couldn't do direct deposit, but that's not the case anymore. They're fully online now, and I like being co-owner of my bank."

Moddie turned to look at each of them as they spoke, as if she were a house cat convinced she could follow the conversation. She tapped her beer bottle and said, "I like Capital One because they're the official sponsors of iHeart Radio's annual Summer Bash."

The man with the Amex looked down at her with an expressionless face, as if to, by soft thought, push Moddie back to wherever she came from.

"And I love their online customer success department," she added.

Tap tap tap.

"Is Jordie still working for Myerson?"

Moddie looked up and saw Craig across the room, who quickly averted his gaze.

She went back upstairs, wondering why she was there and when Nina would arrive.

She had a tense conversation with Kimberly about Facebook. Moddie was happy to elaborate upon her feelings here, and began by saying, "It's the number one worldwide distributor of child pornography, but whatever helps you stay connected, I guess," and then continued by saying, confidently, something half-researched about Cambridge Analytica. Kimberly said that social media had helped her stay politically engaged, and Moddie suggested that the major corporations that were using social media to monitor and influence her every thought and mood had figured out that this notion of the websites as vehicles for radical political engagement was an appealing enough notion to feed Kimberly as misdirection for their real aim, which was mind control, and that it was the corporations that had encouraged everyone to adopt this idea that the websites were radical, so that the users could combine their petty addictions to the jolts of the mind-numbing dopamine of *likes* with the sanctimonious euphoria of imagining themselves as citizens and thinkers of the highest moral caliber, creating an airtight logic for everyone's idiotic addiction to their smartphones, which were made with metals harvested by child slaves in factories with nets outside the windows to catch the suicides, and Moddie was sure if there was anything anyone felt too good about, like for instance their half-formed political stances (at this she curtsied and pointed to her own chest with all of her fingers), it was probably a bad sign, as happiness was usually a bad sign, usually a sign that something horrible was about to happen, if you took a look around you, it seemed true, didn't it?

Oh, she might have said a few other things, but her memory tried to treat her gently. After this, Kimberly's face froze for a moment, mouth open in either true shock or a pantomime of shock, and, as she reanimated to say something about something being "actually unbelievable," Moddie stood still and wondered if this was the kind of behavior that had gotten her uninvited to the annual Oscars party hosted by that hostile, lobotomizingly bland, infuriatingly sour friend group back in dread Chicago. God, how she hated the Oscars, that flagrant display of mediocrity, god how it made her sick, sick to her stomach, how could people stand to watch these awful movies and then on top of that watch hours of these morons grinning their asses off in ball gowns. Ball gowns! Repulsive but more than that so boring it should be criminal, boring enough to be physically painful, just repulsively boring, stupid, and awful.

Kimberly finished talking ("Obviously I'm not an idiot") and everyone in the circle kind of uncomfortably watched where the conversation might go. Moddie looked around the floor, wondering if Bethany owned that dog from the bathroom picture, and if so, what were her chances of seeing it, touching it, getting to know it a little better.

Pam had long since left the circle (she left when they started talking about school, she and Moddie had very different feelings about school), so Moddie was all alone. All alone!

Someone jumped in and changed the subject to a Netflix documentary. Oh yes, they'd all seen that. Moddie let time and something internal and mysterious dictate when she would wander away from this group in search of the next—would the next group be where she belonged? Oh, she needed another drink, and there it went, that was the mysterious inner bell. She broke off and went to the kitchen.

Am I going to cry? she wondered. No, it didn't feel like it, but she did want a cigarette, in fact an entire pack of cigarettes, smoked butt to butt. *Ass to ass!* she shouted in her head, thinking of a terribly stupid movie she'd seen in high school. She might have agreed to spend two years in total isolation if only she could smoke butt to butt with no repercussions.

Later, Moddie received a lecture on white supremacy, as if Moddie had never heard of white supremacy, and then Nina walked in and diverted her attention.

Beautiful, wonderful Nina—her Gypsy bride! Not that she would say that anymore, it was no longer the nineties after all, and she meant no offense to anyone, especially in regards to their ethnic composition.

Moddie walked quickly over to Nina, they hugged, laughed. Moddie breathed in deeply and smelled Nina's hair, which as always was filled with an intoxicating mix of perfumes and pheromones, and then she offered to get Nina a drink and a brownie.

When she returned to the living room, she found Pam and Nina talking. Pam, who had seemed hidden, as if she had been avoiding Moddie, but who now had suddenly appeared again.

Moddie regretted not having a drink and a brownie for Pam, as if this might show Moddie's rude preference for Nina, and thus perpetuate an awkward teen dynamic so early into Moddie's return. She gave Nina the drink and the brownie, and motioned, wanting to explain and apologize, and wanting to offer to extend the same gracious bonhomie to Pam, but Pam held Moddie firmly in her peripheral as she kept talking.

"Obviously I'm stressed," said Pam. "This VAP thing is way more than I can handle, but I want to do something. I'm sure you feel this way, too," she said to Nina, still not looking at Moddie. "I've come to a certain point in my career, and via some crucial restructuring, I'm going to be part of bringing the school into the twenty-first century, so I do have a certain amount of power, and I feel a responsibility to share that power with people who are struggling, who I feel like the culture isn't validating and providing for, including students with wide-ranging backgrounds, of course, but also artists. I'm trying to share what I have, and I'm trying to make sure that universities and institutions continue on in a tradition of patronage. It is a part of my value system. I have a platform, I want to share that platform, but on a personal level I'm struggling with a lot of impostor syndrome—"

"Oh, sure," said Nina.

"—and I don't really have or even necessarily want authority. It's not that I want some high-status position, but if no one else is going to do it," she said, modulating down as if she were depressed, an affect that Moddie had always assumed was taken up to counterbalance her saccharine cuteness, which could have easily gotten in the way of her seeming, as she so desperately longed to seem, like an intellectual of serious gravity (she never liked it, in high school, when Moddie called her "Kewpie"), "I mean, someone has to. I'm really stressed out, and it's taking up all of my time, and then there are all of these other questions of like, okay, but is this how I want to live? By pushing myself at work, am I ignoring something crucial, and maybe perpetuating something negative by example? I don't necessarily believe wholesale in the sixty-hour workweek, but that's what I find myself doing."

Something was ringing slightly false about Pam's insecurities.

"This is all so real," said Nina. "But this is your job right now, you're going to do it, and it's going to take time. I mean, obviously it goes without saying that you're going to kill it, but that almost doesn't even matter."

Pam smile-frowned and said, "No, you're right."

"What's a VAP thing?" asked Moddie.

Pam's eyelids fluttered a little and she sighed and explained it was a visiting artist program she was setting up for the university, and there was really no need for it, but she'd wanted more responsibility, and when Bethany became the department chair after they let Steve Branford go (thank god), it had just seemed so natural when Bethany asked her to stay behind after game night and asked her point-blank "What do you want?"—so natural to say "I want to run a visiting artist program."

"It was just a totally automatic thing," said Pam. "In that moment, I felt like I knew exactly what I wanted, that this would get me out of my plateau, but now I'm totally overwhelmed, and some days it just seems so stupid."

"Sounds cool," said Moddie.

"I really hope it goes well," said Pam with a little shake of her head.

"You'll do great," said Nina.

"We'll see."

The party shifted again. Moddie talked to a few more people. She noticed, periodically, that the woman she'd talked to about Facebook seemed to be glaring at her, her weird little eyes poking at Moddie throughout the night.

Eventually, people started thinning out. One by one, husbands ascended from the basement and whispered into their wives' ears, "*We've got to get the fuck out of here.*"

Pam came over to Nina and Moddie, who were in the kitchen by the food, and said in monotone, "Craig's ready," and then walked back to the door.

Before they could follow, Bethany intercepted them and said, "Nina, sweetie, it's always so good to see you." They hugged. "Do you girls want any of these treats to take home? Thomas and I are just going to chuck it all when you leave, so you might as well make yourselves a carryout."

Moddie wondered where she'd heard the word "carryout" used in this way, and if this was supposed to indicate that Bethany had been to England, a fact she'd included more than once in her essay in *The New York Times*.

"Well, we can't have you chuck it," said Nina.

"Excellent."

Bethany moved to the cupboard and got out a roll of packing tape. She put a pile of brownies on a Chinet plate, put another Chinet plate on top, clam-style, and sealed it with a massive amount of tape from the screeching gunlike dispenser.

"Moddie, I'm so glad you could come," said Bethany, looking up from her craftwork. "It's a pleasure to have you back in town."

It was difficult for Moddie to tell if this was sarcastic.

"Well, it's a pleasure and an honor to return," she said.

"I used to run into your mom at Biggby all the time," said Bethany.

"Ah, yes, 'Biggby,'" said Moddie, using finger quotes.

Bethany smiled warmly, and Moddie laughed a little.

"It's funny, just on a phonetic level, Biggby still sounds like something you might not want to say in mixed company."

"Mmm-hmm," said Bethany.

The coffee shop used to be called Beaner's.

Moddie considered asking Bethany if she had any of the old Beaner's travel mugs in the basement in a locked china cabinet, but she hesitated.

"She's doing well?" asked Bethany.

"My mom?"

"Yes. We always wondered why your parents left, and that *gorgeous* house with all of those funny little lawn projects."

By this, Bethany just meant "plants."

"Just time, I guess," said Moddie. "Retired. Shit like that."

"Well, we always wondered what happened." Bethany handed Nina the snack-object. "I bet she's a little disappointed that you've moved back here just after she left. Where do you live now?"

Moddie told her the address, and Bethany laughed and said, "Oh, my!"

"I'm being frugal," said Moddie.

"I'll bet."

"It's only four hundred bucks."

They whipped through the neighborhoods, the streetlamps strobing the car interior, in silence. Craig white-knuckled the steering wheel and Pam turned to look out the passenger window, her brow furrowed and her hand covering her mouth. It had rained a little during the party. Moddie played with the window, letting in warm streams of fresh air, while Craig called his GPS a piece of shit and reentered Moddie's address, one eye on the road.

When they got to Moddie's house, Nina said, "I'm getting out here, too. So good to see you guys. Thanks for the ride!"

Pam did not move or speak.

Craig said, "Yeah, good night, nice to meet you, Moddie."

"Yeah, you too," said Moddie. "Let's definitely do this again."

The door slam echoed off the pavement.

When they got inside Moddie's apartment, both Moddie and Nina started laughing.

"My, what a lovely couple!" said Moddie.

"Yes, the sexual *tension* between those two!" said Nina.

"Is this Pam's final form?" asked Moddie.

Nina said, "Oh, you know. Pam has her phases."

This was true, and had been since middle school. Moddie and Pam had always run hot and cold. Perhaps Moddie had been naïve to think that this was over with, now that they were adults with a deep history, but of course not all of that deep history had been smooth. There was something warm and welcoming about the problem of Pam's aloofness, something about it that made Moddie feel young again, as if she were thirteen and just discovering that it was in fact Nina who would provide her with the constant stream of admiration she needed in order to feel secure, just discovering that it was Nina who would go along with all of her whims and tirades, propping her up and making her feel an authoritative confidence, unlike Pam, who often bristled when Moddie flexed her opinions, and who often seemed—quite on purpose—to adopt the opposite opinion, as if friendship were a debate or a contest. In this moment, Moddie felt an overwhelming love for Nina, a deep gratitude for her presence, a sense that she was, through Nina, rediscovering a self-assurance that she had buried during her years with Nick in Chicago, and that now she was finally back on the path toward a unified and unburdened self, never to make the same mistakes again.

"Jesus fucking *Christ*, that was a tightly wound group of people," said Moddie.

Nina nodded and said "*Mmmm-hmmm*" while taking off her shoes by the couch in Moddie's small, carpeted, furnished, low-rent apartment.

"Did you talk to, was it Tiffany, in the purple shirt with the little bow on it? She wouldn't stop asking me if I had any 'friends of color.'"

"Probably Kimberly," said Nina. "If I had to guess."

"Listen, Kim, nobody's making any *friends of color* tonight!" said Moddie, and Nina made the *dingdingding* game show noise, and then Moddie said she was going to open a day care called Friends of Color so Kimberly and everyone could brag about sending their fully literate toddlers there. She crossed her arms and laughed, feeling annoyed, aggressive, and misunderstood.

She moved toward the kitchen and got out glasses for water, then turned abruptly and said, "Do you think people would like me better if I told them the story about being sexually assaulted by the six-year-old?"

"Oh my god," said Nina, laughing.

"Then they could be like, 'Moddie's difficult, but it's sad, actually. She's been through some hard things. You just don't know her like I do. She was *sexually assaulted* by a six-year-old. She's just a very sad person.'"

"Yeah, that might work," said Nina.

Over the past year, in an effort to rebuild her identity, Moddie had tried to find the beginning of what she saw as her sexual and romantic history, and had once again landed on this particular episode from the summer she was eight, which she spent at the pool, and during which one of the old butterballs basting themselves on the deck chairs decided Moddie ought to start playing with her grandson, because they were neighbors, and because she believed her grandson to be very handsome and charming and deserving of a playmate. Moddie was polite, so she left her diving rings for the warm, shallow kiddie pool to engage with this much younger boy, who seemed mentally dense, was blond, and had what one might call a very butch kind of jawline. His favorite pool game was "bridal threshold." He would hoist Moddie up in his short arms, walk a few paces, drop her, then repeat, for hours, like a tiny charmless Frankenstein. His grandmother and some of the others would applaud when he did this—can you believe he just turned six, and already such a man? These pool hangouts evolved into unsupervised house hangouts, which included a lot of Moddie awkwardly allowing this boy, a kindergartner, to dry hump her, and which culminated—quite psychotically—in this boy pushing her into a pantry in which he had found a large butcher knife, brandishing this knife, holding it to her throat, and forcing her to put her tongue in his mouth. When she told Nina this story over the phone, Nina had found the story disturbing but the narration amusing.

Moddie started laughing, then turned to the cupboard for the weed. "Oh, I could tell them a thing or two, all right!" she shouted.

"For sure," said Nina.

Moddie raised her finger and said, in an impassioned Mae West voice, "Listen, Mother, I don't want children, because I was *raped* by a child! The mere . . . mere sight of them gives me hives!"

Nina laughed and said, "Jesus."

"I told Nick that story once and he thought it was boring."

"He's a moron, an asshole, and a loser," said Nina. "And I sentence him to death."

Moddie shrugged and started packing the bowl, then nodded her head upward and said, "We should eat those brownies."

"Oh, yeah," said Nina, with baritone enthusiasm.

Moddie leaned against the counter and watched as Nina took the brownie package out of her large leather tote bag and began pulling at the packing tape. She thought about the neighbor boy, his hideous little body, his head nearly a foot below her own, his perverse Dennis the Menace affect, and wondered if Nick had been right, that it had not been a formative experience but a maudlin tale told for cheap sympathy.

"Dude, do you want scissors? This is fucking intense."

"I'm almost there," said Nina, trying to rip the tape apart.

"It just seems like you're directing your intentions at the package, with no real plan or thinking or . . . like what the fuck. This is like watching a raccoon try to get at something."

Nina laughed.

"Jesus Christ, give me that," said Moddie, reaching for the brownies and then getting a pair of scissors from the silverware drawer. "You were just rolling the tape into an impenetrable band."

Moddie cut the tape off and put the brownies on a plate from her cupboard.

They moved to the couch.

Moddie, grimly, "When I try to look nice I look like Baby Jane."

"Baby Jane is a sexual icon," said Nina. She took a hit of weed and a brownie.

"I bought a flowery dress on Etsy when I was drunk last

week, and I got some makeup at the grocery store, and I tried it all on the other night, and I looked like I was in drag and that my bit was that I was a scary sexually repressed little dolly."

"Cool," said Nina.

"What if I'd dressed like that tonight? With my hair curled, wearing barrettes, like, 'Hewwo, will you be my fwiend?'" Moddie made a stupid happy face.

"This outfit has a particular kind of messaging to it," said Nina, waving her hand in the direction of Moddie's blouse. "It's very 'unassailable single mom two weeks after leaving asshole dad.'"

Moddie's hair was unwashed and pulled back and she was wearing a striped button-up with many vague stains on it and cutoff jean shorts with a hole forming in the very upper thigh.

"Emotionally fragile, yet with a quiet inner strength," said Moddie.

"You were too small to help her then, but what about now?" said Nina.

"Nobody mistreats Mother."

"She doesn't have time to wash her hair and get all gussied up like some common *slut*."

"Mother never loses her temper and Mother never forgets her bouncing baby boy."

"But dost she weep? Yea, verily, Mother, she dost weep."

They ate some brownies.

"Yeah, really looking forward to my next boyfriend," said Moddie. She felt like she was about to start crying so she started coughing and raising her eyebrows over and over. "You want to know something funny? I looked up that kid recently, and he's a general anesthesiologist now."

"Oooh-ho-ho, damn," said Nina. "Is this what you're wearing to your *Dateline* interview?"

Moddie laughed and nodded, then paused. "It's like, what the fuck were those people thinking? Obviously no kid is fucking born wanting to put a butcher knife to another kid's throat, that doesn't just happen out of nowhere. If they could have just thought about it for two seconds, maybe they would have been like, 'Hmmm, maybe we should not have a child.'"

"That's not the kind of thing people think about," said Nina. "Everybody thinks their kid is going to be perfect and only embody their good qualities, while erasing and redeeming their bad ones."

"Fucking people and their stupid fucking children," said Moddie.

Nina laughed.

They sat on the couch for about an hour, going over current events and personal experiences. Moddie talked about the summer camp she went to where the owner was arrested for being a child molester and whose wife used to make the sick kids listen to the song "Sunshine, Lollipops and Rainbows" every morning in the medicine line on a loop at six A.M. like a Lynch movie, and then the other camp she attended at fourteen where the twenty-one-year-old counselor, after putting his weird, dry tongue in her mouth, tried to get her to come back to his cabin to "listen to some Dave" and how it was her strict adherence to aesthetic values that had saved her from a gruesome evening, and then Nina whispered that she was the king of the castle, and Moddie the dirty rascal. Maybe Jeff Buckley, but Jesus, god, no, never *Dave*. They talked about the university's new anti-molestation policy, and then tried to remember which of their classmates had been good gymnasts, and Moddie said these places should have government-required transparency like with McDonald's and calories. Pedo Camp, Uncle Larry's Finger Bang Emporium for Physically Gifted Children, etc.

Moddie laughed and whispered, "Take me to Pedo Camp, Mother, take me straightaway!" and then Nina sang an impromptu ragtime song about wanting to go to Pedo Camp.

Moddie said she was still having trouble with her "anger issues," putting those words in finger quotes. Nina said she was too.

"Hey, you seem like you're doing kind of better, though," said Nina.

"Talking about it less, at least," said Moddie, and Nina said, "Uuuuhhhh, no comment."

Then she added, "Seriously. I know it's really hard to set boundaries, and I don't hate Nick or anything, but it does seem like being apart from him has been really good for you."

"Yeah," said Moddie.

Nina's phone buzzed on the coffee table.

"Oh, Tony's on his way."

"Does he want to come in and say hey for a second?"

"Nah, he'll probably just want to keep the car running," said Nina.

"Cool," said Moddie.

Nina had her shoes on before Tony arrived, and when he called to say he was outside, Moddie walked Nina to the door.

"I guess this is farewell," said Moddie.

Nina laughed, and while they hugged, Moddie whispered, "Should I kill Tony and wear him like a skin suit so we can hang out more?"

"Probably not," said Nina, "but let's hang soon. I have a doctor's appointment Tuesday, and I have to take my batteries to the recycling place and talk to my cousin on the phone, so maybe in like a week or something."

"Sounds good," said Moddie.

After Nina left, the apartment still felt inhabited by her, which made Moddie feel less alone, but in a way that underscored her loneliness. The pillow where Nina had leaned was still pushed down. The plate of brownies still sat on the coffee table. She could smell Nina's perfume. She felt slightly jealous of Tony. Maybe his life still had the illusion of continuity.

The apartment felt extra quiet. Moddie put on pajamas and smoked more weed on the couch and watched TV using the antenna she'd bought at Best Buy.

An ad came on in which a shy little anthropomorphized box rang somebody's doorbell and gave a direct address about how all you had to do was take a shit in its head and then you wouldn't have to go to the doctor anymore. He smiled and waved like "Come on, let's go!" The next ad was all about how much food you could get at Olive Garden. There weren't any people in this ad, just an aerial tracking shot of plates and plates of oily food, like the beginning of *The Shining* where he's driving up to the Overlook for the first time. Then the show came on. It was a rerun of a show about government employees solving esoteric crimes while dealing with sexual tension in the workplace. Moddie's face was blank. On TV, they were putting a corpse into a vat of acid and flirting.

Two

When Moddie woke up on the couch the next day, she had the Mr. Bucket theme song in her head. She'd planned to sit on the back porch, drink coffee, and read a book about prisons, but there it was, the unnerving, demonic insistence of the jingle. Balls flying in and out of mouths. She rose and walked to the Mr. Coffee, filled it, turned it on, held her hands to her face, breathed slowly, in and out—[pop] *wheee!*—not knowing if she would be able to concentrate her mind on the book, or if this persistent unwanted thought would have control today.

Despite Nina's initial enthusiasm over the phone, her insistence that it would be great if Moddie moved back to X, Nina was rarely free to socialize, and neither was Pam. It was July. Very little had happened since her return. It had been three long months. Days were harder than nights. During the day, she felt like she should make authoritative decisions about her emotions and trajectory, but this was made nearly impossible by the distraction of her constant, winding thoughts. Nights were easier, because night seemed like the appropriate time to sit and ruminate—at night, she wasn't missing out on anything but sleep. This was what she'd wanted, to be alone, and yet it was not what she'd wanted. There was no great life of the mind taking hold. There was no energetic return to an art practice. There was no clarity, no relief, no escape. The worst parts of Chicago had followed her here, because the worst parts of Chicago had been inside of her.

The cicadas made loud, swelling noises in the yard, merging with and then momentarily drowning out the Mr. Bucket jingle. She stood on the deck, felt the midmorning heat, drank coffee, and looked at the sky. A small bird swooped down, then back up, and for a while, a moment, Moddie thought she could easily reach transcendence through simplicity.

She got her book and sat in the hot plastic chair and put her legs up on the deck railing and read, "... *not to punish less, but to punish better; to punish with an attenuated severity perhaps, but in order to punish with more universality and necessity*..."

She looked up at her legs and rotated them, listened to the sound of the song, *do-do-do do-do* [pop], then looked back at her book.

"... *to insert the power to punish more deeply into the social body.*"

After a minute, she went inside to see if anyone had emailed her.

She had one from her dad.

Happy National Piña Colada Day, sweetheart!

More like Happy Take a Shit in Donald Trump's Mouth Day. The pre-approved Gmail responses to your last email were "Oh?" "I don't know what you mean" and "Okay." Google suggests I respond with barely disguised hostility to your critique of Jeff Bezos's space colony. "I don't know what you mean." My real response is that if I saw Bezos get shot on the street, I'd stand by and watch him bleed out.

Etc.

She Google-image-searched "little dog dressed as british lawyer" and sent the second result to Nina with the message "cheerio, pip pip, allo govnah, right-o!!" She made a mental note to send her parents a slightly tailored play-by-play of the party. One that would amuse them but also not worry them too much about her psychological state.

Moddie lived on the ground floor of a two-story house with white aluminum siding in the "bad" part of town. She was on a small dead-end street just behind the main drag. The siding of her house was streaked with putrid-looking rust, and the patchy, glass-riddled front lawn was surrounded by waist-high chain-link. One of the neighbors' houses was red with a lopsided, moss-eaten porch. One gray house had an Adirondack chair on the lawn next to a dry birdbath. The sidewalk had buckled, and the whole street had a derelict carnival funhouse feel to it.

She passed a bright green plastic bag with a flattened-out old dog turd in it.

The inside of her car smelled good, like hot, dried dust.

She drove down one of the main roads toward the farms, which she thought might be sort of eventful, like a field trip or something. She passed Denny's, the health food store, Kildea Kar Kare, a place that would deep-fat-fry your pizza slice, Tuesday Morning, the karate place, and thought that only a fool or a masochist would have stayed in that relationship, and certainly she was no fool. If you put it all on paper, it didn't make any sense to stay together, and it was probably best for him, too, that she'd ended things. She'd gone through this train of thought several times a day for months. This point in the cycle, where she felt certain she'd done the right thing, lasted about thirty seconds before the return of a lonely guilt and an intense longing for the domestic quietude she had destroyed on what sometimes seemed to her to be some kind of fanciful impulse. She grimaced and started nodding slightly in time with the radio. She tried to imagine, as a consequence of the breakup, that she might never see or speak to Nick again, her friend, her constant companion who she knew so intimately, and who she loved. She could still see him crying. She could feel it in her body.

The radio station became annoying, so she changed it.

In these moments, she found it helpful to recall the things that Nick had done that she'd found hurtful. She reviewed the list of Nick's errors, looping the line items that had made her mom and Nina particularly angry, and looping her mother's words "When he said that to you, that's when I knew it was over."

She didn't like playing the victim, and hated it when other people played the victim, so she didn't feel victimized, necessarily—though Nick had said to her, "I know you think I've really victimized you, now you probably even think that I 'abused' you, but it's not true and you know it's not true. I've been a really good boyfriend. It hasn't always been a walk in the park, you know, sometimes you can be downright crazy," which yes, of course, Moddie knew. Who knew better than she?

She'd read online—instead of looking at porn—that male saliva had testosterone in it, which acted as an aphrodisiac. This was, in a way, what they'd taught her in health class as part of their government-funded abstinence-preferred program. In school, she learned that when a woman had penetrative sex with a man, she released excessive amounts of dopamine and oxytocin, which bonded her to the man irrevocably, kind of like those weird horse things in the movie *Avatar*. This bond feeling led to a further clouding of female judgment, a loss of reason, clinginess, desperation, and erotomania, which were all a real turnoff for men, who found this type of clingy postcoital behavior so unattractive they would very likely leave you for someone more reasonable, someone sweeter and kinder, tell everyone you were crazy, sully your reputation, and doom you to a life of cycling through one unhealthy relationship after another, flailing, never knowing love, never knowing honor, purity, etc.—which was all something to keep in mind, class, ladies, when considering whether or not to have premarital penetrative heterosexual intercourse, and maybe you'd rather go ahead and save your purity and give it as a gift to your husband.

Moddie started laughing—slowly at first, and then wildly.

Isn't life *joyous*?

She turned right down the pretty country lane. This was where she used to make out with her gay boyfriend in high school. She pulled over and got out of the car and looked out over the wide expanse of loamy fields. The damp, pungent summer air caressed her limbs. A group of cows ate from a big pile of hay near a silver barn in the distance. One of the cows lifted up its tail and shat.

She wiped her hands across her face and thought it would make everything easier if only people cared less about certain things. If only some people could lighten up a little, not everything had to go exactly how you thought it was going to go, and it would do everyone a lot of good to lighten up.

Her brows were firmly clenched together.

The cow's anus opened again, and the shit tumbled softly, gently, to the ground.

Life just kept passing out buckets and buckets.

She thought about Nick and Gracie and felt repulsed by the images that came to mind, Gracie's stupid batting lashes. All the phony admiration. Being with someone who liked you too much was like being alone, what a thing to want. That's what Jeffrey Dahmer wanted when he drilled holes into those poor kids' heads—to be alone and together at the same time. Total control.

A burning pain ran through her chest and ballooned out. Waves and waves, a disorienting mixture of anger and regret. He hadn't really been like Dahmer. It hadn't been quite that bad.

The sun was out but it meant nothing.

She got back in the car.

Moddie turned on NPR and got on the highway to do more aimless driving. As she drove, she felt sinless, responsible, mature. Driving on the highway often had this effect on her. A car passed her on the right going much too fast, and she verbalized a lengthy fantasy about the driver's personal inadequacies.

NPR dragged on. A middle-aged man was reviewing a TV show. He sounded elated, almost short of breath. The show had a plot, characters, actors, and someone did a good job using the camera.

Moddie lifted up her hand and gestured broadly to the fields on either side of the road and said, "All this shall be *mine.*"

She passed a billboard that said "Mommy, I don't want to die, at 6 weeks I have eyes!"

The man's voice became unbearable. Moddie shouted, "Oh my god, shut the fuck *up!*" and hit the seek button until she landed on a song she'd heard many times, by design, as there were basically only three radio stations and twelve songs left—the slow death of culture. Rise of the machines. It was a song about intoxication, sexual desire, and revenge. Oh, the song, it worked. It got her all riled up. She was angry, oh boy, and excited, too, by the suggestion of some vague possibility. She felt like something inside of her might spark and ignite and she would be on fire, driving and on fire, and then flying, *flying* over the hilltops and through the towns and over the oceans like a soaring majestic eagle with a forty-foot wingspan. She had nothing holding her back now! Jobless! Sinless! Single! Free! The cord had been severed and now not even the sky, *no not even the sky,* was the limit!

Moddie's head began to spin. She was thinking about the cosmos, the cells, the bloodstream, the cosmic stream, her heart opening up completely in response to the song, completely in its thrall, and then suddenly *she* was passing on the right, what do you know? She was speeding toward the border, north, going fast. Flying. Cheerio pip pip!

CHEERIO PIP PIP!!!

A method of brainwashing, of course. All of the radio songs. You don't have a choice in the matter. It's too strong. Too strong, I tell you! You feel what it tells you to feel!

A sweet tear of release slid down her cheek and in the distance she saw a billboard.

Have fear???? JESUS is REAL!!

She swung her hand out wide again, extended her fingers at the message, made a fist, slowly brought the fist back toward her heart, and whispered, "Yeeeeeessssss."

Yes for Jesus is REAL!! Avast! To Livonia! Onward!

She drove like this for a while.

The cop was in the median about sixty yards ahead in a candy-blue sedan, and when Moddie registered this, it was already too late.

"You sick, twisted motherfucker," said Moddie, pulling over.

The lady cop sauntered up, like in the movies, and when she got to the window, she asked Moddie why she hadn't noticed her. "I've been clocking you for miles."

Moddie felt conscious of the gun and of her rocky history with authority. "No, I didn't see you. I am deeply . . ."

The officer had cosmetically enhanced teeth—a million-dollar smile! Her hair was pulled back into a taut bun and her skin was freckled and tan. The tan skin and the white teeth made her lips look dead, like a gray, dead butthole, and the expression on her face made her look stupid and mean, like a moron, like she'd never had a friend in her life.

"It's not even legal anymore to give you a warning at this speed," said the cop, and while chanting the rest of the predetermined information, she told Moddie she could "plead not guilty in a court of law, or plead guilty online with convenience."

Moddie placed the ticket on the passenger seat, rolled up the window, and got off the highway to collect herself, shaken and ashamed for speeding, of course, speeding was dangerous, under normal circumstances Moddie would never speed, but also angry, in some ways yes quite furious with the cop for having the nerve to make her feel *shame,* considering all of the atrocities committed by the police, it was certainly not Moddie who should feel ashamed. It was only a little speeding, which everybody does. Moddie had an inclination to rip up the ticket and throw it out the window, but she didn't, and this made her feel mature.

"*Disgusting,*" she said in the car, thinking about police brutality, driving slowly to the Beaner's on campus to coddle herself with a latte, which she would drink on her way to get groceries, an errand in which all reasonable adults took part.

Inside Beaner's, there was a long line. Students were starting to move back to town. A kid in front of Moddie shook his head and whispered, "Jesus fucking Christ."

At the front of the line was a stout, panting, elderly man. He seemed desperate and tapped his palms on the bar to get the attention of the barista, who was foaming something. She said, "Just one second, sir, I'll be right back with you!" in a Gidget-like tone, but he only pounded his palms louder and louder, and moaned theatrically, a gentle, plaintive "Ohhhhhhh." He looked confused to Moddie, in a fundamental way that could have something to do with people withholding attention from him in childhood. Everyone in the line kind of rolled their eyes, which gave the impression that this had been going on for a while.

"Ooooohhhhhhhhhhh. Ohhhhhhhhhhhhhhhhhhhhhh," he said, and then put his hands up to his face, lost his balance slightly, and fell forward onto the counter.

"Oooohhhhhhh," he said. "Water. Warm water."

The barista filled a small paper cup with water and his body shook in anticipation. He sipped from the little pee cup and gasped. "No, not hot water, warm hot water! The Double

Burst IceMaker gum, they should warn you," he said. "They should warn you of how cold it really is. I can't feel my face. Oh god I can't feel my face. Warn everyone. The samples of IceMaker gum that they're handing out on the street. Dangerously cold, you have to make them stop, make them stop." The barista gave him three more cups of water, apparently varying in temperature, until he regained feeling in his brain and thanked her in a dry, quavering voice. *"Thank you . . . thank you."*

"Yes, okay, sir, next in line?"

After Moddie paid for her order, she tipped three dollars, cash, into a jug that said (as many jugs did) "Just the tip," which was a reference to a man putting only the tip of his penis into a woman's vagina or possibly anus, she'd never been quite sure.

She got into her car and drove to Kroger, in search of another illusion of normalcy. Moddie loved (past tense) going to grocery stores, and when she got there, she walked straight to a large pile of potatoes, picked one up, and looked at it.

A little barf rose in her gullet. She imagined Nick's delight at opening the grocery bag and a little more nausea took hold because it was sad to cook and eat alone all the time, and to have no one around who really needed or wanted your company, and holding this potato reminded her of how unessential she was to the rest of the world now that she was childless, unemployed, middle-aged, and single.

Gusto. Life no longer had any *gusto.*

The air-conditioning made the tip of her nose and the roof of her mouth cold. She stared at the potato, unable to move.

A song that sounded like the rallying cry for a troop of child soldiers started to play over the loudspeaker. It made Moddie want to deep-throat a shotgun. From the back of her mind, where pointless information lived, she remembered that the band performing this song had chosen to call themselves Fun.

The potato fell from her hand into the basket. She looked up and her eyes landed on the refrigerated shelf filled with nonrecyclable plastic clamshell packages of organic leaves, individually shrink-wrapped and ready-to-microwave sweet potatoes, and other such bullshit.

She felt herself get very, very angry about groceries.

She walked to the open, wasteful refrigerator, and to the tricolor cheese-filled tortellini she used to buy because he liked it, but which she would never buy if she were on her own. Ah yes, "if she were." Well she were now! Her throat tightened up to reject the idea of eating this, this foul fucking *tortellini*—a cozy food, a child's food. Food of fools! Her eyes panned over to the tofu *cut*let. Tor*tel*lini. *Cut*let. God, words she hated. *Tortellini,* said in her mind now like a spit. The more she thought it, the more she hated it. Other words, too, began to churn her blood there in the Kroger. Even "pasta." She imagined someone saying the word "pasta" as if they were admitting something shameful in a coy way, a little wiggling of the shoulders, a little idiotic smile, blush, "pasta" [eyelashes flutter]. Just to stoke herself, she imagined someone saying "pasta" as if it were a sophisticated word. Oh who me yes we were eating *pahstah*. She would no longer allow these things entrance into her body, no, she would not be tainted.

Well what can you eat then, rocks?

She raised her eyebrows in the aisle, frowned contemplatively, and nodded. Yeah, I could eat some fucking rocks.

She had another fantasy of pouring gasoline over her head.

When she got home to her depressing apartment, she put the Fireball whiskey and the Skittles in the cabinet next to the bag of marshmallows, the Twizzlers, the single potato, and the two-pack of green pens.

She looked out the kitchen window into the backyard. A squirrel stood on top of a pile of old leaves, touching different leaves at random.

Moddie put her hands on her face and rubbed rapidly and screamed a little, thinking about Nick.

She pictured him crying. After a certain point, after they'd been split for months, after he was already in a new relationship, she'd had to set his emails to skip the inbox and go straight to a folder labeled "Nick." He wouldn't stop contacting her, even when she asked him to, even when he promised to, he didn't actually stop sending her dozens of confusing love letters, a thing he'd never done when they were together. He seemed to want to date Gracie but keep in constant communication with Moddie, as a kind of hidden girlfriend, or maybe as a kind of comforting ghost whispering to him in the background of his mind. It took so much willpower not to check the folder, especially when she was lonely.

She wagered that if she did call him, there was a 55 percent chance he would let her come over, which meant that just through the simple physical act of dialing him, within five hours, she could be on their old couch in Little Village, and they could hold each other for as long as they needed, and she would feel her old identity, and her old reality, seeping back into her body.

But to call him, first she would have to unblock him. This would take about a half an hour on the phone with Sprint's customer service.

Then she remembered something her dad had said about how even if you take him back, he'll just want to leave again. The best you'll get is one more year, and it won't be pretty. It'll be some Monkey Paw shit.

Moddie went to her couch, sat down, and thought, Jesus I am such a bitch. She looked down at the cheap, rough upholstery and thought about her old, beautiful couch and about how she'd really shit the bed with this one.

Then she remembered what Nick had said to her the last time she saw him. "Do you even want to get dinner with Alan and Jen? Where exactly do you see yourself fitting into my life?"

That had been a particularly cruel comment for him to make. It wasn't her fault she didn't like Alan and Jen. It was hard to like people who disregarded your fundamental humanity.

Moddie needed some relief.

She smoked a little weed. Waited. Stared at the wall.

Almost immediately, she started to feel better, more carefree, as if there were plenty of interesting thoughts left to think in the roughly fifty years she had left to live. She imagined that she felt straightforwardly unburdened as a result of the breakup (phew!) and straightforwardly relieved to be back in X. She put on some music. Paced around. The sky began to dim. The insects grew louder and the humidity lifted.

She took another hit and began an email called "goofy golf, revisit the hole" addressed to Nina and Pam.

Nina, Pamela,

Nick and I had houseguests once who were from Brazil. We were all really high, and I was trying to explain the differences between miniature and goofy golfing. I described the standard features of goofy golf—dinosaurs, bowling pins, small versions of New York—and then I tried to describe how these features were designed to "interact with the hole."

This is when I started to remember Clown Town at Frazier's, which, at the time, because I was so high, seemed incredibly normal to me at first but quickly took on a sinister tone. "You know, there'll be the hole," I explained, "and then there'll be a clown crouching over the hole, and the clown will have a very long tongue on a pendulum and the tongue will go back and forth over the hole so your ball can't get in easily, and the clown is making straight-on eye contact with you, while its tongue is just going back and forth over the hole." Definitely as I was describing this hole, it started to sound obviously and completely perverse to me, bordering on sinister, and I couldn't believe what I was saying, and I couldn't believe what I was discovering about my environment and my memories. I can't really make eye contact if I'm high, so I had no idea how anyone was reacting to my in-depth descriptions of the clown's tongue interacting with the grassy hole, but I could feel Nick becoming embarrassed, and then I started to feel embarrassed and kind of ashamed, like what exactly was I trying to say?

I was trying to say something innocuous about American kitsch, but it went off the rails and I ended up talking for twenty minutes about an anilingus clown, the eye contact, the posture of his crouch. It was embarrassing, because, without meaning to, I felt like I was admitting to something about myself, as if I had had my own butthole licked by this clown.

But how could this be? He is but made of simple plywood!

Anyway, I think it's important that we all return to Clown Town, and to the site of the hole, so that we can all face the mysteries of our pasts for a brighter tomorrow. I understand, and more than that I respect, oh yes, that you are adults with adult duties and full schedules. I throw myself at your mercy, my oldest friends, my last living companions, and hope I have not been too forward in my requests for your time (I am high now, as I was then).

Maybe next week?

Love, blessings, fidelity,
Assalamu alaikum,
Moddie

She read the email a few times over and thought it sounded good, so she hit send, then went out to the porch to sit and wait for night.

Part of her believed that if she could unclench and let herself experience the fullness of these passing moments, life would blossom and feel longer and richer, that this was not wasted time but the true seat of experience, and all she really had to do was surrender.

Pam received Moddie's email while she was working late. She skimmed it for keywords, then closed the tab and went back to the university portal. Her left shoulder was clenched one inch higher than the right.

Hours later, she responded that she was super busy planning this event to welcome the visiting artist and was basically completely swamped and exhausted after work, and might not have much free time on the weekends, which she might need to just recuperate and catch up on rest, but they should both definitely come to the event in late August, and maybe after August, and after the early efforts of welcoming the visiting artist had died down, sometime in mid-to-late September, then, weather permitting of course, because fall could be so unpredictable sometimes, they should "definitely check out goofy golf."

Three

Summer carried on. Moddie didn't get much footing. She talked to her parents on the phone, watched TV, tried to read during the day, tried to engage with ideas. She was lonely.

Sometimes, just as dusk was setting in, she would put her single key into her pocket and step outside and walk the neighborhood for hours, exploring, thinking, and looking into windows lit by television, the vivid purple of the Roku home screen, the flashing patterns of action movies, the yellow-beige waves of office comedies. Dining rooms lit with the overhead, living rooms with a single lamp glowing. People hidden from her, unreachable but near, and when she got tired, she would walk home, put on the TV, and she would feel as if she'd joined them, or she would put on music and pace and continue to think—whipping herself into a frenzy, or soothing herself with silly words about her appealing and forgivable qualities. She thought mostly of herself and her emotions. It felt like her brain was rotting. When she talked to her parents, it was only about herself and her feelings. The boredom was like a cheese grater run gently over her heart, constantly, and sometimes she felt she would give anything to leave her own mind for just one second.

Eventually, she did receive an invitation from Pam to an event welcoming the visiting artist, and when Moddie received the email, she thought she ought to feel excitement, but really she felt as if she'd just been served a large plate of damp paper towels. She did not want to go. She was depressed. A little angry. A little wary of making another public appearance, after the splendor of her debut.

The nights were getting colder. August was almost over.

On the night of the party, she put on a jacket and decided to walk. She hadn't yet visited the newly rebuilt museum, because she hadn't wanted to, because it was completely uninteresting to her. Moddie knew the architect was famous, and that everyone was supposed to feel grateful about it, and maybe that was what made her feel resentful and dismissive—the assumption she should feel grateful to be near fame.

The air was fresh and cool and the sky was a dusty gray blue. On her walk, she could smell that someone had lit a fire. By the time she reached campus, it was almost dark.

A group of men stood outside the museum drinking sangria in plastic cups and one of them laughed and said, "No no, rhymes with *chode*," and then they all laughed and one of them lit a cigarette. Moddie walked through them.

The building's entrance looked like vagina dentata and the lobby looked like if a German Expressionist set designer had used the inside of a Norelco razor as inspiration for a new opera where all of the characters were maybe supposed to be Hitler. Beyond the lobby was an atrium. Placed around the perimeter of this room were a few installations from last year's graduating seniors with a fine arts emphasis. A papier-mâché cow with two radios for tits lay on its back in a kind of birthing position next to a big pile of logs, some of them covered in Saran Wrap, and behind this hung a quilt with an alternating pattern of appliquéd vaginas and guns.

In the reception area in the back of the building, twenty or so people milled around, students, strangers, and some of the women who had attended the party at Bethany's. Moddie considered retreat. The lights were dimmed and some Cialis jazz played over the speakers.

The visiting artist, David Winterbottom, stood at the back of the room, near the podium, scowling at the floor. He had accepted Pam's proposal because he'd recently gone through a divorce and was catatonically depressed, and accepting Pam's invitation felt like a metaphorical suicide, which he thought might be sort of interesting and less committal than actual suicide. He was what one might call a New Media artist.

Moddie spotted Craig and Nina by the bar, which Pam had made by putting a sheet, a giant vat of homemade sangria, disposable plastic cups, and a pile of paper towels on a classroom desk. Moddie felt on display and uncomfortable. Her outfit was odd, like it had been donated to her from an organization meant to help her succeed at job interviews. As soon as she reached the bar, Craig expressed his disdain for events like this, and Nina poured Moddie a sangria and said something encouraging about what Pam had done with the lighting.

"I think Ben's going to be here pretty soon," said Craig.

"Oh, okay," said Moddie.

Last time Moddie had seen Craig—at an incredibly brief coffee with Pam and Nina—he kept mentioning Ben from his department. Moddie was worried this was some kind of a romantic setup, and she was nervous to see who Craig thought she might like. She'd done her best to imply that a setup would be unwelcome.

"I don't know who that is," she said.

A few minutes later Ben arrived. He seemed out of breath, like he'd been running, and he looked about twenty-four years old. She looked at him, nodded, shifted on her feet, and thought about her appearance. She crossed her arms. Everything sucked. She was embarrassed for thinking Craig was trying to set her up. She was waiting for this boy to start talking about his fiancée so that her secret humiliation would be complete. It had certainly been ages since anyone had thought of her sexually.

Ben started talking about a filmmaker who everyone already knew about as if he had made a unique discovery, and then she realized that Ben would have been about six when the first of the director's movies came out, and he didn't seem like he had the kind of parents who would have let him watch movies about gambling and hookers that young, because he seemed like he had at least one Republican parent.

Nina started taking everyone's cups and refilling them with sangria from the giant bowl.

Moddie wanted to raise her hand and say to the group, to interrupt Ben while he excitedly explained a movie she'd seen when she was thirteen, "Just so you know, I'm hardly a sexual person at all and I could happily die alone and untouched, if anyone was wondering."

She wasn't paying attention to what he was saying, no one was, because nobody cared. Poor Ben. He'd understand one day.

But it wasn't necessarily true. Especially since she'd quit smoking, she'd noticed herself feeling intermittently flirtatious, not flirtatious with anyone in particular, but she had been listening to Sade at night, and twice she'd seen herself in the mirror and thought, Well, that's not so awful.

Nina said something that only half-registered.

But this hardly made her a sex-crazed maniac, and she tried not to think about it too much, except she had thought about it, but had made sure, in her thinking about it, to block it out completely, so completely that she didn't even know what she meant by "it" when she acknowledged she had blocked "it" out.

Moddie smiled, thinking, Good, and feeling calm and proud of herself.

Ben responded to Moddie's smile by laughing and saying, "Yes, it's really something!"

She had, one night, *ironically* ordered online the most garish vibrator she could find, a kind of a dildo, if you will. She winced at the word "dildo."

"Of course, I'm still getting familiar with his work," said Ben, chuckling apologetically. He smoothed his shirt and began talking more rapidly and assertively about the filmmaker's importance. Craig hadn't told Ben how old Moddie was, but she looked about thirty, maybe even twenty-nine. She was pretty okay looking. From certain angles. Craig said very intelligent. She could be anywhere up to forty. "No one has ever done anything like this in film, before or since," he said.

Moddie nodded and said, "Mmm," completely disagreeing with what he'd just said.

"N-not that I'm a film scholar," he demurred. "I'm more interested in business and science."

The dildo had some kind of psychedelic theme to it, you can imagine, and it had many confounding protrusions. It was a Day-Glo color similar to some of the rubber grips she used to get for her pencils in grade school. In fact, the whole contraption was disturbingly childish, and she'd wavered for a second, feeling the need to glance side to side before ordering, to make sure no one was watching, but the only person watching was her, not that that helped, because as everyone knows we are our own harshest critics.

"Uh-huh," said Moddie.

Of course she felt uncomfortable about how closely femininity was tied to childishness, exemplified in its extreme by this device, which had smiley faces and baby animals on it, but which was meant to be inserted into the adult vaginal canal for sexual stimulation. Kind of condescending, maybe, unless that was your thing, pretending to be a baby, and she meant no judgment on anyone's fetish. She'd looked at others, but most of them had a corporate, late-nineties Apple look—Scandinavian (probably?) and emphasizing the medical grades of their materials, the technological aspects, the R & D, which struck Moddie as a little too far in the direction of corporatized femininity, like she would take masturbation (even that word made her blush with embarrassment) very seriously, very professionally, another facet of herself to be conquered and forced into submission.

"Yeah, Ben, we all saw that shit out at Celebration Cinema," said Craig. "That and the motherfuckin' *Matriiiix*," he added, with the drawn-out enthusiasm of a sports announcer. Craig had grown up a few miles over in the slightly less sophisticated town—its center being the shopping mall rather than the university.

Nina was looking down and texting and said, "Celebration Cinema!"

Nina and Craig high-fived.

A businesswoman's vibrator.

At this, she laughed, and Ben laughed too.

She was just making changes, acting and then reacting, like Rothko, make a mark and react to it, an organic approach to life, push-pull. Was push-pull Rothko? No, it was German. Hofmann, that's right, Hofmann. Rothko wasn't German? No, maybe Russian or something, but the name didn't sound Russian. Push, pull, blah, blah—when she thought these words, she blushed again, from clavicle to chin, thinking of course of humping and hand jobs and Russians. She wanted a cigarette, just so she could put it out on her face, and then maybe burst into flames, and then maybe her corpse would disappear— poof!—and all of this nonsense would finally be over.

Ordering the vibrator made her feel like a prude. But she wasn't a prude. Nick was wrong, she wasn't a prude at all. She just didn't think anyone should ever have sex. She just thought that any time anybody had sex it started a long chain reaction of gross, stupid things, and that people who had sex were in some way deeply immoral and probably dangerous and should be executed by firing squad in the town commons by a team of masked, randomly chosen villagers.

"So, what do you do?" asked Ben.

Moddie let out a series of incoherent words and noises, not wanting to go into it, stuttering, hearing the silent scream rise again, and Ben nodded and said, "Craig tells me you're coming from Chicago, that must have been pretty cool."

"Chicago was a vast impoverished hell from which I recently made haste to escape."

When the Day-Glo, vibrating, child-themed dildo arrived, Moddie took it out of its strangely bootleg-looking packaging. She hadn't noticed online that it had a suction cup on the bottom of it. She sat on the floor by the couch and looked at her sex machine. She slammed it against the wall, where it stayed for a moment, wobbled, then fell.

Craig had no idea what might make two people attractive to each other, but he'd gotten it into his head that Moddie would like to have sex with a younger man. At coffee, she'd described herself as a "closeted gay man from the 1950s" because she had to get near blackout drunk to admit she was sexually attracted to men and if she ever made a pass at one, she felt horrible to the point of violent tears after, which had made Craig giggle while Pam gave him a stern look. It was good to have someone new around. Lighten things up. Craig liked Moddie and wanted to help her out. Do her a solid, as it were. Ben had an idiotic puppyish quality that Craig assumed might be attractive to an older homosexual gentleman. A bit of a twink, if that was still an acceptable term. Craig approvingly ran his eyes over Ben and his well-fitted outfit, feeling proud of this pairing. Ben responded to authority, so Craig had been pumping Moddie up as a well-connected cosmopolitan.

Craig watched them talk for a moment, imagined them having sex, and then his eyes scanned the room for the face and body of his appealing Bulgarian intern, Petra, with whom he'd recently struck up a bit of a rapport.

"I love Chicago," Ben sighed. "It's such a livable city if you're being practical about things, especially as an academic or someone interested in the arts."

Moddie finished her sangria and started chewing on the ice while she sank into a thousand-yard stare.

"Are you interested in the arts?" asked Ben.

"Oh yeah, I am," slowly, "interested in the arts."

A microphone squeaked, and all attention turned to the

podium, where Pam stood with note cards in her hands. She began her speech with a reverberating throat-clear.

"I think that's wonderful. I'm pretty interested in the arts as well," whispered Ben. "I really like the Museum of Modern Art of Chicago," he continued quietly.

"The MCA?" said Moddie, whispering.

"Yeah, the Chicago MoMA."

Moddie flinched.

"And I've been to the other one, too," said Ben, in his softest voice. "Just great."

Moddie thought about a show she'd seen there a few years ago where the curator had installed constantly looping music that made Moddie feel like she was in a Zatarain's commercial. She stopped herself from saying *Yes, it's been voted Travelocity's Best Museum three years in a row.*

She felt sad thinking of all the things that used to bring her pleasure and how now they just made her want to scream and die.

Pam started to introduce David, who Moddie hadn't really taken note of yet. Moddie had assumed he was a talentless sycophant whose name would surely fade with the passing of time, so she hadn't bothered to google him or ask Pam any questions about him, fearing the tedious conversation that might have—surely would have—followed ("Oh, wow, how exciting!").

"I hear this guy is intelligent," whispered Ben. "Invented a whole new kind of art."

"Hm," said Moddie skeptically, for this could not have happened without her hearing about it, the invention of a whole new kind of art.

While Pam incompetently rattled off a string of David's accolades, her voice trembling as she studiously glanced up from her note cards at metered intervals, David raised his eyebrows and looked at the floor, almost like it disgusted him to hear these things spoken aloud. He was the only man in the room who didn't vaguely resemble Tucker Carlson.

"I'd like another sangria," said Moddie, to no one.

David approached the microphone. He talked casually, showed a few slides, and when he got to the meat of his presentation—something about the stress hormone cortisol—Nina pushed at Moddie's arm very slowly and whispered, "This is the kind of shit you like, right?"

"I can't even tell what the fuck he's talking about," said Moddie.

When he finished his talk, David smiled with blatant disappointment, raised his eyebrows, and said, "Well, that's about it, thanks."

A couple people clapped, and someone turned some of the lights back on.

"He thinks we're hicks," said Craig, clapping.

Pam liked to say that David Winterbottom was an "artist's artist." What that really meant was, even though he was in no way famous, some of his friends were. One of his friends had even been on a talk show. She had plans about what it would mean for him to be there. The intellectual discussions they might have, and where those discussions might lead, either to a profound personal and spiritual growth, or to an expansion of community. They could discuss the complex nature of art, love, and loss, and then maybe he could give her his friends' emails.

It wasn't technically a divorce, since David and Aurelie had not been legally married, but they'd been together for seventeen years, so they were common-law married, he assumed. His ex was a well-liked dancer and "photographer." Despite what David said in his secret diaries, she had aged incredibly well, and was in fact incredibly beautiful, maybe the most beautiful woman he would ever get to have penetrative sex with. Everybody loved her. It hadn't come to this, but if there had been any kind of official division of friends as assets in the divorce, he knew things wouldn't have shaken out in his favor. Not a lot of his friends were talking to him these days. He had no idea what she'd been telling them. He was a scumbag. He yelled at her all the time. There was some part of him ("There was some part of him") that liked watching her cry (he liked watching her cry). It made him feel stable to know that some things were predictable, and in his diary he called her Old Faithful and also sometimes just for fun Old Yeller, from a sex thing.

He liked the crying more and more and for different reasons as the years went on. Once she really started pushing forty (thirty-six), it was like all of the hydration went out of her face during these crying jags, and she looked, no other word for it, dry—she really looked hideous. In these moments, it started to feel ridiculous that he'd ever felt sexually or physically intimidated by her. He'd watch her cry on the edge of the bed until he got bored, and then he'd go to the bathroom and look at himself in the mirror.

Not too fucking shabby! He was getting more and more attractive with each year. He'd been gawky in his twenties—one unkind woman had said he looked like if Ichabod Crane were in a Green Day cover band—but at forty-two, he looked excellent.

He was a little fat from drinking, he had a receding and graying hairline, dark circles under his eyes, a sharp upright line between his eyebrows, strange, random long hairs coming out of his eyebrows and nose, but it all added up to make him look sort of masculine and commanding in a way he'd never looked before. In the bathroom, he placed one hand on his chest and one on the top of his stomach, spread his fingers wide, turned, and examined himself from all angles. Even the button-up shirt he'd been wearing for ten years looked better now. Old Navy. A good lesson in patience.

Part of his unspoken but very likely mutually understood bargain with Aurelie when they'd gotten together when they were twenty-three and twenty-six was that he could have sex with her, use her to raise his social value, have her take care of decorating the house and setting up a social calendar and hosting parties, as long as he would remain single-mindedly devoted to her on a romantic level. Aurelie had intense insecurities stemming from childhood, something about a babysitter, and she could sometimes become so emotionally weak that all she could do was sob and repeat random, confusing apologies while calling herself a bad person, worthless trash, and saying she wanted to die. During these episodes, according to their agreement, David was supposed to rub her on the shoulders and say something like "Nooo, you're smart and good and everyone likes you." One might assume this would be easy.

But he didn't like the implication that he had to do this because she was above him. In some ways, it made him feel like the help rather than the man. He knew he was sort of dopey, but that didn't mean he wasn't the man, with the needs and feelings of a man.

Right around thirty-five, when his face started to harden, he began to notice women in their twenties (and thirties and forties) noticing him. Parties and openings and residencies became a buffet of youth—women he would have blown his brains out for in his twenties, who never would have paid any attention to him, were now leaning particularly close to look at something on his phone, clinging to his elbow, asking him about his childhood and for his opinion on whatever dumb shit they'd been thinking about recently. It was fantastic. Especially fantastic if he got to say "I'm so flattered, but I have a girlfriend" and then tell Aurelie about it, which would make her cry, and he would get to look at her wrecked face, then go into the bathroom and admire himself, then come back out and say, "I don't understand what you're so upset about, I said no. I always say no."

Well, whatever, evil lurks in the heart of man, etc., blah blah.

It was, again, Pam's great good fortune.

David didn't know what the hell he would do in this town. He knew he could probably have sex with the students, since some of them—just like some of them back home—had the impression he had somehow "invented" New Media.

He wasn't quick to disabuse anyone of this idea, but he wasn't totally sure how this impression got started. Uncharitably, he assumed it had something to do with the fact that most young women had no fucking idea about art or art history, and weren't even sure what New Media was, and, further, apparently weren't even clear on how to use Google.

When he'd started sleeping with Kelsey, she had a lot of confused ideas about what the terms "postmodern," "minimalist," and "maximalist" meant, even though she was trying to run an online literary journal for her friends' pretentious and self-involved and ultimately pretty humiliating prose poems that they would no doubt ultimately regret making public. She didn't seem to care that, in a literary sense, postmodernism and maximalism were specific movements, with specific writers and aesthetics attached to the terms. You couldn't just say these words and manifest new meaning.

Kelsey's literary thoughts all came from some kind of intuitive sense she had about what words meant.

These intuitive senses seemed to be based off of something a summer workshop instructor had said to her in high school. No doubt she'd wanted to fuck this instructor too, and he had unfortunately polluted her mind with half-understood bullshit, and also given her an overinflated sense of her own capacity.

Kelsey was very physically attractive. Blonde, for a change of pace.

David was no expert in literature, but one night, after they'd had sex, Kelsey started in on the postmodernism and maximalism thing again, and she was calling Tolstoy a "maximalist" and David's pulse rose and he felt nauseated and angry and he said, "You actually literally have no idea what you're talking about, Tolstoy was a *realist,* William Gass, who was writing a hundred years later, was a *maximalist.*"

She seemed somehow baffled that he might not think every animal sound coming out of her mouth was a diamond.

"Maximalism is a movement from the late seventies and early eighties that came out of postmodernism. Just because something is long and has a bunch of characters doesn't mean it's *maximalist.* Furthermore, just because something comes chronologically after the modernist movement—which I will assume you are vaguely aware of, you've at the very least heard of Faulkner and Joyce, I hope to god—does not make it postmodern with a capital P. No one calls David Baldacci a postmodern novelist, for example. I'm sorry, are you interested in understanding this?" He asked that because of the way she was looking at him. He said she could go ahead and look it up, and that he was willing to hear what she was saying about all of this if it was factually correct.

She looked it up on her phone and said, "It says maximalism is with a lot of characters. . . ."

"Really? Is that really what it says? Let me look it up." And he looked it up and saw something entirely different, something that 100 percent backed up what he was saying (the Wikipedia page where he'd gotten the information in the first place), and then he said, "I don't really understand why you would just outright lie to me about what you'd read just now. If you want to have a real conversation, this is what it's like. If you want me to treat you like a child and say 'oh that's cool' to everything you say, I can definitely do that, but if you want to have a real conversation with me where you don't just lie and make stuff up, I'm open to that, actually I would prefer that." And of course Kelsey started to get upset, and started to pout, and tried to change the conversation to the emotional realm, where she felt more comfortable, because all women did was sit around talking about their feelings, which was how they got into this argument in the first place—because Kelsey was saying shit about Tolstoy based solely on her feelings, rather than on facts, so David just didn't really know what else he could say to her. He certainly wasn't sorry. This was what you got if you wanted to have a real discussion. He said, "I'm just trying to have a discussion."

Kelsey said something about how she thought she preferred Virginia Woolf and David said, "Okay, good, that's great, can you tell me why? Would you like to explain to me what it is you like so much about her?" But Kelsey just couldn't do it.

Which is all just to say that when he thought unkind things about women, it wasn't without reason.

Pam was leaning in close to him, quietly chattering about something and leading him toward somewhere, and when David understood he would have to go pretend to speak with this woman's husband, this woman's friends, he thought that if he had a choice in the matter, he'd rather eat his own fucking corneas.

When Pam and David got to the circle of friends, Craig, Moddie, and Ben were still clapping.

"Welcome, welcome, Mr. *New York City,*" said Craig.

"Aaaaahhh," said Ben, nodding with deep understanding and speeding up his clapping, New York, of course.

David raised his eyebrows and said, "Yeah, actually, I'm not from New York, I'm from—"

"New York City, wonderful city, but not really practical, don't you think? If you're thinking about things like quality of life, it's not really a livable city in terms of real estate and the proverbial price of milk, as it were," said Ben, throwing an expectant glance at Moddie.

David opened his mouth as if to speak, but Moddie said, loudly, feeling possessed by something aggressive, "If you want to live somewhere with a good bottom line, nothing beats our town here."

"Well, I'm . . ." said David.

"I was just telling David what a wonderful talk that was, and how excited we are to have him here with us," said Pam.

A stiff hush fell over the group. Everyone took a moment to admire the architecture.

Lost in her angry reveries, Moddie drank from her new, full sangria and said, "Well, tell us a story about the world, *Mi*ster Winterbottom."

"Uh," said David.

"She's just goofing around," said Pam.

"No she's not," said Craig. "We want to know all about the new man in town. Don't be rude, Pam."

"I'll tell you something," said Nina.

"You guys can actually just call me David."

Moddie laughed.

"One time, I had a student who, whenever I asked her a question, would repeat what the last student said verbatim. She would look me dead in the eye, repeat what the last student said, even if it was irrelevant to what I'd asked her, and I would just stand there like *duuuuuhh,* and then move on without acknowledging what just happened."

"Do you think she's a reptilian who had you in a momentary hypnotic trance?" asked Moddie.

"Yeah," said Nina.

"Anyway," said Pam. "We're so excited to have you here. The students are great, that might just be a onetime Nina thing, I don't know."

Moddie noticed that Pam kept making "sardonic" faces, as if Moddie, Nina, and Craig were a source of embarrassment. Moddie laughed through her nostrils, one quick, dismissive jet.

"Yeah, thanks," said David, not sure who he was thanking or why.

"The students are amazing!" said Ben with a hearty enthusiasm.

"To the students!" said Moddie, raising her glass.

David was floating down an emotional lazy river of absolute indifference. Drifting back and away from this conversation, which droned on and on. If he died, where would he go? Would it be wonderful? Would death truly be the ultimate orgasm?

This could actually be a great opportunity for him, if he thought about it. All the time you saw bios of famous artists saying they'd done their most important work in some place you'd never heard of. He'd made the impossible journey from complete obscurity to the ground floor of public discourse, and now just one last big push.

He thought about it more, how this might be good for him.

"Well, tell us something," said Craig.

"Uh," said David. "I'm reading a book about traffic law."

Across the room, Kimberly stood with Bethany and Chrissy. She looked over at Pam, who was talking to the honored artist and to the disgruntled woman who had called Kim an anti-intellectual pedophile-enabling white supremacist at Beth's party.

Maybe some people would think she was holding on to anger by even remembering this event, but it wasn't so much anger as it was concern for Pam, as it seemed likely that association with this woman might reflect poorly on Pam as she tried to launch her career as an arts organizer.

She knew Pam needed tonight to be a success. Like most people, Pam confided in her. Kimberly was kind and supportive and a good listener, and people came to her with their problems quite naturally. It had always been this way. She was good at listening and good at understanding things from multiple angles, probably because her mother was a therapist.

Her eyes narrowed on Craig, who she'd always thought looked like a loaf of bread. She imagined it might be hard to be in a committed romantic relationship with Pam because of her pathologically warped expectations, which Kimberly knew could put a ton of strain on a romantic partnership, because it was always difficult to foster intimacy with someone who didn't see the world clearly. For example, it just really didn't seem like if your goal was to start your own gallery and residency for internationally acclaimed artists (and Pam had confided in Kim that it was) you could really do it from here. It was a nice idea, but it definitely seemed like you would have to at least be in a major city, or spend a lot of time in Berlin or something, to accomplish that goal, rather than being a homebody administrator at a relatively straitlaced small-town college known for its cow farming program. It was definitely difficult and a little overwhelming for Kimberly to listen to Pam talk about how she'd always imagined one day she'd do something big, or that her life would, quote, "amount to something."

Pam had recently described an "aversion" to sex with Craig, but there she was, standing right next to him, laughing away. If Pam couldn't even break up with Craig, Kimberly didn't think she'd have much career success. She didn't mean any judgment toward Pam, she was just judging the facts, and she did think that if a person routinely behaved in cowardly ways, they did relinquish their right to complain and muse about how things could be, ought to be, or might have been. If Pam chose to remain fearful, the best she could hope for would be to have children with a man she had tepid feelings for in a town and in a job she had tepid feelings for while she sat around and waited to die. Kimberly put her long pale finger into the Solo cup of sangria and removed a bloated apple slice.

Kimberly's aversion was to weakness.

Chrissy began to describe a book Kimberly had suggested she read, responding to it in the way Kimberly had suggested she respond.

"Did you put it up on Goodreads yet?" asked Kimberly. "You have to encourage me to keep logging."

She looked down absently and her eyes fell on the snack

plate in Chrissy's hand, which bobbed up and down as Chrissy forced a laugh and said, "Ugh, I know, it's so hard to find the time," jostling the cookie deeper and deeper into the hummus as she spoke.

But if Pam could prove Kimberly wrong—and Kimberly would love to be proven wrong—the implications would be enormous. It would mean that it really was true, that a woman with only a basic education, no PhD, and absolutely no connections to the incredibly exclusive world of high-end fine arts could just invite these fancy intellectuals who were competing for seats in the canon of eternal memory into their bland town and it would result in the town's learning to "appreciate culture" and the artists' learning to "appreciate the people" and plus would result in Pam becoming famous, the Gertrude Stein of Midwestern state schools, just for writing a couple of emails, which would also prove that the book *The Secret* was real, which would truly be earthshaking, and maybe Pam would even get a Nobel Prize and share a little bit of her glory with her old pal Kim.

Kimberly had begun to grit her teeth, and the whites of her eyes were visible. Bethany commandeered the conversation and said something about the physical appearance of the visiting artist.

Kimberly started laughing gaily. "Bethany Marie, you are *wild*," she said.

"What, he's *sexy*," said Beth, looking over at David Winterbottom, who looked like a man angrily awaiting death.

Kimberly felt sad for Bethany too. Was Bethany's jocular attitude a screen for some deep well of pain? Was her glassy smile indicative of a kind of impotent bitterness toward the world? After the embarrassment of the *Times* piece, it wouldn't surprise. Everyone had gotten together at Panera after the piece was published and confessed they didn't love it. They all had a good, healing laugh and then agreed they should be supportive moving forward. There was probably something in Bethany's marriage, or maybe even in her relationship with her parents, that made her so nakedly desperate for attention—nakedly desperate enough to want to publish something on the national stage that was so clearly inconsequential.

"I'm going over," said Bethany.

"Oooooh, look at you," said Kimberly. "Go get what you want, girl." When she spoke, her voice was a tight mockery of affection.

It was sad to think of Bethany's view of herself as a pillar of the community. Kimberly furrowed her brow and laughed through her nose while her mind wandered to the other issue surrounding Bethany's party last month. That spring, just before the *Times* piece, Kim and Beth had gotten lunch and talked about how important it was to age intentionally, and part of that was to make sure to host and to keep connecting socially with everyone, so they didn't become withdrawn, stagnant, and isolated. They'd agreed that Kimberly would host the first party, but something came up, and she couldn't do June. Instead of waiting for Kimberly to extend the invitation for the July party, Bethany just went ahead and sent out invitations for her own party, without first consulting Kimberly. When Kimberly received this invitation over email, she was actually speechless—the actual speech centers in her brain broke down. She'd felt a little distant and suspicious of Bethany since then, as if Bethany didn't actually want her friendship, like Bethany could just as easily be friends with anyone else—as if Kimberly were an interchangeable nobody, which, to Kimberly, of course, was laughable.

Kimberly rolled her eyes.

"Anyone coming with?" asked Bethany.

Kimberly looked across the room at Moddie.

"Mmmm, no thanks, I'm all good."

Moddie saw Bethany and her friends talking near the podium, not shy of displaying eye contact. It looked like they were all talking at once. Their faces were contorted. Pleasure? Pain? Who knows. Moddie averted her eyes and thought, I'm not here to engage in things like that.

Bethany started walking over. It looked sort of like she was skipping.

"Where is your boyfriend, Nina," said Craig. "We've hardly seen him all summer. I'm starting to feel like he doesn't like us."

"He wants nothing to do with you," said Nina as if it were a joke.

"It's a growing club," said Craig, reaching over and putting his hand on Pam's shoulder and massaging it for a minute before he started laughing hysterically. Pam maneuvered out of his grip and laughed awkwardly.

Moddie started having a lot of anxious and negative thoughts. No one else was talking.

"Yeah, my last relationship was pretty kinky in the beginning, actually," she said, abruptly.

Pam said, "Okay, Moddie," in a *that's enough* voice, and Craig said, "Go on," while making a winding, coaxing gesture with his right hand.

"Yeah, we would do this hard-core twenty-four-seven immersive role-play thing where I pretended to be an attractive but mentally unstable young woman and he would pretend he was really into me and couldn't wait to have sex with me in both missionary and doggy styles." Moddie pulled a deadpan expression and held her entire body rigid, waiting for the next response.

"Lovely," said David.

Bethany arrived and embraced Pam and said how much she'd enjoyed the presentation. "Simply fascinating," she said.

"Thank you so much for coming," said Pam.

"Well of course, it would be strange if I didn't," said Bethany, in reference to herself as department head, the woman who controlled the funds, the woman in whose honor, partly, this night had been held.

David stood there, watching them embrace and talk about how well the presentation had gone.

Moddie looked over at Nina, who was texting again, then back up to Pam, who was talking to Bethany while gesturing at David, and then over to Ben and Craig, who were talking about science. Well here she was, socializing at last. Eventually there was another of those natural silences, during which Moddie asked, after a healthy beat, "If you could have three wishes granted to you by a magical genie, pray tell, what would they be?"

"Moddie," said Pam.

Craig said he wanted a snowblower.

Moddie nodded. Good, good, and, and.

"I'd also like a good angle on the stock market," he added.

David looked around the group and laughed in a wet, disbelieving way that sounded like a dog sneezing.

Moddie looked at him and narrowed her eyes.

"And for my third wish," said Craig.

Nina interrupted to say she would reverse climate change and use the remaining two for sex ones.

"Oh, you've got to have a sex one," said Craig.

Ben looked slightly distressed. Because of where he stood in the circle, by rights it should be his turn next. It seemed like everyone was looking at him and then quickly glancing away, like they already knew he was going to say something stupid, like maybe he'd blow his wish on knowing what other cool movies he should watch. You can just ask that, you don't have to wish that, that's so stupid. Ben began to sweat while Craig contemplatively rubbed what he referred to as his beard.

"This is a tough one," said Ben.

Moddie held up her hand and started counting off on her fingers. "The ability to haunt the dreams of all those who have wronged me, lifelong good health, both physical and mental."

She paused for a moment.

"And for my final, *sexual* wish," she continued, looking over at Nina, "I wish that the 2017 live-action remake of *Beauty and the Beast* had featured a fifteen-minute hard-core unsimulated sex scene between Belle and the Beast, but the rest of the movie was exactly the same."

Nina nodded approvingly.

"And that this was something that nobody talked about, it wasn't mentioned in any of the reviews, there was no comment, no think piece, it was just quietly accepted but never talked about."

Ben opened his mouth and breathed in, ready to wish away the ravages of the climate crisis.

"Or maybe that Neville Longbottom had a revenge-porn fetish," said Moddie, "and it was a major subplot in those books, and some of the scenes of him masturbating to his videos were so convincingly and passionately written they'd make you aroused against your will, but everything else about the books was exactly the same, and when people talked about those revenge-porn scenes it was like it was universally accepted as a brave political and artistic choice."

"These are pretty weird wishes, Moddie," said Pam.

Bethany laughed and clapped, apparently gleeful.

David laughed like *What the fuck am I doing here?*

Pam looked up at him and smiled apologetically.

Nina hated those books above most other things and had since middle school. "Yes, what *grand* wizards they all are," she said, and then went on her usual rant about the racial politics, and the obvious stuff about the "sorting hat" and "how cool it was" that this we-must-eliminate-the-evildoers smorgasbord was what got the *whoooole* globe amped about reading again—*an international phenomenon*! He who must not be named! Is it bin Laden, is it Hitler, is it Trump? Do you hate him? Is there something sexy about it? Take your pick! I won't tell. *Tee-hee!* "And it's just like *so* brave to use a bookish white girl to represent the most despised racial group in the book, I bet this fits tidily into your fucking women's studies thesis."

"Woman is the muggle of the world," said Pam casually, smiling at David, lifting her cup, and laughing awkwardly.

Everyone was quiet for a second.

Craig cleared his throat and drank some more sangria.

"I like Emma Watson," said Bethany in a happy tone. She put an orange slice in her mouth. "She's talented and absolutely gorgeous."

One of Pam's young employees started to mess with the speaker system. That upbeat Feist song played from the beginning a few times at widely ranging volumes.

Everyone turned to the guest of honor.

"What are your magical wishes, David?" asked Nina.

"I'm good, thanks," said David, trying to laugh it off, but everybody was staring at him, cocking their heads slightly like velociraptors. "Okay, fine," he said, and then he choked, unable to think of something cool and funny to say, so he had to immediately switch gears into being completely sincere. He put his chin in his hand and thought.

"The ability to manifest a suitable work or living space anywhere any time I want with no repercussions for anyone. The ability to call upon my creativity at any moment. And the ability to make myself an empty, selfless vessel through which the divine transformative powers of art can be channeled."

"Uh, okay."

A few people laughed.

"Oh, that's cool," said Ben, "they're all kind of the same thing. I didn't know you could do that."

"You don't want a snowblower?" said Craig.

"What's your sex one?" asked Nina.

"What's *your* sex one," he said back, a little loudly.

"My sex ones are my secrets," said Nina. "Every beautiful woman has a secret."

"I've got sex ones to spare," said Moddie, and David looked at her.

Two men passed by on their way to the bathroom and one of them said, "No, she's just being a cunt, you don't have to enroll this early in any pre-K program, that's so fucking stupid."

Nina raised her hands, palms up, arms out, and she began to speak in a chanting manner. "You can see into the hearts and minds of men by way of their wishes, for we should all be careful what we wish for, yea verily." She moved her fingers in an eerie way. "I hereby grant your wishes," she said, glancing around the group while moonlight streamed in through the big windows. "I truly hope you have chosen wisely."

For a second there was something unnerving about this to David, as he realized he was surrounded by strangers and living in a strange place, with no one to come and help him, but then he remembered he really just thought this was stupid.

"So," said Ben to David, reaching across the conversation circle to pat him jovially on the arm. "I think it's really cool how interested in art you are, man. That's solid."

Over the next hour, everyone had a few more drinks and loosened up a little, and despite everyone's best efforts, a bit of mild camaraderie began to form. David even laughed a few times and told a joke. Ben was trying to get his opinion on the filmmaker, and David kept making equivocating gestures and asking Ben if he'd seen *Nashville*.

Even Moddie was hesitantly enjoying herself, watching Pam and Nina as they discussed work-related frustrations.

"Oh, Jesus, here she comes," said Pam. "Sorry, Nina."

Bethany took a swill of sangria and said, "Ah, yes, this old *slag*."

"You know, it's actually totally fine," said Nina.

"What?" said Moddie.

Pam jerked her head in the direction of a woman who was approaching them and mouthed, "Chipper."

"Ooohhh," said Moddie.

Moddie had learned about Chipper during one of her two solo hangouts with Nina over the past month and a half—a hangout that she treasured as a rarity and a throwback.

Apparently, Chipper Jordan was a woman who, according to Nina's boyfriend, "no women liked," which, according to Nina, was not entirely comforting. Nina first met Chipper at a coffee shop on the ground floor of a parking garage. Chipper didn't make any kind of eye contact with Nina or even say hello, instead she locked in on Tony and spoke to him intensely in a breathy way about a long-standing email thread between them about poetry, life, and emotions, touched his arm twice, and pointed out, dolefully, that he had a "little rip" near his shirt collar. During all of this, she edged over slightly until she was standing directly in front of Nina, "like in a De Palma movie," she'd said to Moddie as they drove aimlessly last week, "where one guy is standing in front of the killer, and you can only subtly kind of see the killer's earlobe or a little hair or something."

"You mean like *Raising Cain*?"

Moddie put on her turn signal.

"Yeah," said Nina. "So picture her quoting an email from Tony and then she laughs and is like, 'Oops, I dropped something!' and when she bends down, I'm standing there with a psychotic expression staring straight into the lens."

"Cut to black," said Moddie.

Nina tried to let it go, but she was like a paranoid schizophrenic, putting the pieces together, unearthing the conspiracy. Chipper was the friend who Tony had seen doing Bob Dylan covers at the open mic downtown. Chipper was who he went on the river bike trip with. Oh, Chipper was this, Chipper was that. Chipper was who he was on the phone with whenever he got up and left the room, speaking gently and very carefully, as if to an invalid. "I'd always thought it was his grandma."

Moddie laughed and pulled into the Meijer parking lot.

"'Hey, how *are* you?'" said Nina in an embarrassing mannish whisper. "And then he comes back into the living room and tells me not to be jealous, which is insane, it's not that I think he's going to fuck her while we're together—obviously I have eyes and a brain, I can tell the difference between the two of us—it's more that I'm like considering if I want to continue to develop intimacy with a guy who is so easily taken in by this Fleshlight–meets–Tiny Tim routine, because honestly I find it repulsive, and I've already made peace with dying alone on my dog ranch, so if he can't get it together I'm of half a mind to just kick him out of my apartment, which he's not even on the lease of, and which I can absolutely afford on my own. It's not like I'm dependent on him. I'm hardly fighting for my food source when I bring up Chipper." She packed the bowl with strong weed and they each took one big hit, then another.

"Fuck, let's get this bitch," said Moddie, who was excited to hear about Tony's flaws and Nina's dissatisfaction with her relationship, as if the whole dog ranch idea might have been approaching more quickly than she ever could have dreamed.

Nina recounted more things Tony had told her about Chipper and then said, "I mean, what the fuck?"

"Can I tend the rabbits on your dog ranch?"

"No . . ." said Nina. She closed her eyes. "It's not that bad yet, it's fine."

Moddie blew out smoke and sang an impressively accurate impersonation of the most passionate part of Marvin Gaye's "Trouble Man" at the top of her lungs and then started laughing.

They got out of the car and walked toward the Meijer doors. Nina had gotten into Tony's phone and read some of Chipper's text messages ("Let he among us" etc.), which she promptly memorized and texted to Moddie, who recited her favorite one in a trilling Edna St. Vincent Millay voice as the doors opened and closed around them in the vestibule of Meijer—"In this morning's readings of Rumi, I found a most ponderous passage—truth surrounds us! As does love." Moddie held out her arms and gestured at the grocery carts, the coin-operated pony ride, and the extra-large gumball machine.

"People are so fucking humiliating," said Nina.

They walked.

It had been a few years since they were together in the Meijer, and their return felt grand and fated. Moddie handed Nina a Very Cherry Jelly Belly scented candle and Nina closed her eyes and huffed.

"It just makes me feel like my closeness with Tony is cut in half. If I feel one hundred percent sure I'm not going to break up with him and he gets a text from Chipper, or her name comes up in any way, I immediately drop to fifty percent sure, and once it's forty-nine percent, that's when I do it, that's when I'm gone," said Nina. She snapped her fingers.

Moddie took the candle from Nina and switched it for a new one.

"She's like *House of Mirth*," said Moddie.

Nina's vision went red around the edges, red framing the Ocean Breeze Yankee Candle. Her stomach plummeted and she lost touch with the feeling in her limbs.

"I love that book," she said.

"No no, me too. I love punishment," said Moddie, "because I'm such a bad, bad, guilty girl, and I deserve to pay for what I've done, et cetera, but Lily is a fucking cunt." She picked up a candle that was supposed to smell like a Douglas fir and considered this again.

"No, she is a fuuuuuhhhhcking cunt. She's Queen fucking Cunt." Moddie was using her outdoor voice and some shoppers took note. "Her whole deal is that she just runs around this group of couples, flirting with the men and taking money from them, while being super fucking haughty and fakey with all of the women—like, 'Oh, your married life is so fucking bleak, blah blah blah, I'm the jewel of the whites, I shall wait until I'm ready,' thinking that she's fucking hot shit, vulnerable, pretty, better than everyone else, and once her whole idea of being loaded fades away because her aunt or whatever is cutting her out of the will, I don't remember, she gets like fixated on marrying some aloof artist who's clearly not even half-in, because what, then she'll have clout or something? It's actually fucking stupid."

They started walking, arm in arm, toward a large gazebo made of Doritos.

"I get the feeling Edith Wharton didn't like Lily, like I'm imagining you writing a novel from Chipper's perspective, but then you slowly start to identify with Chipper, so you get to use Chipper to mock your friends, but you also get to do something sadistic to her in the end. Like, no shit Edith Wharton was getting off in her castle writing about Lily working in that hat shop, I mean, no homo," she said, enjoying the comforts of old friendship, "but I was definitely getting off on that, too."

Moddie had to stop for a second because she was feeling a little high and she couldn't remember if she actually had a personality or opinions or if she was just a vessel through which bullshit passed. A woman whose style resembled the worst and most punitive type of all third-grade teachers walked by and frowned.

"And another thing!" Moddie mock-shouted. "But no, seriously," she continued quietly, "that book is fucked. In your mind recast Simon Rosedale as young Jeff Goldblum rather than middle-aged Anthony LaPaglia because then you also have this asshole doing all of this look-at-me-look-at-me bullshit, but she basically commits suicide so she doesn't have to have sex with a *Jewish guy*." Moddie whispered this, in case the walls had ears or something. "So, if you picture it. You're like our age, well okay younger actually, and Jeff Goldblum is like, 'All of your friends are cunts, your wishy-washy boyfriend is a tool and a fuckface, I just bought his apartment, I'm his fucking landlord, I'm fucking loaded, baby, let's shake things up'—and Lily is like, 'Actually I want to go cry and commit suicide over Eric Stoltz.' I mean, this is a thing of madness!" said Moddie, that last part kind of loud again.

"I fucking love this book. But I do not remember that part," said Nina, remembering an early erotic experience watching *Earth Girls Are Easy* on VHS.

"I know, I fucking love this book. I mean, I'm certainly misremembering or misinterpreting—maybe Edith Wharton and I have the same idea about things, and I'm doing that thing where my little cousin was like, 'I don't like *The Social Network* because Mark Zuckerberg seems mean,' like no duh, Jill, that's the point of the movie, but I don't know, because Victorian people were stone-cold psycho."

Nina reflected on the insanity of Victorians as she stared at a rack of children's T-shirts. One of them said "Mama's little psycho" and had a sloth on it, smiling back at her like a cozy pervert.

"I haven't read it in forever, so I know I'm messing up some parts, so don't quote me, and I also have a huge history of lying and making things up just because they feel true, but all those wealthy Victorians were basically weird torture people who were really into eugenics and vivisection and creating mutants and the idea that white Anglo-Christians were the only *people*-people, so they didn't have to feel so guilty about all of the shit they were doing and benefiting from. Totally anti-Semitic, really not crazy for Asians, totally pretty much sure that Black people weren't actually people, but some kind of like fascinating animal hybrid—I'm pretty sure *The Island of Doctor Moreau* wasn't too far from what these nutjobs were actually trying, and it's really easy to imagine Wells being like, 'Well, it's a complex issue, actually, I don't mean to necessarily condemn making weird little cut-up animal people.' And all of this shit was the talk of the town, like in the same way everyone is kind of thinking about global warming and police brutality right now, so it begs the question, like . . . was Lily Bart passively psyched about eugenics and mutants?"

"Fuck, probably," said Nina. "Yeah, that does change things."

Moddie and Nina were by then stoned out of their minds. When Moddie got too high she had a hard time telling if she was peeing or not.

"Oh my god, that really fucking changes things," said Nina as her eyes scanned the lingerie and, behind it, the basketballs. "Everything is starting to make sense."

"The thing for Lily was the power, she had no capacity for love," said Moddie in a quiet authoritative voice that sank Nina deeper into her gothic reverie.

"Holy shit."

Moddie kept whispering crazy things about mutants and the foundations of culture while they looked at hamsters in terrariums near the bulk cereal, and Nina said, "I'm picturing that photo of Edith Wharton with the dogs on her shoulders and reimagining her as someone who was into Dr. Moreau-style vivisection and how maybe she was kind of a furry but for mutants and maybe she wanted to be fused with those Pomeranians and fuck a guy who also had dogs fused onto his shoulders." She started laughing but in a psychotic way, like she was about to start weeping. "Oh, god, no, you have to make it stop. Now I'm picturing Tony and Chipper having sex with a bunch of Pomeranians tied to their shoulders."

Moddie confessed she couldn't tell if she was peeing or not. Nina looked at Moddie's crotch and said, "I don't think you're peeing."

They walked for a while, each ate a banana, and regained their composure. A half an hour later, they left the store.

"The reason I like *House of Mirth*," said Moddie in the parking lot, "is not because I think it's a morally pure feminist examination of patriarchal structures, in fact I know Edith Wharton said point-blank she wasn't a feminist. I like it because I'm a fucking masochist with a weak ego, and I love being emotionally manipulated by a master pervert, duh."

"Yeah, duh," said Nina.

"No duh."

"Yeah, no fucking duh," said Nina.

They got into the car and Moddie started the engine.

"My sexuality? Let me tell you," said Moddie, "I read *House of Mirth*, masturbate, and then donate a hundred and fifty dollars to the Anti-Defamation League."

Nina laughed and said, "Jesus Christ."

"No, I don't masturbate to Jesus Christ, that's my aunt Helen."

Nina paused for a second and then said, "People like Chipper with low self-esteem are like little toddlers just smearing their caca all over the walls for attention. She's smearing her shit all over me, all over my friends, and the guys are just a bunch of fucking coprophiliacs, eating it up, and I'm honestly within a fucking inch of my limits."

Moddie nodded solemnly and said, "Live like a bitch, die like a bitch."

"Fucking truly," said Nina.

With this in mind, Moddie began her examination of Chipper as she approached their circle. True to form, she didn't acknowledge Pam, Beth, Moddie, or Nina, and instead promptly started breathily whisper-talking to David about some article of his she'd read. Her voice was strained, her words somehow both loud and clear and faraway and throttled. It was like listening to a gas leak. ". . . really interested in your thoughts on concepts of utopias in alternative arts communities and I read an interview with you in [online art journal], where you were just, you were talking about . . ."

David tilted his head to the side and noticed how chilly the group had become.

Moddie had a historical tendency to be overly protective of Nina, sometimes to the point of jealousy, so when she looked over at Nina and saw how rigidly she was holding herself, how uncomfortable she seemed, Moddie couldn't help herself. She took a step forward, held out her hand, and said, "You must be Chipper."

When Chipper took her hand, the first skin-to-skin contact Moddie had had in months, Moddie looked into her eyes and said, smiling, "Your reputation precedes you."

Chipper flinched briefly. Craig made a slight *oh damn* expression. Nina raised her eyebrows.

They released the handshake, and Chipper turned to David and continued to ask him about his presentation. Nina and Pam stood there silently with their arms crossed. Bethany sent an email on her phone.

After about three minutes of this awkward interlude, Chipper gave David her number, offered to show him around, and then left. After she left, David looked over at Craig, who rolled his eyes and shrugged.

Chipper walked through the crowd and imagined everyone was glancing at her, shunning her. Over the summer, she'd invited Tony to the lake house twice, and when he said he couldn't make it, she knew it was because Nina was jealous. Even though she'd grown to expect this, she still felt annoyed, disappointed. There wasn't anything between her and Tony anymore, but there had been at one time, and she liked to honor the bonds with her past. Most of her friends were men, but she'd never made a pass at someone who was taken. What she liked was the secret tie, the feeling of an unspoken possibility. She knew her friends' girlfriends didn't like her. She wasn't clueless.

She walked out into the hall and suddenly felt queasy. The hall was lined with lockers and lit harshly by fluorescents. She leaned against a locker that had a My Chemical Romance sticker on it and grounded herself by entering her Bob Dylan masturbation fantasy, the one where he heard her doing covers at the café and asked her to sit in the corner booth with him and then decided to leave his wife for her.

"I like you better than her."

"R-really? You know, I don't want to get in the way of any—"

"It's been over for years."

"Because, you know I've always . . ."

And then he wiped away the tear that ran down her cheek with his gentle, legendary fingers.

No one understood her like Bob. Because it was true, she did ache like a woman (vaginally) and break like a little girl (emotionally/intellectually). She was just a thirty-seven-year-old little girl.

"I break like a little girl," she whispered, sticking out her lower lip, trying to coax herself into crying.

She started to feel angry that she and Bob couldn't be together and she stomped her foot over and over, thinking about how she was just a child, pure and empty and ready for Bob. She banged her head gently on the locker, thinking, I break like a little girl, I break like a little girl, and because it felt a little good, she started doing it harder and harder, louder and louder, chanting to herself in a silent scream, I'm a broken [slam] little [slam] girl [slam] an achy [SLAM] LITTLE [SLAM] GIRL [SLAM SLAM SLAM] LITTLE [SLAM] GIRL [SLAM SLAM SLAM SLAM *SLAM SLAM SLAM*].

David finished his sangria and Moddie drank the vaguely Kool-Aid–tasting water from the melted ice cubes in her cup and they watched Nina and Craig talk.

Moddie had no desire to join in, and was aware of standing very close to David, like she was leaning a little toward him, like maybe if she were left to it long enough, she'd end up just smashing her face against his arm and letting out a low monotone sound and then would start humping his leg. She really wanted to go home, but she couldn't make herself do it. Instead of saying "I have to leave," she turned to David and said, "Did you do something at the Renaissance Society a few years ago?" which made her want to shoot herself in the face and let her corpse fall against his large, warm torso.

"Oh yeah, I did. Like nine years ago."

"I thought so—I remember it, my friends and I really liked it."

She shook her head and frowned because she'd lied and said the word "friends."

"Oh, thanks," he said.

David started to get antsy. He was looking around, over Ben's head, toward the exit.

"You know, I'll be right back," he said.
"Shitter's that way," said Craig.
"I'm going to go smoke, actually."

Moddie's eyes went around like a ventriloquist dummy, landing briefly on Nina, who was scowling in an understanding way. "Do you mind if I come with you?" she asked.

"You shouldn't do that, it's a disgusting habit," said Craig.

"No, I don't mind," said David.

"I'm telling your father," said Craig.

"Yeah, but you don't know my dad, Craig," said Moddie as she followed David toward the door.

They walked quickly through the lobby and out the front doors and Moddie said, "This building looks like vagina dentata." David said the name of the architect and Moddie said, "RIP," and David shook his head and laughed and said, "Jesus."

Once they were standing outside, Moddie said, "Sorry, I don't actually have cigarettes, could I bum one?"

"Yeah, but they're menthol."

Moddie opened her mouth.

"I'm just fucking with you."

"Whoa," said Moddie.

David got a cigarette out for Moddie and handed her the lighter. After the first drag, she leaned her head back and said, "Oh, fuck that's good."

"Did you quit?"

Moddie nodded.

"So this is a good one for you."

"Yes it is," said Moddie.

"It's great to have something you want after a long wait."

Moddie curtsied and said, "I thank you for this pleasure," and thought, You have no fucking idea.

Moddie forgot how she'd gotten home and then felt relieved to remember she hadn't driven, Pam had driven, and Nina and Moddie, from the back, had whined about how Pam should let Craig sit in her lap and steer, because he'd been such a good boy all night.

She'd definitely have to round out her interests, start reading heavily again, start watching better movies—what you put into your brain is what forms your brain, everybody knew that.

Everybody knows that!

She thought about how every idea she'd ever had, someone else had already thought it, and then someone else had already thought it was fucking stupid.

She turned on the TV.

A Terrence Malick–style tracking shot followed a little boy wearing a cape made out of a towel as he ran through a dust-mote-dotted atmosphere of warm, angled domestic lighting, knocking into things and jumping onto furniture, while his youthful attractive white mom ran after him, cleaning things with paper towels and putting things in Tupperware and snuggling the boy. The ad was for the Koch brothers and how their products were deeply embedded into every corner of your private life, which was a good thing. It wasn't that she'd *never* liked sex. It was more like it had become kind of complicated and frightening for her and made her feel like she was doing something wrong and was somehow in trouble, and in bracing for the blow of sexual contact, all of her muscles tensed up and she felt like she might vomit.

The show came on. It was about a family of good-looking men solving crimes for the FBI using the power of math. The voiceover in the introduction told the audience to relax because logic was there to solve life's biggest mysteries, and it reminded her of another TV show she sometimes watched late at night about another group of government-employed crime fighters that usually began with a shot of all of the characters flying in a private jet like the Justice League, and one of the characters, usually the one who used to do Broadway, would quote something from history, like "There is nothing to fear but fear itself" or "The only thing I know is that I know nothing."

Well, maybe the men on TV weren't exactly good-looking, except in a saccharine, Care Bearish way.

She was glad she hadn't in any way made her horrid animal feelings toward David known. Everything was still a big secret and she would probably never see him again (even the words "see him again" made her recoil, she theoretically felt more likely to rip the flesh from his bones and keep that flesh in a plastic tub in the basement than to have any soft feelings about "seeing" or "again" or anything), which was her preference, honestly—to never see him again. Never ever ever (she thought this over and over, her eyes glazed and pointed at the TV, never ever ever).

She didn't like the math show that much, but only because she hadn't watched enough of it yet for the Stockholm syndrome to kick in, so she flipped around looking for the private-jet-Socrates-quote show and found it within forty-five seconds.

Moddie had the feeling of being a squirrel trapped in a roof drainage system and all she could do was scramble until she died.

It's not like . . .

Well it wasn't exactly like she really wanted to kill everyone and keep them in sealed plastic tubs in her basement, but maybe life would be less embarrassing if she did, that's all.

She fantasized about breaking up with David a little. He took it like a champ. Didn't care at all. If we get too close, I'll just let you take complete control of my brain like a parasite and you'll use me for whatever until you're bored and then you'll force me to act so horribly that you start threatening to break up with me so many times that eventually I'm forced to break up with you. He got it. He was fine with it.

An image rose in her mind of Nick in ten years, single, shattered, and living back in Tulsa near his family surrounded by all of those terrible Evangelicals. She saw him as a Nick Nolte type, driving a pickup, living on the edge of town, sullenly hiding his broken heart and his troubled past, but that image didn't really seem right, and was quickly replaced by another vision where he was more of a late-stage Depardieu playing a sad, insane mama's boy. She imagined this creature crying and rocking himself to sleep and whispering I'm sorry, I'm sorry, I'm sorry, forgive me, forgive me, forgive me.

I forgive you! she thought, and then felt racked by strong, opinion-altering guilt.

He's going to have a string of unsatisfying failed relationships based on living out this breakup over and over, she thought, and what a horrible thing, to condemn a man to endless hollow searching like that. What she had done was unforgivable, she'd caused him so much pain, the person she loved best out of all people. Nick had been supportive and kind. He trusted her taste, encouraged her, and at first seemed to really adore her. When Moddie started to rant about an idea, back in those early days, Nick would laugh—laugh with delight—then lean back and nod slowly, absorbing her company. Sitting in his living room, warm midafternoon light coming in through his thin orange curtains, dust motes catching in the air, drinking coffee and talking. In those days, she didn't feel she had anywhere else to be, and for Moddie, these were the only days in her life where she had experienced pure contentment.

This is the great love story of my life, she'd thought at the time and many times after, feeling herself letting go and feeling herself and her life move toward him with almost no resistance, as if she were moving toward the inevitable, but now everything was over.

The impulse to call or email Nick was strong, and she worried he was out there alone and in pain.

"I'm such a fucking bitch," she whispered.

She tried to remember what had been so bad about Nick. At that moment, it all seemed like a two-way dynamic between two people who were just doing their best and she was real scum for leaving him, her baby, alone with no one to help him.

She remembered him again in those early days, trying to help her when she couldn't stop crying, always asking her, "Why are you crying?" and she would just sit there, holding her face, confused, underwater, not sure why she was crying, saying, "I don't know, I don't know," while thinking it was because she was bad, so bad, such a fuckup. Oh, what a sweet, good guy. She'd definitely taken too much in the beginning, and set a precedent for an unstable emotional dynamic between them, and then abandoned him in part because of this dynamic, which she herself had created.

She could feel herself lying in bed with him, she could hear the rhythm of his heart, the rise and fall of his breath, as he explained his thoughts on love. Of course, pity was the highest form of love, that's what Nick thought.

Something twisted around in her and made her feel like something was wrong. Usually when something felt wrong, she knew she was on the right track. For many reasons, Moddie associated self-confidence and happiness with danger. It seemed very clear to her that any time she thought she was at the beginning of something wonderful, it turned out that she was only at the beginning of some massive humiliation, or some kind of terrible disappointment, and any time she felt free and easy, like she was at her best, she was actually at her worst, and the way she'd learned to avoid this was to pin herself in a low-level brooding depression—the devil she knew.

Any time she'd tried to process these feelings in her work, it felt trite. Before they got together, Nick said her work was "kind of funny." Senior year, she'd made a series of Japanese-style woodcuts of her dogs eating poop in the yard, and a collection of offset-printed baseball cards of all of the celebrities and strangers she'd had sexual fantasies about, complete with stats, but Nick didn't think anyone would want to hang the woodcuts and didn't think anyone would really "get" the baseball cards, unless they knew her already, and since she only knew about fifteen people, she probably should have used silkscreen, rather than offset, which was typically for print runs of around a thousand.

After college, she moved away from printmaking and started doing a series of grotesquely exaggerated portraits of their friends, which Nick liked, but when she tried self-portraits, or portraits of people she identified with, he thought there was something a little overtly self-pitying in them. She and Nick had many conversations about what made work good and what made it embarrassing, and in the beginning they had disagreements, but eventually they settled into an agreement. She'd gotten him to embrace a kind of anger in his work that she felt had been buried too deeply, and he cautioned her against making "crazy lady" work, saying that he always found it disappointing and kind of "Okay, and . . ." when a piece ended up just being about a woman's mental health, or a woman being crazy, saying it was just sort of cheap and embarrassing, maybe even sexist, and ultimately not very thought-provoking. "Everybody thinks they're insane, but nobody's actually insane, it's just drama," he said, speaking to her indirectly in the beginning, in the honeymoon phase.

A local commercial came on. God, how she hated people! Their endless quest for dumb shit. Mattresses. How many fucking mattresses can one nation buy? She stood, turned the heat on, and slapped the wall like she meant it.

When she got back to the couch, she said, "Pfff, I actually don't have to ever have sex again if I don't want to," and then made a facial expression that a character from a movie in the nineties might make, like *Get real*.

Sex? Never heard of it.

She imagined herself as incredibly desirable for a second and took pleasure in the thought of withholding herself from the unfit masses.

Nick had called her disgusting a few times, but she hadn't always been disgusting. He had made her disgusting. She started laughing, suddenly enjoying her own company for the first time in a while. He wasn't alone, he was with Gracie.

They were playing the ad again with the box that wanted to be shat in. She wasn't tired, but she was always exhausted. She knew she should try to sleep, but was too agitated, and remembered that she had a pack of cigarettes in the bottom of a suitcase in the closet. She went to the refrigerator and got a beer and then went to the closet, found the cigarettes, and then sat on the back porch, wrapped in a blanket, drinking and smoking for a while. She could see stars. The air was gentle and cool. In her head, she could hear a constant, unbroken scream.

When she finished, she showered, put on pajamas, grabbed a loaf of bread, then got her laptop, a pillow, and a blanket, set herself up on the couch, and started to watch a show she didn't really like but had started watching as a way to prove to herself that she could have some fun and ease in her life, and that she wasn't a snob, but a common, salt-of-the-earth type of person. A relatable, likable civilian.

It was a network comedy. She'd felt virulently opposed to the show back in 2015, for political reasons, and had been drunkenly vocal about it at a party, maybe more than one party, unleashing her opinions in a voluble, bilious way, and further alienating people who already had a low opinion of her.

It turned out that she was in many ways right, which was a comfort, she didn't agree with the politics of the show, but she did understand the show's appeal more now that she spent roughly half of every waking moment praying to become more stupid so that she could bear the crushing tedium and confounding horrors of her life.

Such is the way of the Tao, she thought, and laughed.

Four

Finally, the semester had begun, and with it came the good weather, and the shift from all the summer's strategy into action.

Pam sat in her kitchen, looking out the window. She had recurring intrusive thoughts of a hooded executioner or Klansman whose hood was made out of jute, like something you'd see at Pier 1 or World Market.

Things were not going well with Craig. The intensity and frequency of their fights had increased and they weren't having very much sex at all, but perhaps that was to be expected in any long-term relationship.

Over the past year, Craig had woven in and out of differing opinions on marriage and commitment. Sometimes he would threaten to propose, try out the word "wife," and imagine who might come to their wedding. Other times, he said marriage was the thing that drove the final nail in and made you an automaton, because it meant your freedom was over, and the rest of your life would have to do with working not only for a boss but for a wife and children, and you'd never get to do anything fun or interesting again, and undoubtedly you'd grow to resent your wife and children, but probably especially your wife. Nobody asks to be born.

Sometimes he would call Pam the love of his life, and sometimes he would talk so much about Petra the intern that Pam would just start looking at her phone, thinking about putting a gun to her face. It wasn't that Pam minded Craig being open. She had always valued open discourse. It was that Craig's mind seemed to Pam to be increasingly dull.

Once a week, Pam left the office after lunch. This was when she did her chores. Years ago, she'd stopped asking Craig to help, preferring instead the simmering resentment. He often complained while she cleaned, as if she were behaving in an accusatory way toward him when she brought out the mop from the front hall closet.

Craig had even asked if they could just get a maid. He said they could afford it. He could afford it. He would pay for it himself. Then he said if Pam wanted, she could keep cleaning, and the maid could just be for his half of the chores. Or maybe the maid could come to do a deep clean once a month, and he could take the trash out sometimes and keep an eye on his own things. And then he said, since she was looking at him so intensely, that of course he'd be happy to get a maid to do all of it. He wasn't trying to add work for Pam, he was trying to save some precious hours for himself, hours he needed to recuperate on weekends. The more she kept glaring at him, the more he kept talking, trying to make the case for a maid.

"There is no way in hell we are getting a maid," she said after what she felt was a meaningful pause. To Pam it was unseemly and shameful to hire servants to do what you could easily do yourself, which is what Craig's proposal boiled down to.

"Well, they have to have jobs," said Craig.

"*They?*" said Pam.

"Yeah, Pam, *they*—the maids."

They did not get a maid. These were crucial hours for Pam's sanity where she could be at peace before going back on duty with Craig, listening to his constant ticker tape of observations and criticisms, not saying anything to contribute to the conversation—his speeches were not conversations—because if she ever did say anything to interrupt his constant flood of talking, Craig saw it as an attack, an attack that he enthusiastically countered with pouting, needling, and meanness, so Pam had learned to just sit there, bathe in the flood, because it usually lasted only an hour or two, and it was what they did these days, as a couple, instead of sex.

Pam walked to the living room with the rag and spray cleaner and thought something was deeply off. The arrangement of the furniture was depressing. She moved an armchair, but it only looked worse.

She got out her cell phone and wrote to David, asking him if he'd like to get lunch or tea on Friday after his class to discuss the semester, a request she knew he would be unable to decline for professional reasons.

Craig got home around five-thirty while the light was still out, the windows were still open, and the apartment was fresh from cleaning. Pam was finishing dinner. When she heard Craig walking up the stairs, she went over to her laptop and turned off the show she'd been watching, *It's Me or the Dog*, and put on a playlist of psychedelic world music so as to seem unassailable.

"Fucking cold as shit in here," said Craig, setting his bag down on the chair by the door and taking off his coat and shoes. "Can we close the fucking windows? Jesus."

He walked over to the refrigerator, opened it, and said, "Brrr!" while Pam watched his coat slide from the chair onto the floor directly beneath the jacket and bag hook she'd installed last month. Craig started eating a piece of cheese and looking at his phone. He farted a long, three-tone fart. "Smells like a salad in here," he said. "Did you clean with vinegar again?"

Pam blinked rapidly and asked, "Uh, what are you looking at?"

Craig didn't respond.

She could feel the anger sliding into the driver's seat and she asked him, almost without being aware of the words leaving her mouth, if he was talking to "that dumb cunt Petra."

Craig took his time responding, not looking away from his phone and breathing deeply and slowly, not as if to calm himself, but as if he were already in a state of extreme calm. He looked up indifferently and said in a neutral tone, "No, I was reading an email from that dumb cunt my mother."

Relief filled her, partly. "Ah, yes, the source of all error," she replied.

"She dislocated her toe," said Craig.

"How the fuck did she do that?" asked Pam.

Craig shrugged and shook his head no, set his jaw to the side, not looking at Pam at all, as he walked into the bathroom.

Pam turned up the music for privacy and went into the other room to look at a decorating website on her phone.

When Craig came into the living room he said, "What's for dinner?"

"Enchiladas."

"Cool."

Craig went to sit in the kitchen and Pam followed. She made a salad while Craig talked through the minutiae of his day.

Craig sighed and said, "I wish you wouldn't chew like that, Pamela."

"Like what?"

"You know," he said. "Chomp chomp chomp chomp chomp."

Pam swallowed.

"Anyway, I never learned a goddamn thing in undergrad, grad school was a fucking joke, I'm not learning a goddamn thing at this job, they never let me do anything interesting, and I don't see any way out, so I'm in the fucking cage. It's over, I fucked up. I just walk around all day pretending to be alive. Nobody gives a shit what I do. My life is a fucking prison, just like everybody else's life is a fucking prison. I think you really need to push yourself to read all of the great books by the time you're twenty-three, you just have to learn everything you can by the time you're twenty-seven, because by then, your life is pretty much decided. If I think about learning something new, at this stage in life, all I want to do is laugh in someone's face. Not happening. And, of course, if you didn't push yourself to succeed in your early twenties, which I certainly didn't, by the time you're in your thirties, whoops! You chose what you chose, and life is basically over. I'd do a lot of things differently if I could go back, and then maybe I could have a more interesting life. Maybe I could even have a house in Spain."

Craig put a large handful of chips in his mouth.

Pam's parents had told her, "Whatever relationship you're in, you're going to have the same problems, so you might as well try to figure out how to make this one work."

"I had an interesting day today," said Pam.

Craig raised his eyebrows and his eyelids fluttered and he breathed out, looking punched. His mouth turned down at the corners, and his upper lip curled, as if something revolting had just been said.

Pam put her elbow on the table and rested her head on her hand and sighed. Craig leaned back and crossed his arms and started tapping his foot like he couldn't wait to get it all over with.

"I don't know what to do here," said Pam.

"I don't know what you mean," said Craig impatiently, gesturing with splayed fingers. "I don't know what you mean when you say things like that, with that sort of esoteric and foreboding melodramatic air you take on sometimes."

Pam looked at him, at his face.

"Well, you seem to hate me," said Pam. "That's what I mean when I say I don't know what to do here."

"I was in the middle of a sentence, and you cut me off to say something completely generic and unrelated. It's just rude. I would think you would be able to sympathize with how I feel, since you're always complaining about how I don't listen to you when you talk, and how I'm always 'gaslighting' you. Now I feel gaslit since you don't seem to think you're being rude, and I would just think you could relate to this feeling I'm having right now. Is there some kind of double standard where you're allowed to be rude, and not me?"

Pam held the bridge of her nose and breathed in and out slowly. She pictured herself screaming and slapping him across the face with both hands.

"Oh, come on, don't be so performative," said Craig, holding the bridge of his nose and panting in and out.

"When's the last time you took the trash out?"

"I think this kind of conversation is beneath us."

"Or washed dishes, or did laundry, or went grocery shopping, or made dinner, or gave me a foot rub, or asked me a question about my life? I don't want to be having this conversation either. I find it tedious too you know."

"I get the majority of the Grubhub, I buy you tons of presents, and the rent gets paid out of my account," said Craig.

"But, Craig," said Pam, "the food in this town is not very good. I don't like it when we eat Grubhub because it's going to make me fucking fat. And I don't really know if a new stereo system is necessarily a present just for me. I feel like there's a lot of stuff that goes into living that takes *time*—chores take time. And I'm putting in all this time, but all I get back is sitting here listening to you say how much you hate your life."

"If it takes so much time, Pam, then really, you don't have to worry about it. You know I don't care about chores as much as you do," said Craig in an aggressively upbeat voice.

"I don't think you're totally getting what I'm saying," said Pam. "You are benefiting from this relationship more than I am."

Craig laughed loudly and insincerely.

"I can't handle this anymore," said Pam calmly.

"What can't you handle anymore?" said Craig. "You know, this really feels like an act. Why are you always trying to embarrass me? When I'm with my friends and my coworkers, I never feel embarrassed and ashamed of who I am. Other people make me feel good about myself, and then I come home and you're here glaring at me. What am I supposed to do? I'm trying to tell you my thoughts on things, and you interrupt me to ask me a pointed accusatory question about the garbage? It's just fucking stupid. You have no fucking right to tell me you 'can't handle this anymore' when I can barely breathe in here. You obviously have no respect for me. It's humiliating. It makes me want to fucking die."

"It's hard for me to hear you talk about how much you hate your life," said Pam, "because I thought this was the life we were building together."

"You always do this. It's pretty egotistical, if you think about it. Not everything in my life is about you, and when you make my problems about you, I think it makes it really difficult for you to empathize with me and give me the patience and support I clearly need."

"That doesn't seem right," said Pam, shaking her head slowly and looking into space. "I've been so supportive. I don't know anyone who has been more supportive." She kept shaking her head. "No, that doesn't seem right." Pam started breathing heavily. "I feel like I'm the only one who is trying to do something about our relationship and it's driving me insane."

"Maybe I'm just not in the mood to think about our relationship right now," said Craig.

Pam looked up at him and glared.

Craig started shaking his head briskly and raising and lowering his hands. "I'm not going to let you do this to me." He laughed.

"Are you really not aware that you're refusing to help me with the basic functioning of our lives, and on top of that, you're trying to make me feel bad for asking? And on top of that you're blatantly ambivalent about our relationship?" said Pam. "It's incredible, actually."

"Well, what about every time I try to have sex with you and you start crying? How do you think that makes me feel?"

A sloshing mix of guilt and anger filled Pam's stomach. She felt like she'd been caught. There was nothing she could ask for if she couldn't have sex with him, but Jesus god did she not want to have sex with him. Tears formed in her eyes but inside she felt a strong resistance and did not want to cry. She brought her hands up to her head, squeezed, and made the sound of a teakettle, and Craig said, "Here we go again!" in a jaunty voice. "Ladies and gentlemen of the jury!"

He left the room and started laughing so that Pam could hear. She put her fingers over her eyes and whispered, "Oh my god, get the fuck out of here, get the fuck out of here, I need to go. I have to go. This is no good, no good, go go go."

"What's that in there, Pamela? Muttering to yourself again?" said Craig.

Yes, she was. She whispered, "I fucking hate you so much." All she'd done was ask to be treated more kindly, that was all she'd done, I fucking hate you so much.

They wound down their fight as they always did. These fights had become routine. They stood facing each other making angry "I feel" statements until one of them heard something that sounded like an apology and felt vindicated, softened, and gave a little ground, which led the other person to feel vindicated, which led them to soften, so that Pam and Craig each felt that the other saw themselves as the wrongful aggressor. From there, they each assumed that the other was about to make some fundamental changes to their behavior, but of course they were both mistaken.

This process took several hours.

After, they got ready for bed.

Pam was putting on hand cream, which somehow felt like obtuse stage direction. The side-table lamps were on. Craig was talking about stocks.

"Are you going to get in bed, or are you going to just stand there rubbing your hands together?" he asked.

"Oh, sorry," said Pam. "I was spacing out."

"No, I know you're not interested in any of this, I'll shut up," said Craig.

"No, I'm listening, I'm listening. I'm interested." She turned off the lights and got in bed and spooned Craig, and when he came to a lull in his monologue, Pam counted to three in her head, in case there was a thought he was in the middle of, and then said, "I love you."

David had responded that he'd be "down to meet for tea."

That Friday was a motivating kind of day. Sixties, clear blue sky. The leaves on the trees were beginning to turn. All of the colors were vivid, and the combination of warm sun and cool air did something good to the psyche. It was the kind of day that, in her youth, would have made Moddie feel ambitious and alert—back-to-school weather.

She was on the couch in the clothes she'd fallen asleep in, letting her mind wander. She'd gotten drunk alone again last night.

Once, on a plane, Moddie and Nick had been seated behind a woman with two loud toddlers. Moddie rolled her eyes and sighed melodramatically, thinking again that children should not be allowed on airplanes, in restaurants, or in theaters, and that mothers and children should be kept in a separate society until the child was at least ten. This was a speech she'd given before, and it hung between them unspoken in the way common understandings often hang between old couples. To Moddie's alarm, the mother in front of them began to slap her two toddlers with her large, ringed hands. The children wailed in angry panic, but their cries died down into whimpers, then into calm silence. During this scene, Moddie had wanted to turn to Nick and say *What the hell, are we witnessing a kidnapping?* but before she could, Nick leaned over and said, in a way that seemed completely genuine, "Now, that's how you do it," which had startled her at the time, like she was sitting next to a stranger.

Moddie sat up on the couch. Enough. Today, she was going to properly unpack and arrange her apartment, be more forceful about social plans, and knock off all of this freaky nighttime solo drinking.

She decided to start with the boxes in the closet.

One of the boxes had papers and photos she did not want to see, because of their connection to her past life, but also a few interesting things. She found a printed-out microfiche clipping from a nineteenth-century newspaper about her ancestors, which Nick for some reason wouldn't let her put on the fridge in their old apartment.

She read it over.

Elward Cappell of Chestnut, Wisconsin, suffered injury this morning between the hours of three and six o'clock A.M. when he slit his throat in the family barn and was discovered by his son, Elward Junior, aged twelve, who recalled there was a great amount of blood at the scene which had splattered in great quantities on the hay which surrounded the prone and unmoving body of Cappell Sr. Happily, Mr. Cappell is well and enjoys great financial success, owning several prospering farms and businesses, his wife and three children are in good health and he is well liked and active in the Community Country and Golfing Club and in the Church. The accident is believed to be due to excessive discomfort in the recent heat and no mental disturbances are believed to be present.

She put the clipping on the fridge, dressed, and left her apartment, aiming for campus by way of Quality Dairy, where she planned to ease her hangover with a long john, a LaCroix, and a cup of coffee. She texted Nina to see if she wanted to take a five-minute stroll on her lunch break.

She ate the long john in the QD parking lot, eyes closed, with reckless abandon and a lot of nose-panting, and thought, This is junkie shit, when she noticed how she'd eaten the donut. She was wearing sunglasses. A cool breeze moved the heat from the sun. She drank the LaCroix, wiped the frosting off of her face, panted, belched a few times, straightened herself, and kept going. Nina was busy.

To get to campus on foot she had to cross not exactly a highway but a huge road using an overpass, and then after not too long, she was in the nice residential neighborhood where she used to live in her teens with her parents. She intentionally skirted her old house. It would have been too weird for today, which was already weird enough, like she was dreaming about walking around in a skewed version of her childhood.

In another twenty minutes, she entered the campus, which was filled with young eager people who all looked good and full of sexual, if not intellectual, promise. She passed a teenage boy who was holding a wallet, some keys, and a crumpled wad of paper, wearing nothing but basketball shorts, a T-shirt, and sandals.

A sharp breeze hit Moddie and she felt buoyant and close to stretching out her arms and making some type of operatic pronouncement about the song forever in her heart.

The campus was very beautiful. Rolling hills, green lawns, tall pines, oak trees, maple trees, gardens, streams, ponds, old buildings covered in ivy, large gothic libraries. Moddie felt protected, as if she were in a perfect zoological habitat created just for her happiness by a race of aliens who thought she had no soul or subjectivity and that she was simply an object of mild amusement for when they went on vacation with their children—look, honey, look at all of the stupid little people.

She walked for a while, feeling peaceful, happy, and optimistic, and then sat on a bench to warm herself in the sun. She stared vacantly at the coeds, who laughed and screamed, blissfully unaware of what boredom and anguish were to come a mere decade later in their lives.

There should be an Aesop's fable where a little ant jumps back and forth eternally between two spinning plates to teach us about the pitfalls of getting stuck in two conflicting and endlessly circular trains of thought, thought Moddie, but the only Aesop's fable with ants, as far as she knew, was about how you deserved to die if you enjoyed your summer vacation.

Her optimism cooled.

She remembered one of her high school history teachers, a vocal Lutheran, who once told the class that the existence of Noah's ark had been proven, because archaeologists had found a piece of wood that was 120 cubits long. Moddie had asked what a cubit was. Nobody knows what a cubit is, we don't use them anymore. Then how can you know the wood was 120 cubits long? Because the wood could be divided by 120, etc., etc. The woman's name had been something like Miss Tinkle. Moddie couldn't remember.

She heard something in a bush that sounded like small screaming.

The scene around her looked like *La Grande Jatte* by, as her high school art teacher would say, Sir Rot the Dot.

Life was a disappointment through and through and pleasures wilted by the hour.

At her feet, a little off in the distance, a squirrel sorted through a pile of leaves. He looked focused on his craft. Moddie admired him. He looked up, they locked eyes. He started flirting with her, posing and edging closer and closer, until he stood two feet away, with his front paws draped over a tiny plant sign and his little ass in the air, fluttering his eyelashes. *Blink blink blink.*

The art department at her high school had been an absolute joke, of course. It was housed at the back of the building near the rooms where remedial classes were taught to aggressive delinquents, one of whom did a thing he called "rigging," which consisted of walking up behind the art students, putting his hand around the back of their necks, and pulling as hard as he could while he shouted "rig" for some reason.

The art teachers were central-casting nutcases, middle-aged divorcées, some of whom wept during class in between vitriolic outbursts. She remembered the head of the art department wouldn't let them use blue tempera paints, because "cobalt is from Afghanistan, and we won't be getting any more of *that*," which was honestly fine with Moddie, because who outside of a mental ward wanted to work with tempera? All of this had sent a clear message to Moddie that, because of her interests, she would always be seen as pathetic and incompetent, and that art was to be merely—barely—tolerated as a pitiful inconvenience to functioning society, and that throughout her life—unless she were to make great sums of money off of her art and prove that she was smiled upon and chosen by god to re-create his infinite beauty for the betterment of man—people at parties would call her "artsy," "creative," "funky," and "special" with a certain kind of high-pitched hostility in their voices, as if they were talking to someone who believed something fucked up, stupid, and lame, but their Christian charity had taught them to always be gentle and kind to mental and spiritual invalids, which they certainly thought Moddie was, when in fact they didn't know the half of it, they didn't know they had it twisted around and opposite, and they were the ones with soft minds and talking to them was like slowly taking a hand-crank drill and boring it into one's temple.

The squirrel dove back into the leaves and continued his search for whatever it was, some nut memory that haunted him and drove his days slowly toward madness.

At the far end of the quad, David walked out of one of the lecture hall buildings after his first class, feeling heightened and excited and optimistic about this whole endeavor.

The clear blue light cut straight through him and made him feel pure and clean and new. He passed a beautiful tree that was beginning to turn bright red, and the pleasure of this image loosened his muscles and quieted his paranoia, and part of him felt so gentle and so grateful he almost let out a small gasp. Not everyone spent as much time thinking about the things he spent his time thinking about, and now he was being put to use. At last!

His head swam with fragmented thoughts of how he could encourage the students to adopt his viewpoint on art, and he imagined them receptive, and he imagined how good it would feel to enlighten them, and he imagined this could be part of a cultural change, that maybe everywhere, students could be enlightened.

The students in his seminar had a limited understanding of culture, and some of them had seemed angrily threatened by some of what he'd shown them. One student kept asking how much everything cost and who had paid for it. "If you're saying you agree that none of this is marketable, could you explain the benefit of spending time on things that won't help us in our careers as artists?"

He would have to start with that girl. He wasn't entirely sure what kind of an idea she had about what was to come in her future. "Career as an artist" sounded aggressive to David. To be totally honest, no real artist thought the word "career," because none of them really thought about the "job advancement" aspect of it, they were thinking about the work itself, the ideas, the craft. "Careerist" was a pejorative among all of the artists he knew and admired, and he imagined this student comparing Vito Acconci's *Seedbed* (which he'd just introduced them to) with the hideous painting hanging in the coffee shop across the street (priced at two thousand dollars), and flinched when he realized who she would rule in favor of, and was depressed to understand that his was the minority view, and then suddenly David started to feel bitterness creep into his fleeting optimism, and then remembered where he was, a place that would never be like Europe, in a life that would never be satisfying, among people who would never understand him.

His shoulders were up around his ears in a brittle cringe.

Approaching him on the path were four young men, slightly chunky but undeniably muscular and healthy, all wearing basketball shorts. He threw the boys a side glance and angrily thought of them as "the beef boys." He anticipated that one of them might make some passing comment about him or try to shoulder-check him. He started to think about himself as "Grampa" and became overly conscious of his receding hairline and his right kneecap, which would need medical attention if he ever got into a fight.

Without incident or hostility, they parted around him on the path, and just ahead he saw Moddie sitting on a bench, twitching slightly, gesturing at a squirrel.

Pam was hurrying to the center of the quad to meet David for tea. She had been really looking forward to this. Sometimes all a person needed was a little change of pace. She was a little nervous, and tried to breathe slowly and to appreciate the nice weather as a way to calm down.

When she spotted them in the distance, she thought, Oh, but no fucking way.

She knew anger didn't flatter her or do her any good, so she let go of the language, and thought that she was happy to run into Moddie, her dear old friend, and was still looking forward to talking to David about the upcoming semester, nothing was spoiled, and she was not in the least bit annoyed to find him talking to Moddie, of all people, who apparently lived here now.

"Well, hello," she said as she approached them.

"Hey, Pam!" said Moddie. "Shit, it's my lucky day. I was feeling bored and depressed, and now I feel like the mayor."

Moddie stood to give Pam a hug.

"The mayor is never bored and depressed?" asked Pam.

"He's popular," said Moddie.

"Hello, David," said Pam.

"Hello," said David.

"What are you two up to?" asked Pam.

"Oh, just reviewing the catalog of our sorrows," said Moddie.

"Okay," said Pam. She laughed.

"For example, is it an actual, inherent moral flaw not to work and 'earn' constantly, or is it cultural grooming for the masses that we feel this way?" said Moddie.

Pam nodded and tried to estimate how long this might take.

"I was in Barcelona once," she continued, in a way that wasn't looking so good to Pam, time-wise, "at the National Museum, and I saw room after room after room of medieval Jesus statues, and I was really struck by the repetition of it, and they started to seem like mass-produced government objects, and I imagined them placed strategically around town in order to remind the peasants that their suffering and their poverty were actually really great and that they should keep at it, because it made them holy. So, I'm sort of idly thinking about the cleverness of greed—and how the elite use their intellect to misdirect the masses from their swindles. I have a healthy anger toward billionaires, but do you think that an open disgust for privilege, which seems to be circulating on Facebook and elsewhere, is a kind of misdirection, and that maybe Zuckerberg and co. are algorithmically encouraging us to avoid the taint of leisure and to take pride in our slavish work schedules, and that there's not something ironic and almost amusing about that?"

"I'm not totally sure what you mean," said Pam.

"Ah, well. Me neither," said Moddie. She smiled at David and shrugged. "Can you believe this day? It's so nice out."

"Yeah, it's great," said Pam. "David, I've got something at

two, are we still good for today? Should we head out now, or do you want to do next week?"

"Yeah, sure," said David. "I'm good for now."

Pam turned to Moddie and hugged her again. "I would invite you, but it's work related. We're just going across the street for tea," she said.

"Ah, yes, the English vice," said Moddie. She looked over at David, who gave her a curious microexpression, and then she looked away.

"Well, let's catch up soon," said Pam, and then she and David walked off to the café.

The gorgeous weather continued on into the early evening, where it touched Kimberly's heart and made her feel hopeful about repairing some of her friendships. There had been things she'd left unsaid, fearing rejection, but that evening she felt clearheaded and strong enough to communicate. This was the way fall weather always worked on her, giving her a renewed sense of purpose and a desire to cultivate follow-through.

Her husband, Bobby, was in the kitchen sautéing onions. She decided it was time to send some emails.

Bethany,

Hey. I'm really not sure if this is the right thing to do or not, but I am thinking about the seven-year cycles of the body, and I'm in the tail end of the throat/philosophical chakra, so this felt like something I ought to do. I hope it lands on kind ears, because being honest in this way is of course outside of my comfort zone, but I still think it's worth doing. I think you know what it's like to be a Midwestern woman. We're peacekeepers, and sometimes that can lead to burying unexpressed emotions. I do think it's good to be open. I'm really sorry if this comes off as aggressive in any way, I don't mean it to.

When you and Thomas hosted the last get-together at the end of summer, I was very hurt, because when the idea had been presented months prior to start a regular get-together, we'd agreed that Robert and I would host the first one. I put on a good face, and so did Bobby, and we didn't say anything, but it doesn't feel right to hold my tongue any longer. I know this doesn't sound like a big deal, but it's not the first time I've felt undercut by you. You have a tendency with me and with others to be slightly patronizing, which just really isn't necessary, and makes you look a little foolish because we're all adults here and we're all perfectly capable of hosting get-togethers, so this attitude just gives the slight impression that you think you're above the rest of us, which really doesn't compute.

I know you recently had a think piece published in *The New York Times,* and I know that must come with an enormous amount of pressure to be on the national stage in such a way, and I have such sympathy for that, but what I think you need to recall is that I have nearly ten years' more experience than you as an educator, and have actually published much more than you, have been on three speaking tours at academic conferences, and occasionally appear on radio. So when you make little comments about how you might "help" me in my career, or when you give me unsolicited advice, it's not so much hurtful as it is confusing. I don't really need your advice?

I don't mention this to put you in your place. I just think there's a chance there are areas of your life that are unhappy, and if so, there might be some value in getting a fuller picture of yourself and your behaviors from the outside. You might want to think about whether or not there are areas where you are unnecessarily exerting authority, and whether or not this is alienating you.

Phew! Ok. Thank you for your ear. I hope you'll bear with me as I learn to cast off the oppressive mantle of culturally learned, gendered interpersonal accommodation in exchange for a perhaps more male but hopefully more open type of directness.

With true respect,
Kim

She sent it without hesitation and began her next message.

Pam,

I'm feeling a little miffed about something, and I'm hoping it's ok to bring it up with you over email so you can have a chance to process and think before you respond. Don't worry, it's nothing horrible, but I'm worried it might spin out into something more if I don't say something now.

I was hurt that you were spending so much time with Moddie at the art opening, and that you didn't even bring the new visiting artist—which I was so proud and excited about for you—over to say hello to me. I think I've been supportive, right? I think you remember the very vocal and uncomfortable disagreement that Moddie and I got into at Bethany's party. She was shockingly aggressive and personally attacked me and called me a bigot in front of all of our friends. You and I have been close for the past two years, and I had thought we had a true friendship forming, and now I'm feeling a little silly about that, and a little embarrassed that I put so much stock and faith into our connection. Now I'm feeling wrong in my interpretation of things. I'm feeling hurt. In my opinion, friendship includes a certain level of loyalty. It just makes me sad that you don't have my back here. And, further, it makes me sad that you were prioritizing keeping Moddie company at the opening, and even though I was the one who had been publicly verbally abused, I was the one who was being left out. I've given a lot to keeping this friend group alive. Maybe we have different friendship styles, but I still feel owed an apology or some kind of reparations in order for me to feel comfortable moving forward.

I hope this falls on open ears.

Sincerely,
Kim

Then another quick one while she was thinking about it.

Janice,

I am in receipt of this email. I am unable to take on additional projects at this time. Perhaps contact Morgan for best practices on getting this completed.

More soon,
Kimberly Johnson

Kim had meant to include something about how Moddie's elitism was triggering in the way that it seemed to be a flaunting of class privilege, but had forgotten to.

"Shit," she said.

Bobby stopped banging pots and pans together and asked, "What?"

"Well, I just sent an email to Pam, and I forgot to mention something, and it's kind of a sensitive topic, so I can't really write it in a PS before I hear back from her."

"Damn, I'm sorry," said Bobby.

"Yeah, it's just that it was about that girl from the party. Do you remember I told you about that?"

"Oh yeah," said Bobby.

"It's just sensitive," said Kimberly.

"Yeah," said Bobby.

"It actually makes me pretty mad, so I'm just trying to talk through things with Pam about it, because I feel like this girl really accosted me, and I feel like Pam was giving her preferential treatment at the opening," said Kim, not having a better word for the museum party.

"Sure," said Bobby. "She sounds like a bitch."

"Yeah. It was really insulting, but particularly insulting to be publicly accosted by someone who I assume has the luxury of having her parents pay her rent for her, since clearly she did not come here with any kind of job offer in hand, and that was the part I forgot to bring up in my email, was about that wound, and how that was extra triggering for me, because even though my parents are fortunate to be middle-class and have savings, they definitely didn't grow up in wealth, and their savings is one hundred percent absolutely for them and their retirement, not to subsidize my every whim. I don't feel entitled to my parents' things. I actually find that notion physically repulsive. I work for things, and when my work is done, then I deserve my things," she said, moving her pinched fingers around in a bee-like pattern and jutting her chin forward. "If you have the extra funds to support yourself for a year, and you are able-bodied, but you are not working, and you choose not to think about the people who could be using your extra funds to survive, and you are not donating those funds, but using them for your own directionless leisure—which for some reason includes coming here and coming to Bethany's and insulting me—then you are greedy, you are lazy, you are stupid, and you are selfish, point-blank, end of story."

"Yeah, for sure," said Bobby.

"And her fucking outfits, I mean come on," said Kimberly, "like, buy a clean shirt. You're not fooling anybody."

Kimberly's mother, Cindy, was a psychiatrist, or psychologist, whichever was the one that didn't prescribe medication. She used to say, "Some people choose to look down on me for my choice, but I'm not a drug dealer."

Cindy's parents were low-verbal churchgoing people from a town well-known for its outlet mall and Klan presence. Cindy categorized their treatment of her as emotional-neglect abuse. The jewel of Cindy's collection of anecdotal evidence was an incident in which Grammy left five-year-old Cindy at the grocery store for twenty minutes after Cindy was being too cute and getting too much attention from the other shoppers, which made Grammy jealous. Grammy took her out of the cart and said, "Maybe you'd like to walk, since you have so much energy today," set her down, and moved quickly to the end of the aisle while Cindy was tying her shoe. "Stop, Mama! I'm going to try and tie my shoe!"—she thought if she could tie them real good, her mama would be proud—but Grammy was gone, and Cindy desperately searched the aisles for a long,

long time. From this and other incidents, Cindy knew her mother didn't love her, which is a terrible emotional burden for a small child to bear, one that most certainly would leave a lasting negative effect on the psyche of the child, but Cindy did like to tell this story a lot, and she definitely used little baby voices for herself and husky Big Bad Wolf voices for the adult characters, especially the grocery store manager, and sometimes would whip herself into theatrical tears when telling this story, which was as confusing for Kimberly at thirty-two as it had been for her at eight, though Kim's interpretation of her confusion had morphed over time—morphed so many times as to become meaningless, and now when she heard her mother tell this story on the phone or at family gatherings, she felt an extreme, to-the-marrow numbness, sometimes accompanied with legitimate temporary loss of hearing.

One day, though, as the legend went, Cindy finally stood up for herself. "And it was you, my little girl, who helped Mommy."

Kimberly had been sitting on Grammy's lap, telling an animated story about going to the zoo with her day care. Grammy was brushing Kim's hair, smiling, asking attentive questions, and there was something about it—something about how sweet and vulnerable Kimberly looked—that just triggered Cindy so deeply that she finally snapped and decided to go no contact. She took Kimberly home and wrote her mother a letter. She gave her mother one more chance to atone within one week, and if she did not, that would be it.

"Sometimes it's just time to know the firm truth about how someone feels toward you."

After Cindy got her mental health professional certification, she leaned into this idea of the bluff call. She thought most intimate relationships were predicated on a lie, and to test for love, you needed to tell the truth. She'd skimmed *The Dance of Anger* a few times. She got it. She challenged each of her clients to tell the truth and to see if their bridges were made of wood or steel. No matter what it was, Cindy always told her truth to her children and to her husband, because society was too uptight about other people's feelings, and she wanted to be part of the emotional revolution.

Cindy liked to talk about her and her children's superior intelligence, which was evident because she was a mental health care professional, which was one of the intelligent professions—doctor, lawyer, etc. If Kimberly's grades did not fit with Cindy's idea of herself as intelligent and therefore the breeder of intelligent offspring, she would ground Kimberly and sometimes sit on the couch weeping and lamenting, wondering very out loud where she went wrong as a mother.

Since high school was incredibly facile, it was simple for Kimberly to stay in her mother's good graces and prop up her mother's ego, and when her mother's ego was full to the brim, sometimes it would splash over onto Kim, and, thus drenched, she would walk, smug and sure of her ultimate intellectual domination of the other students around her, through the halls of school, spiteful of both jocks and burnouts, fiercely competitive with anyone she considered a near equal, and obsequious with her superiors to a degree that prompted her acquaintances to do viciously accurate impressions, thinking of Kimberly as not so much a friend but a passing amusement. But, in the end, she showed them. Graduate school, world travel. Marriage, home ownership, publication. She was on the golden path.

She scrolled through her phone. The last text Pam had sent to Kim was "Yeah, let's!" but then weeks of silence. She raised her eyebrows, quietly furious. All of her furies were quiet, because Kimberly was in control. Control was not easy to obtain.

She'd developed it through deliberate training and discipline. Sometimes when women were deliberate and assertive, people called them bitches. But she didn't want to have to see what might happen to the next person who called her a bitch. No, no, that was something she would not want to have to see. Oh, no. No, no.

The overhead lights were on, which made the dove-gray paint on the walls look more institutional than sophisticated. Kimberly was crammed into the corner of the sectional, her legs curled under her and her neck curled toward her phone, which she gripped in her fist. The muscles in her body were clenched and the force of her jaw was subtly pressing one of her molars up, up toward her brain, the synapses of which were carving dark, difficult pathways with each repetition of these angry thoughts.

Later, eating dinner with Bobby, cutlery resonating in the open-concept living and dining area like a tolling bell, Kimberly continued to express her position on people like Moddie.

"I hate these pretentious snobs going around telling me what to watch and what to read and what to think, honestly it makes me feel fucking attacked, and even if it's women doing it, maybe even especially then actually, it is deeply *deeply* sexist to police people in this way, especially if you're policing a woman. Honestly, no woman actually likes to read these dense, stupid, complicated books, and none of them actually like to watch foreign films, they're just doing it because they think that's what a certain type of guy wants them to do. And I *like* television. There's nothing wrong with my liking television. I think everybody knows we're in a television renaissance, nobody was looking at cave paintings for entertainment after the printing press was invented, and anyway I think everybody knows the most exciting writing is happening on

Twitter, and I think everybody knows that the best works are those that are completely accessible and maybe working on multiple levels at once, and honestly to say otherwise is to reinforce a kind of classist rhetoric that is actually responsible for a lot of fucking poverty and actual violence against actual bodies, and if we want to dismantle the fucking patriarchy, we need to start by dismantling culture. And I'm just honestly done hearing shit from people who want to look down on me just because I prefer nonfiction that teaches me something, and just because I prefer TV over nonsense and because I prefer a novel with a fucking likable, relatable protagonist and an actual fucking plot that I can follow. I'm also sick of people making me feel like shit just because I want to have a family. I just feel like everybody thinks I'm so lame or square or I have no sexual power or like I'm resigning and not taking my career seriously just because you and I are living in a home—*that we paid for and that we worked for*—and we want to have a baby, or maybe two babies. I feel like when I've mentioned this to Pam, she looks at me like I'm like Chrissy, which is a real laugh, like I'm just going to turn into some kind of a fucking loser if I get knocked up, but obviously that's not going to happen, if you take one second to look at my track record. That's what I want to say to everyone. Like, think about who you're talking to before you give me that look. I can't even imagine what it's going to be like when I'm actually pregnant and fucking fat and hormonal and have to take time off from my career and those fake friends of mine just completely stop talking to me and make snide little glances at each other and then they'll slip off to go do drugs and watch art films with that girl Moddie or whatever the fuck it is they want to pretend to enjoy doing, it's just fucking horrible to feel so . . . I don't know, like I'm a fucking outcast just because I actually understand my own belief systems."

Bobby's ears were ringing and he was hearing Kim's words like "Wah wah wah boop boop boop lalala, meow meow meow." He moved food from his plate to his fork, from his fork to his mouth, and watched the color white leak across the circle in front of his eyes as the food slid from his mouth into his stomach and he felt like bwoop bwoop bwoop bwoop and in a tiny giggling voice in his head he thought, I'm gonna go get my dick sucked. I'm gonna go get my dick sucked. Yep, that's me, going out later to go and get my dick sucked!

Bobby said, "Fuck, yeah, what a bitch," but his tone was flat.

"I'm sorry, are you even listening to me?" said Kimberly. "I'd rather you not give me a halfhearted response here."

"I'm listening," said Bobby.

"Well, I guess I'd just expected a little more sympathy from you as my partner when I'm here pouring my heart out to you."

Loud in Bobby's mind were the tantalizing words "Go sleep at your mother's, I want a divorce, fuck off, fuck you, you don't mean a thing to me, you're just a body, a stranger, and I want a divorce," but of course he'd said "I want a divorce" before and so had she, what couple hadn't? These thoughts were the subterranean babbling brook coursing through him day and night, at the sound of her voice these were the words that whispered up close to the barrier of his lips, "Divorce divorce, I want a divorce."

She'd lost almost all features except her passion for shouting unflattering things about other women. Her hands looked like tiny little gremlin paws. Her mother was a sour-looking asshole and spending time with Cindy was like looking into a scary crystal ball.

"You don't have to shout at me, I'm listening to you," said Bobby.

"Shouting? I am not shouting."

"I'm sorry, I'm listening. I'm so sorry you're dealing with this."

"Thank you, it does suck. This woman literally point-blank called me a fascist and then said it was 'weird' to try to be friends with Black people." Kimberly scoffed. "I really just feel the need to let people know what type of person she is. Like, right now." She got out her phone and started texting.

Bobby had forgotten that that's what they'd been talking about.

The voice inside his head was whispering to him.

I know I don't want to have children with you. I hate you.

I know I want a divorce.

You hate her, that's what the voice said as it leaned casually back in its armchair smoking its pipe and cleaning its fingernails by the fire, chuckling, the pops and flashes of the fire lighting up its face, you hate her, it said, if you let yourself knock her up you'll hate the children too and you'll leave and that's the kind of life you'll have, one haunted forever by anger and resentment. The rosy golden little man laughed and took a drag on his pipe and in a strained post-hit voice said, Obviously the choice is yours you can be a throttled little coward your whole idiot life [long, slow exhale] but you know you'd feel so good and so light and so free if you just tell her how you really feel and grow enough balls to follow through.

If you say you need to talk and you keep your voice calm, she'll know you're not kidding, and then you get to go sleep at Stan's, wouldn't that be nice, and find a lawyer, every step is just a mechanical action and you're already living your life as if it's one big mechanical action, why should this be any different? The man's face started to stretch lengthwise and turn green and as he talked his teeth drew down into sharp points and the rest of the room he was sitting in began to shift and blur and melt away until it was just the wide sharp green face saying there's no difference if you keep your voice calm and firm it'll be real how can you live like this like a coward such a coward such a little boy little crybaby you think if you leave her no one will suck on your stupid little wrinkledick so you might as well stay with Mama none of the girls want your stupid crybaby *wrinkledick wrinkledick WRINKLEDICK!!!*

Bobby's palms were flat on the kitchen table and he breathed in and out as slowly as he could manage and looked around and saw all the things Kim had bought for their house, the way she had arranged it without allowing him to have an opinion, and he felt so sorry for her, so very very sorry, she'd never had a fighting chance, with a mother like that, she would never be normal. He watched her angry little face move around as she talked about all of the stupid nonsense she'd brought on herself and then he felt pity, then anger, then disgust.

Five

Moddie had tried to make the most of her ambitions for the day.

She returned to her apartment that beautiful evening and set the bags of useless bullshit from Target on the kitchen counter. Target had been what one might call "triggering" and she'd had another emotional episode in the cleaning products aisle, thinking of how many dishes she used to do for Nick and wondering how he was getting along without this service—this "wonder" manifesting itself inside of her as multidirectional suffering.

She didn't understand how she could fully know a person and in the end reject him. She saw Nick in his greater context (shitty mom), and even though she knew he'd made mistakes, she felt like she understood and forgave those mistakes. But thinking about forgiving Nick made her hysterical. Of course she wanted to forgive him, had he not been the object of her love? When she'd forgiven him before, nothing had happened except more mistakes—more and more mistakes, more and more forgiveness, until forgiveness seemed like a poison inside of her.

Nick's voice ran through her mind. Maybe bring it down a notch. You can be really intense, you know.

And then she thought, Yeah, well that's because I have this poison inside of me, but he never let her talk about it. While crying in the Target bathroom, she'd pictured Nick crying and muttering about how she was rejecting him, and she'd felt in that moment like she would do anything to be transformed back into the type of person who believed in enduring love and the power of forgiveness, but each act of forgiveness had seemed to cram her deeper into hell, and the last time Moddie saw Nick, she'd given him the opportunity to be deserving of her forgiveness, and he'd thrown it back in her face, like a challenge to a duel.

Moddie knew she hated Nick. Nothing was more clear.

But the muscle memory of loving him was too strong, the reality of her last reality was too alive, too vivid (my baby!), and that's where the confusion began.

She'd talked about this with her mom so many times that her mom had started to sound bored on the phone, like, Moddie, what is it about this that you're not understanding?

He cannot say that to you.

What he asked you to do when you were twenty-three was cruel and stupid. And I understand, he was a boy, but he's not a boy anymore. This is who he is.

She changed into the new sweat suit she'd bought at Target, thinking the sweat suit would make her feel as though she had her life together, which now seemed like a very stupid idea, but what's done is done, the sweat suit was stupid, the walk to the quad had been meaningless, getting the "courage" to leave Nick hadn't done anything tangible, hadn't released her from anything, just another lateral transfer.

She lit a few candles, sat on the couch cross-legged, closed her eyes, and tried to counterbalance her rapid-cycling feelings of frustration, hopelessness, and shame with a clarifying anger by reviving dead memories of her friendships in Chicago—thinking that perhaps, through this, she might be able to reach the emotional synthesis of cool indifference.

She'd been friends with these people for over ten years, but not one of them had reached out after the breakup to see if she was okay.

Moddie smiled, disgusted, as Nick's voice ran through her head again. These people are your friends, they love you. Why are you so weird about them?

She laughed. Hate to say I told you so!

None of them had really liked her. No one really wanted her around. She was usually an afterthought and was only invited to parties where everyone was invited—just to get the numbers up and make the host feel like they had a wide network of friends. She was just a prop, *Weekend at Bernie's*. Nobody gave an actual shit about her.

In the beginning, of course, she was invited to everything, but slowly she was only invited to one or two smaller gatherings a year. The whole dynamic of everything changed. Even her dynamic with Nick, which had seemed so promising in the beginning, faded into stupid shit.

Nick had been very ambitious. When they got together at twenty-three, he'd already had two solo shows, and his work was good, so when he said he thought Moddie's work was good, and when he started to invite her to hang out with his friends, she felt as though she'd arrived on the doorstep of her future, which she had, but not quite in the way she'd imagined.

In the beginning, she and Nick's friends got drunk and talked about ideas. Sometimes they would hang out in someone's studio and look at new paintings, sculptures, whatever, and talk and smoke, acting cocky and happy. People seemed to value Moddie's opinions, and everything felt fated, like this was definitely the right direction. There were about three years of equilibrium, and then many things shifted at once. Jen began to date Alan, some of their older friends got married, some friends moved, and Nick began to think about money. Moddie told him it was ridiculous to think about money, nobody makes money off of their art, but he didn't want to turn thirty before he'd gotten recognition. Moddie thought he had been recognized, but he said, "Please, none of that counts." Then he would get depressed about it, sometimes for months on end, so she started to give him pep talks and tried to reassure him that he was talented, undeniably talented, in a way that was sure to bring him success, eventually, success or whatever power trip he was after, and then once he was soothed, once he was convinced that this was true, then she would sit with him for hours, days, however long it took for her to help him find the perfect balance of esoteric intellectualism and irresistible visual charm so that his work might be shown and commented upon favorably by some nebulous money-granting "public"—a phantom Other who he both loathed and yearned for equally.

But at first it had been fun—a thrill. She'd loved being part of this group in Chicago. It felt like the first step toward the life she wanted, a life free from ridiculous convention, a life in which art would be at the center of everything, a life she had made a few sacrifices for already, but once things started to go south, they never went back.

Moddie recalled a conversation. Walking down the street at night next to Nick, balmy and energizing spring air on her cheeks, she said, "I think I want to take the next few months to really hunker down and finish these drawings," but instead of saying "Cool" or anything encouraging, Nick said something about how she was abandoning him just like everybody else, and he'd thought she was going to be around to help him with all of these grant deadlines, this was a really crucial time for his career, but fine, go ahead, leave me just like everybody else, which had been too difficult for her to hear, so she'd said no, no, I'll help, it can wait.

What a fucking doormat.

She thought about those early days, everybody united in the priority of art, and she felt a compounded sense of loss for the life she had imagined but would never lead. Now here she was, back at home, defeated, and she would probably stay here and work at 7-Eleven, die before she turned forty, never draw anything again. Moddie was loath to admit she even liked Alan's early work, and in it, saw her own ideas made real (though perhaps this was a result of her ideas getting filtered down to him through Nick, who knows).

"Disgusting," said Moddie. "What a bunch of assholes."

She thought about all of the work she had done for Nick, critiquing, workshopping, literal mark-making, canvas stretching, grant writing, taking him to museums, bringing him to Europe, dressing him, coaching him on how to talk about his work, slipping him things to read and watch, completely redecorating his apartment, all of which had been mistakes, and then laughed, finding it ironic that it was this shit that had attracted Gracie, so, in effect, Gracie was actually in love with Moddie.

That girl had no fucking clue.

Do you want to get dinner with Alan and Jen?

No, I don't want to get dinner with Alan and Jen—like, what are you not understanding?

Why, though, they're so nice to you.

Why? Oh right, I guess it's because I'm a stupid fucking bitch and I can't stand that I'm not the center of attention, so I'm throwing a weird temper tantrum to make everything about me, is that what you'd like to hear?

Jen and, of course, Alan were Moddie's focus when it came to the spiritual torments of camaraderie, the hells of social engagement, but there was something sadistic about the entire group of them, the core clique, Nick, Alan, Jen, Chelsea, Nelson, Elmyra, and Stuart, the smug pleasure they seemed to take in giving up. Their tedious, time-consuming jobs as teachers and administrators. Safety, validation, retreat.

Chelsea, perhaps the third-worst of them, thought of herself as a kind of leader. She made tepid work and had been the first of the group to fold and get an art-adjacent job. Chelsea adored Alan, doted on him in the way of a mother with weak boundaries, and by sheer force, she placed him at the center of the group's identity. Everything he said provoked her to let out a sick peal of delighted laughter, afterward letting her hungry eyes linger on his stupid face. She referenced things Alan had said and done, as if he were a celebrity—Alan, the special one with such an irreverent sense of humor, and such a shining avant-garde talent. Well, Chelsea was too fucking stupid to realize that every time Alan said something "funny" he was saying it with the cadence and rhythm of a character from a sitcom Moddie had seen at her parents' house (*It's treat time, baybeee!*)—so much for everybody's conceptual art degrees, turns out you just like TV like everybody else—and any time he said or did something that made him seem like an asshole, he wasn't doing some kind of irreverent, sophisticated, post-sarcasm *bit*, Chelsea, he was just being a fucking asshole, but Chelsea and the rest were too fucking stupid to see this, and too stupid to see that Alan's work was getting worse and worse (just like their own work was getting worse and worse). More opaque, and leaning heavily on his dense, incompetently written artist statements, which Moddie had a sneaking feeling Jen had ghostwritten—but everybody loved Jen! So vulnerable, so sweet, so "hardworking." Three cheers for industry!

Jen had the air of a fucked-up Chihuahua people doted on for being so ugly—tremulous and egotistical. Look at her quiver. Look at her hateful beady little eyes, how precious. Jen was always glaring at Moddie, always rolling her eyes whenever Moddie talked. Nick never believed it. Even after Moddie found photographic evidence on Facebook, he still said, "I don't see it."

Moddie heard Chelsea's laugh ripple through her brain again. Oh, Alan, your work is so *charmingly* bad, how counter*cultural*! Ah-hahahahahaaaah, how *droll*.

One night, years ago, as Moddie sat at the table with the group at a dinner party, feeling her brain slowly leaking out of her body, she heard Jen say, "I don't understand why anybody would smoke. Obviously it kills you, but what it does to your skin is just disgusting. You get all of these gross spots on your face, and when I think about the smokers I know, their pores are enormous and their skin is basically yellow and it *sags* over time, the toxins destroy your collagen, and your hair and clothing smell so bad, and, just, when I see somebody smoke I think to myself 'That person has *no* self-control,' " and as she kept talking, Moddie stood up and said, "I'll be right back," and went out to the porch and smoked, drunk, always drunk, and her friend the cigarette told her, "It's fine, don't listen to her, what the fuck does she know about *self-control*," and since when in the fuck did any of them give a shit about pores? When she went back inside, Jen was talking about an essay she was writing about female masturbation. *Female* masturbation. She said some incomprehensible shit about how this had something to do with socialism, the pleasure labor we perform on ourselves.

And where was Nick in this? She could barely remember him being there, much less defending her.

The thing I liked best about those nights was being drunk, thought Moddie.

Jen talked, everyone talked, but nobody talked as much as Chelsea, who went on ad-motherfucking-nauseam about the intriguing difficulties of her bland existence. On and on and on, these people were always talking, talking, talking, but not about anything interesting—god, what a prison, what a swindle.

Every once in a while Moddie would get too drunk and snap, let something out like in the old days when everybody was still interesting, and then she'd spend the next week or two sending humiliating apology letters, "I'm sorry, I've been under a lot of stress. I'm so embarrassed for what I said, it's just been difficult," but she hadn't ever actually been sorry.

Every time she spoke, it was like Russian roulette.

Every time she spoke, Alan and Jen would get quiet and their faces would assume the wooden, schoolmarmish affect of the turd sniffer.

Oh, if I told any of them, asked any of them if they noticed that Alan and Jen didn't like me—Chelsea, Nelson, Stuart, Elmyra—I'm sure they would say they didn't even notice. Oh, no, they would say, we never noticed anything strange about how Alan and Jen treated you, no, that's what they'd say.

What are you, paranoid or something??

Did they ever say anything about me?

No, now let's move on.

That's what Nick always said whenever Moddie would try to talk about it. They *love* you. I don't understand why you get so weird about them, they didn't do anything wrong. Are you projecting? Are you jealous? I don't get it, let's move on.

Jealous? No. He knew. He knew what her fucking problem was.

Sitting at the table with these people, drunk. The overhead lights were always on, another sign of their twisted sadism. Just sitting at a fucking table with the overhead lights on, no music, getting trashed and listening to these simple people talking.

"Oh!" Jen would say. "I booked us that house in Door County," and by "us" she would mean everyone but Nick and Moddie, who had not been invited, and then Chelsea would say, "I'm so excited, let me double-check my calendar," like she might be booked.

Ah-hahaha-*ha*!

Door County.

And what was worse, Moddie and Jen had been friends, and it had been Moddie who introduced Jen to everyone—just another fucking mistake in this circus of error. Just another lesson for Moddie that her actions had consequences.

Early on in their friendship, Jen wrote Moddie a long email about how Moddie was a bully and an asshole. They'd had a disagreement over coffee about an artist, which apparently had made Jen feel "small, ridiculed, and unsafe." Moddie invited Jen over to her apartment and consoled her. Jen wept about how mean Moddie was while Moddie made her tea and said she hadn't meant anything by it, this was just the way she liked to talk about art and movies. Moddie tried to explain that this was an essential value of their friend group, that open expression of ideas was nothing to take personally, and that everyone was allowed to add their own flair to their arguments, because everybody had passionate opinions about art. Jen said she didn't think that was right, and that she didn't think bullying and ridiculing people had anything to do with making art.

Of course, Moddie always wondered about the timing, since this schism came a few weeks after Jen and Alan started hooking up ("Guess what, *III* just kissed Alan *Tree*bag"), and one week after Jen went up to Moddie at a party (back when Moddie was still invited to parties) and said, "Alan told me that you guys used to date, and I want you to know, I'm totally cool with it."

Oh, was that what had happened between Moddie and Alan? That was an interesting development. That was a development that made some of Moddie's hidden resentments tiptoe toward the surface.

After this, Moddie noticed, increasingly, that she was disinvited from group outings, to the beach, to the movies, to dinners, and that it was always Jen who mentioned these outings in her presence, always Jen who seemed to be organizing these outings—the proverbial car always seemingly full, and Jen, like some fucked-up Pied Piper, leading everyone off the cliff into the middlebrow banality of weekend apple-picking trips, recipe swapping, antiquing, and "really trying to take your career seriously—I mean I can definitely help you with that."

Jen was the end of an era. A poison.

Moddie put her hands on her face and rubbed rapidly and screamed a little. Then she started laughing.

She had been rude to Jen several times. It was all true, mea culpa.

Why are you so obsessed with her? Are you jealous? That's kind of awkward, you know.

If Moddie and Alan had truly dated it would make sense to interpret this as Moddie being jealous (and maybe it was a kind of jealousy) but that was not what had happened, of course—every once in a while Moddie would try to remind Nick of this, but he really didn't want to listen, and, as he often said, he preferred to "just try and get along."

So, naturally, because Nick wouldn't let her talk directly about her anger toward Alan, all she could do was express herself adjacently, pointing out things like "Hey, when you get texts and emails from Alan with all of those typos, does it make you wonder if he's had some kind of brain damage?" or "Do you think it's embarrassing that Alan applied for a Guggenheim, when all he does is pour glitter on pine cones and tape pictures of Matt Damon's face on them, like he's the smelly girl at summer camp?" to which Nick would just scoff, like Moddie would never get it, never belong.

Fuck, so be it.

Moddie thought about the last time she'd seen Nick, the night she went to their old apartment to reconcile, the night she learned about Gracie, and learned that she and Nick would not be getting back together (though, of course I'll always love you).

That night, he told her that when he saw her walking down the street toward the apartment, all he felt was dread in the pit of his stomach, like he could actually see the depression and animosity radiating off of her, and "I just really can't have that energy in my life right now. Do you have any idea how much you hurt me? I'm kind of confused about why I'm supposed to feel sympathy right now. I mean, obviously, I do feel sympathy toward you, and if you feel like you're really mentally unwell, or like you're about to harm yourself, you can stay here for as long as you need to, of course. Of *course*. But, think about it. Do you even want to get back together? Like, right now, tonight, do you feel like going out to dinner with Alan and Jen? Because that's something I would like to do tonight, and I don't think I can do that with you, so I'm just not really sure where I see you in my life."

That's what Nick had said. That sick bastard.

"I cannot even fucking believe you," said Moddie at the time, and again right there in her new, horrible apartment. She was so angry that her hands began to tremble, and she did not feel in control of the words coming out of her mouth, and she could hear a light ringing in her ears, and the colors in the room changed, a few shades paler.

"Alan is a very dark person," she said, perhaps dramatically. "And I would be very careful around him if I were you."

Nick leaned back on the couch and looked bored, like *Jesus Christ, calm down,* while Moddie reminded him in detail of what had happened senior year of college, when Alan had, "forgive me for the histrionics," forced his way inside Moddie's apartment.

Nick averted his eyes and bounced his foot a few times to express impatience. He raised his eyebrows, like you might when you've decided not to dignify something with a response.

This was quite a humiliating, painful memory.

Before going over to see Nick that night, for the first time since the split, Moddie had gotten things clear in her mind. She wanted to try again, but she needed to be able to have one or two conversations about Alan and Jen. She'd started to think that maybe her history with Alan had negatively impacted her mental health, and that Nick's refusal to take her seriously, plus his constant, almost performative taking of Alan's side, had stopped her from being able to deal with it, or perhaps the word was "process" it, straightforwardly, and that this might really explain a few things—the crying, the anger, the dread, the loss of sensation from ribs to knees. When Nick had seen her walking down the street, glowering, anxious, she'd been rehearsing what she would say. She'd imagined herself speaking calmly, she'd imagined Nick listening, she'd imagined a difficult conversation, perhaps the first of many, but instead of this, she learned that Nick was seeing someone new, that he found her depressing and exhausting, and that—true to her worst paranoias—one of his main qualms with her as a girlfriend was that she was not friendly enough toward Alan and Jen. The information about Gracie was a shock, but the comment about Alan and Jen was obliterating. After he said it, Moddie started trembling, and then she started gibbering out the details of the night that Alan asked her if she wanted to grab a beer. She'd almost said no. He was sort of funny in class, but also a little odd, a little off, but the reason she did say yes was that he was friends with Nick, and Moddie trusted Nick's opinion, so she said yes. They went to a bar where you could drink beer out of a glass boot, the conversation was halting and awkward, and then after a few drinks, after maybe about an hour and a half, Alan got up the nerve to "express himself" about how great he thought Moddie was, how attractive, and how much he would like to be her boyfriend, and even after she said she wasn't interested, he kept pushing and even asked for a list of her ex-boyfriends, which Moddie thought was weird, but she listed them off and then he seemed relieved and said, repeatedly, like a tic, that he was way cooler than all of those guys, so "this shouldn't be a problem" (at this point in the story, Nick began looking bored, like *Yes, Moddie, we know, you were so dazzlingly attractive back then*, and remembering that look on his face made Moddie ill again right there on her new couch). Alan was definitely embarrassing himself, so, in order to save him some dignity, Moddie kind of laughed and said, "Yeah, sorry, dude, I'm not interested," and indicated it was time to wrap it up, but Alan really wouldn't drop it, and he began to really insist and to really dog Moddie, saying more than once, as if she gave a shit about his reality, "No, you don't understand." She told him she did in fact understand, and reminded him that they were both drunk, and that it was time to go home.

Alan followed her out of the bar, walking quickly next to her. He kept putting his arm around her and holding her hand, and each time, she would shake it off and say, "Dude, you need to go home," and when she said this he would say, "Nope, I'm coming over," in a happy and cheerful way, as if she had caved to all of his dopey pleading and somehow transformed this annoying outing into a lovely first date.

"Dude, you need to go home."

"But we're having such a nice time."

He put his arm around her waist again and she could feel his hot, moist palm pulling down the corner of her shirt. She moved away and said, "Brother, what do I have to do to get you to go home?"

"Come on, don't be dumb," he said, and then giggled.

They walked like this the half mile to her apartment, and when they got to her building she told him again, "Go home, nighty night!" and when he said she needed someone to tuck her in, she got goosebumps.

She got her keys out and said, "Seriously, knock it off, go home."

"Let me hold the door for you," and he slipped in and Moddie started to laugh nervously. He saw that she laughed and his face lit up. She could see his eyes and beneath them his teeth.

"This is fun," he said.

"Well, not for me, please leave," she said in an annoyed singsong, while walking up the stairs, Alan trailing her by one step.

"Nope, I'm definitely coming inside," he said, a bleak double entendre that didn't escape her, but which likely escaped him as he was not exactly a man of letters, and every time he talked, he sounded like a happy boy on Christmas morning, dazzled by the bounty of Santa, and of course he slipped inside again, and as soon as he was in, he pushed her into a corner, pinned her shoulder to the wall, and put his tongue in her mouth.

"I kept pushing him off and saying no, but he kept coming back." This should have been so clear, but somehow it hadn't been clear to Alan, and had never seemed quite clear to Nick, either, the man whose opinion she trusted as if it were her own.

She pushed him off and asked him, "What the fuck?" but he came right back, like he was the ball on that stupid paddle game, or like he was a brain-dead dog she'd have to shoot, like a drooly, toothless Cujo. She pushed again and said, "Stop it, *Jesus,*" but again he came back (he always came back). She pushed again, and while he was off of her, she tried to raise her arm to hit him, but it felt heavy, like when you try to run in a dream, but your legs feel like they're stuck in thick water, and that's when she knew things weren't going to turn out so well. There was nothing she could do to get him to stop, and soon his hand was beneath her shirt, then beneath her bra, where he tried to do something *erotic* and *sensual* with her nipple— some complex twirling and flicking bullshit with his fingers—

and back then, unlike now, Moddie's body was sensitive to physical contact, so she could feel this motion everywhere, head to toe, and a wave went through her of revulsion, fear, frustration, and scorn, and when the wave reached its peak and crashed, she felt hollow, hopeless, and alone. At first she tried to scream, but nothing would escape her throat, and when she wanted to collapse into tears, she found that something inside of her wouldn't let her do this either. She pushed him off again and said no in what she thought was a decidedly un-coy manner, but he came right back again, predictably, his hot, grubby little face right up in there, breathing on her, smelling of damp hot dog buns, mustard, PBR, and Parliaments. This vile eternity would not end. There was nothing she could do.

She blacked out and came to on the floor, and was surprised to find herself kissing him back, and she immediately moved her face to the side, trying to bury it in the vintage shag rug she'd bought in Ravenswood with her mom. She knew it was no good that she was starting to black out, but it was too much, and she blacked out again, and when she came to, she tried to pull away again, but he grabbed her by the nape of the neck and stuck his tongue in her ear, and when she tried to get up, he pinned her to the ground with his leg. She tried to put her ear to her shoulder to block his wriggling tongue from penetrating straight into her brain, but then he just started licking her neck and doing things to her nipples again. She could feel his dick on her leg and she thought, *No no no no no no no.*

All of this was exhausting, and Moddie wove in and out of consciousness. Nothing would stop him—words, actions, it was all the same. She felt an indifference come over her, and a kind of boredom with the situation—how much time had passed? Shit, I dunno. Every time she saw that he had made some kind of advance—the undone button on her shorts, her shirt and bra hiked up over her boobs, the grunting doglike sound he was starting to make after every time she said "No, seriously stop it, *please,*" his slimy mouth's progress down her torso, as if he was going to try to go down on her (for what?), some insane tickling shit he was trying to do to what he must have believed to be her erogenous zones—she imagined herself crying, but she didn't do anything outwardly, until she felt her underwear move to the side and she felt something slide into her, something like an eel or an accusatory finger, she couldn't tell what it was, some kind of a penis or what—*nobody actually likes you, nobody cares about your opinions, any time you talk it's just goofy nonsense, a secondary opinion, barely tolerated, stupid, silly, you've been so fucking stupid, very very stupid*—and she felt herself click out of her body and her elbow lifted up and came down on his orbital cavity, bone to bone. She heard him whisper something like "fuck" or "shit" and then she heard herself say, "This is over, I am going to sleep now, and you are going home." When she got up and walked toward her room, she looked down at him on the floor while he said, "Hey, it's cool, it's cool. All good."

"Go home."

She slammed the bedroom door behind her.

She stood by her door with her palms against it and waited to hear him leave. She heard the front door open, and after a pause, she heard the front door close. She changed into a nightgown (a weird choice) and got into bed. Then she heard the bedroom door open, and after a pause, she heard the bedroom door close.

Alan got into bed with her. He started to run the tips of his fingers up and down her back, from her tailbone up to her scalp, while he whispered, "Hey, hey. It's okay. Shhh, it's okay.

I just want you to know that I really, really care about you and I think you're an incredibly special person. I think we could be really good together, and we can take this as slowly as you want. We don't have to do anything you don't want to do. I just wanted to come back and make sure you were okay. I really care about you. This was really great. You are very, very special." All while running his fingers up and down her spine.

In the cheerful morning, birds chirping, when Alan tried to kiss her in the kitchen, she sidestepped him and asked him what the fuck he thought he was doing. She stared at him. He didn't try it again.

She went to get coffee across the street, and Alan came with her, but he was "out of cash" and there was a five-dollar minimum on cards, so she bought his coffee, and when they were outside she said, "So are you finally going to go home?" and he told her his plans for the day like she gave a shit.

She called her mom and some of her friends to tell them what had happened. Her mom was quiet, and then said, "Jesus Christ." Nina said, "What a freak." She called Nick too and said, "Hey, your buddy Alan is a real fucking asshole."

"Oh, yeah, what'd he do?"

She was really mad about it. The gall of some people! Like I would ever fuck or date Alan *Treebag*.

Alan emailed her and called her and texted her so often—seven to twelve times a day—that she had to block him on her phone and on MySpace. She never planned to see him again, but then she fell in love with Nick—after years of friendship, some kind of switch went off—and Nick's first request when they started dating, the first concession he asked of her, was that she bury the hatchet with Alan, because Alan and Nick were tight and were thinking of renting a studio together.

"I fucking hate that guy" had been her first response, but,

as Nick pointed out over the course of a few weeks, Moddie could be pretty harsh on people and "anger burns the vessel that contains it."

To Nick, Alan seemed like a cool guy who just had a crush on Moddie, which didn't make him so different from Nick, if you thought about it. He'd had a long-unrequited crush on Moddie, too, "and you like me, right? *Riiiiiight?*" [jostling her knee and being playful]. "I think he's a little jealous that we're together, and maybe a little embarrassed, but he wants to bury the hatchet, so I think you should." And plus, Alan's work was really cool, they were trying to put a show together, so if Moddie could just smooth things over, "then we can all hang out."

And wouldn't that be cool?

Well, at first it was kind of cool, but eventually it was decidedly uncool, and she could not believe that Nick would throw it in her face like that, she could not believe that he would say that the reason he was choosing Gracie over her was that Gracie could get dinner with Alan and fucking *Jen,* especially in the context of the last five years of Alan's work, which was objectively aesthetically hideous, this was not the agreement—stewing over being slighted on a trip to Door County, slowly beginning to view herself as Alan Treebag's jealous and clingy ex-girlfriend in a group of mediocre adjuncts who sat around talking about emails, no, this was not part of the bargain—she had been promised something much better in exchange for her lacuna, but she had been deceived.

She stood still, breathing heavily, looking into the center of the basil-scented Target candle. As she stared deeper into the candle, she traveled back to their old couch and could see Nick sitting there passively with his legs crossed, looking so lethally bored, looking like she was playing him those Sarah McLachlan anorexic dog videos or something—crying and begging and shouting for him to help her save the dogs.

It was so humiliating, so confusing, and she could feel herself saying, could remember it as if it were now—could feel the vibrations of the words inside her, feeling genuinely insane—"I told you what happened right after it happened, and I've told you about this several times over the years, and you asked me to bury the hatchet with Alan, and I tried, but it didn't work, and I can't stand being around him, and I can't stand being around Jen, and it's all so embarrassing and weird, and I don't think I did anything wrong, and I just want someone to tell me that this wasn't okay, *please*."

God, that wretched, squeaky "please."

But he just couldn't do it.

He just looked at her. He took a long pause, and then slowly, calmly (wanting her to leave so that he could get dinner with Jen, Alan, and Gracie), "They say that one in three women have been sexually assaulted, but if you talk to any guy, none of them know a rapist. So, I'm pretty sure that's not what Alan thinks happened."

This was the thing that had really pissed her mom off ("Honestly, sweetheart, he's a fucking jackass"), and the bottom fell out and all of Moddie's nights were like an atonal accordion, compressed into one space, and then expanded out across a great distance, compressed again, and then pulled apart again, and, Fuck it, she thought, crying, her head on the counter, fuck it, yes, I do feel sorry for myself, fuck it, who cares, yes, fuck it, fuck you, whatever—repeating whatever, whatever, and trying to evade the thing she really knew, which was that Nick had never really loved her. In the beginning, lust, and in the end, utility, but never really love.

Boo-hoo-hoo!
And what does that mean about me?
It means that I am fucking stupid.

The moon was almost full. It was large and yellow and the sky was a rich dark blue. In the quiet neighborhoods, you could hear katydids and crickets and the far-off sounds of cars. Downtown, kids stood outside of bars flirting and chain-smoking. Every once in a while, someone slammed a car door or shouted.

A girl in a hoodie pointed at her friend and said, "I've got some plans, biotch," and her friend said, "Yeah, have another drink, Annie," and Annie felt, deep within her, something burning and rising, and she wanted to say it again, to hold her friend by the lapels and scream "I've got *plans,* bee-*yotch,*" as if this cry might reach the heavens, and fate and fortune would smile and give her a life exceeding all expectation.

Her friend started to tap-dance and sing a song about how she was smoking weed.

She doesn't understand, thought Annie, she won't understand until I make her understand.

Annie looked up at the sky and saw the moon, and then her eyes traveled down to the streetlamps and traffic lights. The light changed from green to red, but there were no cars at the intersection. Annie felt celestial. She wanted to drink every last drop of liquor in this town, smoke every last cigarette, fuck every single one of her teachers, then fuck their teachers, then dig up their teachers and fuck them, make a million dollars, and then jettison herself into outer space, burst into flames, and rejoin the universal consciousness as the ultimate supreme being.

Annie looked over at her friend and slapped herself once on the face, quickly, but hard.

"What in the fuck, dude?"

They both started laughing.

In the surrounding neighborhood, where the adults and parents lived in professorial midcentury-modern and tasteful colonial-style homes with casually abundant, wabi-sabi gardens, a family of three attractive, educated, upper-middle-class people watched a Swedish crime movie on the couch.

The daughter, Evelyn, was fourteen. She was just starting to think about love, and how it might intersect with her sense of self-respect.

She'd recently told her parents she was having trouble with math, not because she couldn't understand it, but because it didn't feel urgent or interesting to her. Volleyball practice, English, and history were providing her with, quote, "so much delight," it was hard to find the motivation to prioritize something she didn't care about, like math. She asked for their help figuring out the right way to identify the things that should be important in life, and asked them to support her while she learned how to communicate effectively with adults and authority figures.

When it came to Corey, she knew she needed to process her hurt feelings and move forward. Of course it was his right not to be her boyfriend, and even though she wished he'd handled it differently, she didn't know his situation. She did a tarot reading and then gave herself a makeover. She'd been letting others dictate what she wore. It was okay to be fashion passive, of course, and fashion wasn't the center of her world, not at all, but she liked the way it made her feel to look a certain way. She took her normal clothing to the consignment shop and then took the extra cash to the vintage store and bought a few dresses, and then her mom bought her a few sweaters and a jacket. She'd been drawn to a suede jacket with long fringe but decided on the corduroy, as the fringe felt appropriative, or maybe like it signaled passive approval of the genocide of Indigenous peoples. She gave herself a new haircut, which looked surprisingly good and gave her an artistic, alternative presentation. This was good. She wanted anybody who was going to become interested in her to know that she was artistic and alternative, likely to speak her mind, and that there was a kind of bravery to her.

Work was going just fine for both of her parents, who were both doing yoga three times a week at the Pump House and making an effort to keep trying new things. When they had problems, they tried to confront them openly, but of course they were as subject to emotions as anyone else and sometimes experienced sadness, irritation, and fear. They were impressed by their daughter, and tried their best to remain calm and allow her to make her own choices about things. If we get in the way of her individuation, she'll resent us, and we so want her friendship.

Everybody fucking hated these people.

Up the street, a woman finished reading something for her book club. The book was dumb. She didn't have anything to say about it. She put the book on her desk and then logged on to Facebook to read posts from her close high school friend who had become very conservative.

She went downstairs into the living room to read the posts out loud to her husband, who had been lying on the couch eating cookies and watching a comedy TV show. They talked for forty-five minutes about authoritarian personality types, then went through their friends deciding who was authoritarian, who was antiauthoritarian, and who was too dumb to know which they were. "Who the fuck is an undecided voter?" asked Gerald. "If you don't know who you're voting for, you should be taken to a field and shot." Mary pointed at him and said, "Authoritarian personality."

Next door, a man played Snood on his computer. He had been playing Snood since 1997 and could not stop, and sometimes while playing, he imagined he heard a quiet voice in his mind screaming "Help me!" Downstairs, his wife was asking their son's tutor what they could expect, in terms of outcome, from her services, as his grades were still not great, and they were considering the idea he might in fact have some kind of dyslexia, rather than some inherent inability to comprehend science, so what did the tutor think about this idea for a diagnosis, that maybe it was a chemical, or rather a physical, deformity—or, not deformity, but disability or medical issue that was to account for the grades, did she have an opinion? The tutor held out her hands, equivocating and feeling slightly surprised that the son was sitting on the couch between them, the tutor and the mother on each end, the son in the middle looking straight ahead, emotionless—like when a rabbit goes limp in a dog's mouth, the tutor would say to her boyfriend later—and the tutor didn't know what was best for her, which response would lead to her continuing to get a paycheck from this family, which she did need, looking for income was such a hassle, so she gambled and said, "No, actually, I think, well, of course he's bright, and I think he's starting to get it." The tutor calculated for a minute. "I think in about two months he should be up to speed." The tutor's eyes ran over the brass sculptures of nude women on top of the mantel and down to the large original Prairie-style coffee table, then back up to an oversized painting on the wall behind the mother. "Yeah, two sounds good."

David was staying in this neighborhood, in a small house owned by the university. He was drunk and watching TV.

A little farther out from campus was the more conservative neighborhood. Their lawns were more trim, and their houses were newer or more thoroughly rehabilitated, because the general consensus was, it seemed, that it was dirty to live in a used house. Bethany lived here ("We liked the size"). A little out from there was a small neighborhood of unremarkable homes with unloved yards. One might call these starter homes.

In one home, the overhead light was on in the kitchen, blasting down on a drop-leaf table, which was piled with circulars and unopened mail, a bag of cat food, and six dirty coffee mugs, each with its own sassy and confrontational slogan.

The woman sitting at the table was texting with her friend about another friend of theirs who was on a diet after gaining twenty pounds from emotional eating. They were both saying they hoped she wasn't going to develop an eating disorder. It made them both very uncomfortable when women wanted to alter their bodies to conform to a norm, and they thought it was unfair to expect that natural changes wouldn't just happen within the body. They were both angry at the implication that they were somehow unhappy because they were not on diets themselves, when in fact they were both incredibly happy and satisfied career women. It seemed to them like their friend was a striver, the way she always set herself goals and then cheerfully expressed her progress in public, either on the internet or in person. It was pathetic and shallow. Their friend was maybe even a gender traitor for being so concerned with physical fitness, turning herself into walking pornography for men.

Farther out from that, close to Moddie, on the literal fringe of society, were the very cheap apartments and rental houses. Young pseudopolitical men scoured the internet for things that made their lives, their senses of isolation, make more sense to them. One of these guys, Jacob, had been hideously bullied in Moddie's high school, in ways that sounded right out of *Carrie,* and whenever he thought about it, the shame and the anger felt like hot puke.

He couldn't stop thinking about pedophiles. All these liberals with their liberal academic parents, he hated them, and couldn't believe they were too fucking stupid to see the obvious truth that what they believed in and what they supported was textbook evil. Johnny Gosch, the original milk carton kid, it was on the record that he had been sold into an establishment-politician child prostitution ring. It wasn't even a conspiracy theory, it was just openly true. The Democrats and the establishment were kidnapping and raping children, then murdering them once they were past what they saw as their sexual prime, right around puberty. He wasn't completely convinced of reptilians, but he was open-minded about it, and felt like it was also openly and abundantly clear that the aliens had arrived—the lights over D.C. in 1952, all of the military eyewitnesses who seemed very credible to Jacob, Bob Lazar, all of those South African children, why would they lie? What he didn't understand was what they wanted, or if and how and to what degree they walked among us.

Moddie had calmed herself down, smoked some weed, and was lying curled in the fetal position in her comfortable Target sweat suit watching *All About Eve* on her laptop and telling herself she would get better about groceries and physical fitness, and she would definitely drink more water.

Three miles over, Kimberly was still thinking about her,

and what an entitled bitch she was, and then she started to think about privilege in general, all of these entitled bitches without any jobs. Who the fuck did they think they were, and weren't they ashamed? You should be ashamed. Kimberly would make sure they were ashamed. She could tell someone was rich by the way they acted, like someone with a lot of *free time*. Languid and comfortable opinions, very vocal, as if they'd always been able to say whatever was on their minds, without fear of consequences. Moddie was just like that, like some kind of trust fund kid, it was so absolutely disgusting. But, she wasn't even a good trust fund kid, or she wouldn't be here in this stupid little town. If Kim were rich, she'd be better at it, live more interestingly, find a way to make something out of all of her free time. Of course she wanted free time and she wanted luxury, but she didn't feel entitled to it like some people, she knew she would have to work for it to have it, and then when she had it she knew she'd deserve it, because she'd earned it.

Kim had known a lot of rich people. When she was younger she knew some rich people, when she was in college, at the university, they were the ones who had the unpaid internships, they had no idea what it was like to be working-class like her. They didn't know they weren't real people, they didn't know they existed just to be objects of scorn, they thought they were charming little carefree special people, like babies, but they were scum, and Kimberly was excited that people like that were being publicly exposed as scum. When they talked about their summer internships at museums, they didn't know they were living in an extended childhood and that their jobs were an extended day care and that even if they did end up having high cultural positions it didn't mean they deserved it, it only meant that culture was turning into a kind of adult day care system for unchecked privilege, and if these rich white women had any sense of shame or morals they would not be taking these positions, but rather would be offering up their positions to people of color or people of a queer disposition or white women from working backgrounds like her, because they had no idea the amount of shame and anger that came from being condescended to constantly by people who had grown up with cultural access, grown up in private schools with good stupid fucking summer art camps, with loving parents and educated neighbors. They didn't understand how much cultural capital they had and how little of it they deserved. You had to go through the proper channels. You couldn't just have things handed to you, that wasn't the way it worked. Kim did well in high school and she went to a good college and then she went to an Ivy League university for her master's, and she took out the money to do so using the proper channels, and she had worked incredibly hard to be where she was, not like someone entitled, and she knew she wanted to keep rising, but she knew it wouldn't be handed to her, and she made decisions and had thoughts based on this feeling that she wanted to rise, she took this starter job so she could be on the right career track, and she thought she could write papers that would be read within the academic community, but also—like how she'd been on the radio—she could write some things that were not academic, that were in more of a mainstream style, published in more mainstream places, which would be great because then she could put those things on her résumé and she could then use that to rise, and then she would maybe get a sabbatical and she wouldn't have to work all the time, forty-plus hours a week, and she could take some time off, but it wouldn't just be handed to her, no, it wouldn't just be fucking handed to her like it was for some people, she would have to work for it and she would have to earn it no matter how many people didn't understand who was who and what was what, she thought, her mind mounting the ladder, now palpitating crazily on the sectional in the living room in the house that she and her husband owned in the manicured tree-lined neighborhood, TV on, swaddled in the blanket of things, *still I rise*.

Craig was in bed when Pam got Kim's annoying email on her phone. Tea with David had gone well and restored some of her confidence. She wanted to say something that would defuse the situation on paper but would also serve as a well-earned chiding.

She typed quickly on her phone.

Kim!!! I am so sorry, yes, that was incredibly awkward at Beth's, but you have to understand, Moddie's been through a lot lately. I know she can rub people the wrong way sometimes, but we've been friends since we were 12, and she's really loyal and funny and smart and when it comes down to it, super, super generous. Give her a chance! Even if you have to think of her as a crazy person or something—when she says stuff that makes me mad, sometimes I just think of her as a crazy person and it helps. But I promise she's one of the good ones.

There will be more parties this semester, and I will definitely introduce you to David! We just had a lunch date, actually, and he's definitely game to do more community stuff. I was really overwhelmed that night, and was really sleepwalking or of course I would have introduced you two. I'm really glad you think we have been getting closer, I think so too. You are definitely a real friend to me!!

Ah, sorry if any of this sounds manic or sloppy, just wanted to write you back asap because you sounded upset! Talk more about any of this soon if you want!

xx,
Pam

Pam stood by the bed, refreshed her email compulsively a few times, and decided she should invite Moddie over for dinner. It wouldn't be so bad. What was she afraid would happen?

A flock of geese flew by, honking. An outdoor cat ran across a major intersection. Traffic lights changed. A man filled up his SUV with gas. Someone smoked weed behind the bowling alley and thought they saw something moving in the bushes. Someone's mom lay awake in bed having a sexual fantasy about a colleague.

Crickets chirped. More geese. Moonlight.

Six

It was sunny out, warm but not humid.

"I bestow upon you, child, *grace,*" said Moddie, gesturing benevolently. Moddie and Nina were on a bench behind Beaner's, and Moddie was in the middle of railing on Gracie. It was Nina's lunch break. Nina kept saying "Oh my god, haha" while glancing down at her phone.

She checked her phone again and said, "Fuck, I gotta go back."

They'd been together for about fifteen minutes. Moddie stiffened and then nodded agreeably.

"Oh, hey, you know," said Moddie, "I'm going to Pam's for dinner later, if you want to come. I could ask, I'm sure she'd say yes. It'd be cool to keep hanging out."

"Yeah," said Nina.

"Awesome."

"I just can't really do weeknights. I have to work in the morning. Sometimes I can do it, if I have like a week or two to prepare, but right now everything is so stressful with work, I don't even want to get into it, and also there's been this huge piece of tape on my living room window since I moved in, and I keep trying to get the management company to come remove it, but they refuse, so at night I have to kind of litigate that whole mess. I just really need my nights."

Moddie nodded and tried to arrange her face to say *I understand these reasonable things you've just said.*

"Cool."

Later that evening, Moddie put on a dress and some makeup, then washed her face and put a shapeless sweater over the dress so she wouldn't frighten anyone with her sexualized appearance. She was never quite sure if she and Pam were still friends. She decided to drive instead of walking, and in the car, she felt nervous and weird, sort of bummed out and disoriented, but in a way that was beginning to feel normal.

When she got there, she hugged them both and set a six-pack and a two-pound bulk bag of gummy worms on the coffee table.

"Huh, that's *quirky*," said Craig.

"I have PTSD," said Moddie.

They sat around the living room and drank beer while Pam's eggplant thing finished baking.

"Fuck, that smells good," said Moddie. "Pam, you're the best cook. When we lived together, you really took care of me."

"Aw, thanks, Moddie. Well, you certainly needed all the help you could get," said Pam.

"What do you mean?" said Moddie. She laughed abruptly.

"Oh, just your cooking. Remember how you basically lived off of sandwiches? Even if you made a curry or roasted vegetables you would put it in a pita pocket. Everything was a sandwich."

Moddie was quiet for a second, raised her eyebrows, and said, "Nothing wrong with sandwiches." Then she smiled.

Both women were talking at a slightly gentler, higher pitch than normal.

"Oh, but you remember when Nina made us dinner and she started that grease fire in the skillet and when we came in from the porch she was just standing there crying?" said Pam.

"Yes, I do," said Moddie. "A very memorable day and a very memorable time."

"Memory lane," said Craig, raising his beer.

Eventually, they moved to the kitchen and the conversation turned to work and to David, who Craig disliked vehemently, and who he routinely referred to as Mr. New York City.

"Like my grandfather used to say about Paris, wonderful city, hate the people."

Pam gave him a look like *Who are you, why have you come here?*

"New York, New York, it's a horrible town, the people rot in a hole in the ground," sang Craig, confidently and loudly in a deep vibrating Broadway voice.

"Craig, I think he's actually from Connecticut or something," said Pam, faux delicately.

"I am loath to admit that I find him vaguely attractive," said Moddie.

Pam glanced at her quickly, then reached for her beer and took a few swills.

"Yeah, if you're attracted to slightly flabby brooding middle-aged men," said Craig, putting a fistful of bread in his mouth and pouting.

"Men and women might be into slightly different things," said Moddie. "This was something Nick and I used to fight about. When I would make fun of whatever some dumb girl was reading, and we're talking *Eat, Pray, Love*–level shit, not just like *The White Album,* he'd be like, 'Duuuh, I don't think that's what men care about.'" She shifted. She'd said that last part in too doltish an imitation, and it hung inside her. She preferred it when her imitations were more nuanced and less mainstream. She shrugged and shook her head rapidly a few times.

"I guess, candidly, having cultivated taste and being cultured makes a woman seem educated, which makes her seem maybe wealthy and well-bred, so if she's hot plus cultured, plus into you, that's a nice double self-esteem-confirmation thing, but it's not totally necessary. To be honest, if a really beautiful girl who's even marginally socially acceptable is into you, that's just like win-win. And you have to remember most people don't care about reading, so your *Eat, Pray, Love* could be another man's," Craig trailed off, having trouble thinking of a book to complete the comparison, "Machiavelli."

Moddie gave him a wtf look.

"So, you don't care about being with a well-read woman?" asked Pam.

"You're the double self-esteem confirmation," said Craig with a crack in his voice. "You're the win-win-win." Craig raised his eyebrows, and stared at his food and ate in silence for a second. "A rich ol' broad."

Moddie looked out the window and into the neighbor's window, where someone was watching TV.

"I had a really insane nightmare last night," said Moddie, "if anyone cares to hear."

"Yeah, sure," said Pam, wiping her mouth with a paper towel.

"I was in the bathroom—it was my grandma's bathroom, but instead of being beige it was kind of aqua and silver. I had somewhere to be. The person who was going to drive me was waiting out in the other room, and I felt very aware of their impatience and very responsible for it. I was squatting over the toilet in this weird position, almost standing on the toilet, and I was pooping, but I couldn't get the turd to sever from my anus. I don't remember if there was toilet paper or not, but in the dream I realized I was going to have to reach down and pull the turd out of my ass myself."

"When you're here, you're family," said Craig, setting down his fork.

"Somehow in the context of the dream," Moddie continued, "this was the polite thing to do, and I remember being hyperfocused on being polite. I felt like if I didn't get it off of me, it would follow me wherever I went, which, obviously, that would be terrible. Even in the dream I knew that. So I got the turd out of my ass and into the toilet, but then my hands were covered in shit. There were a bunch of white towels and white terry cloth robes, but I didn't want to get them dirty. I kept trying to wipe the shit off my hands, but it was getting everywhere. It was getting on my clothes and in my hair, I was spreading it all over the walls. On my face. It was just fucking everywhere. The room got completely covered in shit. I was frantic about making the person in the other room wait, I felt really guilty and weird, totally panicking, and then I woke up."

"Poop dreams," said Craig, in reference to the documentary *Hoop Dreams*.

"That's obviously a Nick dream," said Pam, reaching for the salad bowl. "He's the turd."

Moddie nodded in a noncommittal way, sort of side to side.

"You know you need to flush him out of your life, but he's still just getting all over everything, and making it hard for you to go out and be with other people. And you've been polite with this turd, you've anguished yourself about whether or not you've been considerate enough with it, and all it's done is gotten you covered in shit, so it's time to yank the turd and deal with the bathroom next. I hope you're not talking to him."

"No . . . no no," said Moddie.

"Good, because frankly he's toxic, and I would venture to say slightly emotionally abusive, or at least incredibly manipulative from everything you've told me. He's not your responsibility, he made his choices, and if he's suffering or if he hurts himself, frankly that's his own fault, and I really don't care," said Pam. "Who cares? You shouldn't, either. He made his bed."

Moddie examined a piece of the lasagna and thought about asking *What is this, basil?*

"I don't know," said Craig. "Maybe you're painting with your shit." When he said "painting" he gestured broadly in an arc. "The turd is not your ex, the turd is your anger. You're trying not to express your anger—your turd—but it's impossible to stop, because it's your nature to express it. It's going to come out. And you're pretending that you don't want to get it all over the nice clean bathroom—telling yourself you're a polite person—but you're still wiping shit all over the walls and your face and the towels. You could have just washed your hands, but you're like an action painter. You're like the fucking de Kooning of turds, just," Craig put his tongue in his cheek and then pretended to paint something, "let it out, baby."

Moddie laughed. "Yeah, maybe."

"I don't really think that's it, Craig," said Pam.

They all ate and drank for a second until Craig stood up and said, "I have to pee," and left the room.

Moddie shook her head and said, "Fuck, I was so obsessed with him."

"You were not obsessed," said Pam. "You were in a relationship that was incredibly imbalanced and you were taken advantage of, and now you're healing."

"But he was like the only thing I ever thought about day and night. I like . . . *worshipped* him. That's fucking crazy. This is fucking insane, what the fuck?" said Moddie, laughing.

"Moddie, I just don't think that's true," said Pam. "Don't say that about yourself."

"I don't know if it's a bad thing," said Moddie. "I'm just reviewing my feelings. 'Tis better to have blah blah blah."

Pam speared some salad. "I just really hate the way he treated you. It seems like he completely blocked you from maturing and developing and pursuing your own goals. It doesn't seem like he cared about you at all."

"I don't think that's true," said Moddie, looking down, listening to the sound of running water in the other room.

Craig came back in, wiping his hands on the bottom of his shirt.

"What are you guys talking about?" he asked.

"Whether or not my ex cared about me at all," said Moddie.

"Oh my," said Craig, sitting down.

"I just think he's an asshole," said Pam, "and he had every opportunity to address the problems in your relationship, but he just kept making selfish decisions and treated you like shit up to the point where you had to break up with him so that he could end the relationship without any of the guilt and get everyone else to feel sorry for him. They say you learn a lot about a relationship from the breakup, so, that's all I have to say."

"I mean, yeah," said Moddie. "I know."

"It's not that simple when you're in love," said Craig.

Pam rolled her eyes and laughed by blowing air out of her nose. "I'm sorry, I thought she wanted us to interpret her dream. And I'm not sure it's helpful for her to think about love right now while she's in this delicate phase," said Pam. "Just because you think you love somebody doesn't mean they get to walk all over you and treat you like their servant."

Craig raised his eyebrows.

Moddie shrugged. "She's not wrong. I was his love slave. His stupid, mindless little love slave. I made no choices, simply obeyed my tyrant's every decree," she said, holding up her fist and shaking it at the sky.

"Okay, that's not what I'm saying," said Pam. "I don't know why you guys are ganging up on me."

Moddie looked over at Pam and their eyes locked for a second, before Pam looked away.

"Frankly, I'm impressed," said Craig. "You seem like you're really holding it together."

"Thank you," said Moddie. She thought about going for a high five but didn't.

After a little bit of silence, Pam shifted to the Supreme Court confirmation hearings, which apparently she'd watched at someone's desk at work with a small crowd of sympathetic women, all of whom had felt buoyed by the bonds of sisterhood.

"Yeah, I didn't really watch that much," said Moddie. "I looked at some of the pictures."

"You have to watch the news, Moddie," said Pam. "This is major."

"I watch the news. I watched it for a second. I got what I needed."

Moddie wondered how much of what she'd told Pam about Nick had stuck, and how much of it had been misremembered and rearranged to reflect her disappointments with Craig. She reached across the table for a piece of bread and ripped it in half.

Pam described how everyone in the office had felt like this event was both retraumatizing because of the reckoning at work and how much care and concern they had for the students—they were all acutely aware of how dangerous these years were for young women—but also poignant in a solemn way, as if the pain of these things' being brought to light was a necessary part of everyone's healing. She said she found the woman's testimony incredibly moving, and she found the woman herself to be incredibly brave. "I mean, I can't imagine having to be in a room with someone who had done something like that to you, it's disgusting, and it's disgusting to think of him sitting next to Ruth Bader Ginsburg, too, of all people—I mean it all makes me sick, and I'm so angry on her behalf but also so grateful for her testimony and her strength and for what this will do in terms of moving the conversation forward. But, yeah, it was just a hard day overall," she said, smiling sadly and breathing out in a way that Moddie found slightly theatrical.

Moddie had very much wanted to have a nice time at this dinner, and to look forward, not back, but the way that Pam was speechifying was beginning to get under her skin, was beginning to seem self-satisfied, and was beginning to seem like dangling bait. Moddie had liked it when Craig said she seemed to be holding it together, and she wanted to keep her shit together, but each borrowed and obvious statement from Pam was like a turn of the crank on an emotional vise, until it seemed as if she had no choice but to abandon this fleeting idea of herself as a calm, strong, and proud presence, because hearing Pam describe these as desirable attributes in the abstract—strength, bravery, etc.—made Moddie want to take a hammer to the stupid mental statue Pam was constructing, this sort of benevolent, martyred, middlebrow Venus, and smash it until it was dust.

Pam kept reciting her prerecorded feelings.

Moddie ate some of the strawberry rhubarb crumble and said, "Obviously the pageantry of everything is totally disgusting. Lindsey Graham is a little fuck, we knew that, but even the 'good guys' are putting on such a show—just trying to force this damaged woman to tell her dirty secret on TV so they can try to get votes or whatever, audition themselves for glory. Everybody knows he's going to get sworn in. It's like watching the fucking *Hunger Games*. It's cosplay. What's the point of it all? To put on a show so we can all feel good about ourselves and then go back to not paying attention? I mean, no shit, obviously, but nothing's going to come of this except that he'll get sworn in and DeVos will be able to use this to roll back Title Nine protections using this 'witch hunt' as a precedent, and then Ginsburg will die, and then abortion will be illegal and we'll slide slowly toward a fascist dystopia, but no one will wonder why the fuck Ginsburg didn't just retire when she could be certain she would be replaced by someone reasonably sane, no one will wonder if it was because of the intoxicating ego trip of that egregious 'Notorious RBG' bullshit, or some stipulation in her Netflix contract, and no one will look at her as a corrupt, narcissistic, and responsible old crab, no, they'll put her face on their flags as they march the streets shouting stupidly about something they don't fully understand outside of 'I am angry, someone said something mean about *me*, and I am *important*, and I defy anyone to say otherwise.' Shout, shout, shout, scream, scream, scream, while nothing gets done about climate change and the pot keeps getting hotter and hotter but we're all too self-centered and egomaniacal—with our egomaniacal heroes—to do jack shit about it but complain, I mean though honestly what the fuck are we supposed to do anyway, the Republicans are too strategic and their constituency too batshit to be leveled with, and then we'll die, all of us in an orgiastic catastrophe, but maybe that's how it's supposed to be, I don't know."

Her eyes roamed over to the refrigerator. A rectangular magnet with a photo of the Golden Gate Bridge held up a flyer with the words "Vote No on 14" and a long receipt.

Pam breathed in quickly, as prelude to her response. She wondered how many of these ideas had come from Nick.

Moddie felt disgusted as she drove home, thinking to herself that she was surprised by how dumb and simple Pam seemed now, almost brainwashed. She'd been trying to get Pam to hang out for four months. Gee, that seemed like a long time, long enough to send a message—one that Moddie had finally gotten tonight. Pam used to be a good time, she used to be able to have a spirited disagreement, but now she took everything so personally, as if Moddie were some kind of idiotic bully who should be treated with calm, condescending politeness. When Moddie thought about listening to Pam talk, hearing her catchphrases from the internet, "men are going through a reckoning," etc., it was like a faucet turning off. Where once flowed friendship now flowed nothing but the petty drips of cool indifference. What did Pam know about "the reckoning"? And for the love of god, why did everything need to be cased in such corny biblical language?

Moddie pulled up in front of her house. She slammed the car door. When she passed the mailboxes that were nailed to the front of her house near the doors, she rolled her eyes and whispered, "I fucking hate people." Her neighbor had just put an Iron Cross decal on his mailbox. Fucking people. She jabbed it quickly with her fist.

She threw her keys on the couch and fantasized about bringing this up at dinner. She would have said, There are like seventeen Iron Cross decals up in my neighborhood now. Craig would have asked what a decal was, and then Pam would have told him it was like a bumper sticker in that voice of hers that's supposed to humiliate him but really only makes her sound boring, and then she'd have turned to Moddie and said, I don't think you need to be so dramatic about it, Moddie, I'm pretty sure the Iron Cross is just a symbol for motorcyclists now.

You mean like biker gangs? is what Moddie would have said, and there would have been a provocative tone in her voice.

Well, maybe not *gangs*. I don't think we need to be alarmist.

Well, I don't know if you've ever watched any movies about biker gangs, but all of those old bikers have just straight-up swastikas tattooed all over their faces, so I don't know if I'm totally comforted by the idea that the Iron Cross is now, as you say, "just a symbol for bikers" because I'm pretty sure the history of bikers is mostly that they were roving bands of psychopathic serial rapists, not decent hardworking Americans trying to cut back on their carbon footprint.

Yeah, that's what she'd say.

Are you sure he's not just a skateboarder?

Well, Pam, no, he doesn't have the lithe, lean body and carefree spirit of a skateboarder, so I'm pretty sure it's a straight-up Nazi medal of honor.

And then Craig would get his phone out and offer to look up Nazi symbols and Moddie would start screaming about how there should never be any phones allowed at the dinner table, then she would pick up Craig's phone and throw it at the window, where it would bounce and fall to the floor.

Moddie let out a little scream and then turned on some music.

Suddenly it was like, Okay, what the fuck now? I went to fucking dinner and here I am again in my stupid little room, guess I'll sit on the couch and think about my stupid life.

She crossed her arms and sat on the couch, scowling.

All shall be punish'd, thought Moddie.

She knew a thing or two about the Nazis.

Moddie grew up in a very small Midwestern town one state over. Her family had something vaguely to do with the founding of the town. The town itself would have you believe that it had something vaguely to do with the ending of slavery. These things were taught as a general part of the indoctrination into civic pridefulness at Moddie's elementary school, and there were annual field trips to the former Yance estate, which was now a museum, which put her at uncomfortable odds with some of her elementary school teachers, many of whom seemed to openly dislike young Margaret, much to her confusion at the time, as she was used to being liked and accepted at least to some degree. Maybe it had something to do with Moddie correcting the docents on school tours through the mansion, which she only did once or twice.

The elementary school had been built in the 1800s. It was

a beautiful building. According to anecdote, the principal during the fifties and sixties was what one might call a history buff. He owned a full, authentic SS uniform and when the children were studying World War II, he'd wear the uniform and goose-step down the hallway, busting into rooms and shouting "Heil Hitlah!" over the din of fearful and titillated squeals. Later, as his interest in history intensified, he hired a local musician to reset the school's anthem to the "Horst Wessel Lied," with new lyrics that championed the themes of childhood bravery, strength, and loyalty, and eventually, after the students sang this new anthem in the school gymnasium, all erupted in the frenzied, exuberant ululations of the North American Indians, hand to mouth, screaming "*Wooowooo-wooowooowooowooowoooo!*" What joy!

By the time Moddie was in school, this man was dead, but his presence lingered in the form of the anthem and in the forms of the teachers he had hired, Moddie's second-grade teacher, Ms. Schmidt, among them.

Moddie didn't like to think too much about Ms. Schmidt, but when her mind did wander back down the stream of time, looking for some original source of her suffering, she often arrived here, as if at some ancient shrine to human stupidity and cruelty.

I went to Nazi school, she thought, on the couch, and then imagined Pam rolling her eyes and saying *No you did not,* but yes I did, I did!

Schmidt wore outfits with little teddy bears and sunflowers on them, a smiling appliqué worm poking out of a fresh, red apple, as was customary in her profession. Her hair was a soft, white, unfuckable swirl around her head. Her classroom was filled with teddy bears in different outfits. Among the rewards given by Schmidt to the good students was the privilege of holding one of these toys. Due to the intensity of Ms. Schmidt's feeling for the toys, Moddie was under the impression, at the time, that they had been given to Schmidt by either her father or her lover, but now Moddie understood that Schmidt had bought these dolls herself, and this filled Moddie with delicious, scornful pity.

Among the weird shit they were asked to do as children was to administer lengthy massages during story time. Moddie recalled the sensations of her young fingers sliding around on Schmidt's ancient shoulders, the skin like a lubricated dental dam laid over a piece of dry chicken.

Moddie assumed that no one else liked giving these massages, a safe assumption, they were mandatory, they were repulsive, Schmidt had a mean streak (Moddie had overheard her mom say that Schmidt had suggested Moddie might have a "learning disability"), so when it was her turn, because Moddie liked to make people laugh, as she was massaging Ms. Schmidt's shoulders, she crossed her eyes and made the silent, universal "blah blah blah" expression with her mouth, thinking she was speaking the will of the people, giving voice to the voiceless, but two hands shot up—Clark the "class clown" and an unremarkable dishwater-blonde girl who always got A's and who always told everyone she loved bumblebees, and sure, who doesn't, but shut the fuck up about it already.

Moddie was sent to the corner (before she could even finish her massage!), and Clark and whatshername were given candy for helping Ms. Schmidt maintain moral order. Candy was given to students who best conformed to Schmidt's idea of how children should behave. She was delighted by loud boyish boys and soft-spoken fastidious (non-Asian) girls (she hadn't seemed so fond of Yui), and above all she loved obsequiousness.

The mass hoarding of candy seemed to be the main point of the class.

Soon after the massage incident, Moddie passed by a shelf and accidentally knocked over a teddy bear. Not with her hand. Just with the breeze of her passing. A casual, victimless accident. Ms. Schmidt screamed like an annoying neighbor you secretly hate reaching shrill climax, and when Moddie looked up, she saw Schmidt holding her trembling hand up to her face in pantomime horror. She gasped! She pointed! Her finger was arthritic! From her wrist hung a golden hearts charm bracelet!

"Jimmy Toes!!!" she called, as if to the heavens in an incompetent local production of something Greek. "Children, look, Jimmy Toes has fallen seven stories! His arm is broken in six places! Maggie has broken his arm through her carelessness, oh everybody pray for his recovery!" And then she brought the children together in a prayer circle while Moddie was instructed to stand in the corner and make a cast for the doll, which everyone but Moddie was allowed to sign, because Jimmy Toes was still angry with Moddie but most of all afraid of Moddie's violent temper.

Jimmy Toes was a bug-eyed bear with a torn-to-shit straw hat, a corncob pipe, and a green gingham vest that didn't quite button over his fucked-up little tumtum, and the sight of him in that moment tapped into such a deep wellspring of hatred that Moddie felt faint as she wrapped the expertly crafted cast over his undeserving fat-fuck little arm.

When Moddie told her parents about this, she made a joke about which one of them had the learning disability now, "Uh, that bear is not *re*-al, lady," which made her parents laugh and try to say, sternly, "Moddie, you cannot say things like that outside of this house." Things did not improve. Schmidt started making fun of Moddie's bladder control every time she asked to use the bathroom pass, and we all know where that sad story leads, yes, yes, to public pee-pee pants.

One day, near the end of the school year, when it was nearing Moddie's birthday, she brought up a drawing to give to Ms. Schmidt that she thought Schmidt might agree to pin to the bulletin board next to the other students' drawings, since maybe she knew it was almost Moddie's birthday. It was lunchtime and Moddie had come in from recess to have a moment alone to submit her request. The lights were turned off. Young Moddie held the paper in her hands. She approached slowly. Schmidt did not seem to notice her. She sat there, slowly eating a soft, white sandwich, staring at the back of the room, rocking gently, quietly humming the school's anthem to herself.

Each year each teacher was a little weird. In fourth grade her dope-faced farm-enthusiast (what, pray tell, leads someone to become a farm "enthusiast"?) teacher threw a kickball at her face and when she said "Ow" he shrugged cartoonishly and said, "Ooops, I'm sowwy. Did I hurt your wittle facey?"

Uh, yeah?

Just kind of slightly off shit like that, and there was probably something about the way Moddie was acting that was making these teachers so angry, but even as an adult, she couldn't think of what it could be, and then after they moved and Moddie went to high school in X it was the Calvinists with their anal obsessions with daily planners—*did you get your li'l fuckin' stamp on your daily planner? Because you know if you don't have your stamp you're actually not authorized to be here on the premises*—and then in art school the Satanists. Jesus Christ. The Satanists!

Moddie was on her back on the couch looking at the water stain on the ceiling, percolating, reviewing the events of her education. Everybody thought she was so whiny and annoying and entitled when she said she hated school, and when she suggested that maybe being too proud of doing well in school might in some ways be a bad sign, and might mean you were, unbeknownst to yourself, some kind of a fascist. Moddie thought about her worst boyfriend (revenge porn, roofied her as a joke) and how he, even in his twenties, bragged about having been in a Montessori "gifted and talented" program. She wanted to make a where-are-they-now brochure for Montessori. He could be on the cover, which could be a lenticular to show his DTs.

Moddie laughed and said, "Whoo dawggies."

She stood and began pacing in circles around the apartment, rubbing her hands together and sometimes touching her face.

Methodical control of students. Each student would be perfect and raised according to perfect principles. There was a standard of measurement. Certain standards each child would have to meet in order to pass on to the next rank. If a child were defective, the child would have to be disciplined, and if the child were still defective, the child would have to be isolated so as not to negatively affect the students who were advancing well and properly and in an orderly healthy admirable manner. Like prison! And if someone came along who didn't fit in and who didn't do what she was told, she would be assigned extra work to do in isolation, because teacher and students were all on a mission of correct improvement.

When whatshername and Clark raised their hands that day during story time to let Schmidt know Moddie had been misbehaving, Schmidt sent Moddie to the corner, and then went to Clark and the girl and gave them each a Dove chocolate, because good boys and girls got Dove chocolates, and as the chocolate melted in the mouths of those two children, they felt comfortable, content, safe, good, and all across the room in little minds, associations began to form, personalities began to form—compliant or deviant—alliances and feuds began, alliances and feuds that would play out in so many different configurations over the years, different actors, same story, over and over—Clark and whatshername, Ms. Schmidt, Moddie in the corner, Clark and the girl swimming in a bath of dopamine and serotonin, Moddie steeped in adrenaline, and Schmidt high on a cloud of control so strong as to almost certainly be sexual in nature, the skin-tagged turkey wattle dangling from her neck like a sucked-out teat, placed there by her maker as a signal loud and clear, if she were creative enough to see it, that she was a goat, an abomination, a farting creature on the sidelines of a Bosch-like fantasy, what a *bitch, FUCK!*

Moddie laughed again.

To succeed in this system would be a grave spiritual failure. Pam was an A student. She went to Oberlin and grad school at U of C over Columbia, but only because of a boyfriend (she told everyone this thing about Columbia and the boyfriend so that everyone knew she could have gone to Columbia, whoop-de-doo, nobody gives a fucking shit where you went to grad school).

It wasn't exactly that Moddie was saying all people who got A's were in some ways similar to Nazis, but she also wasn't not saying this.

Pam, Pam, Pam.

Moddie was furious, and opened up Photoshop and made a design for a travel mug—"travel" for when she had a job again—based on that Notorious RBG design. It was identical, the crown and everything, except underneath where it said "Notorious RBG" Moddie added the line "Beating motherfuckers like Ike beat Tina since 1993."

She placed the order on Shutterfly, since they were more lax about using copyrighted images.

"Spread love, it's the *Brooklyn* way!" said Moddie in a cloyingly peppy voice, her whole body bubbling over with revulsion at the idea of "Brooklyn" as a culturally accepted marker of "success" for all of these corny milquetoast careerists pumping themselves up by thinking that the Supreme Court (and what, therefore, *they*??) had something to do with gangster rap—and who didn't like feminism, and who didn't like *Ready to Die,* but just because you like peanut noodles and bubblegum, doesn't mean you put them in your mouth at the same time.

Oh, and what is your job?

My job is eat my fucking cock, dumbass.

Be careful, you're going to need a good GPA! Bull*shit* I need a good GPA. Lies, lies, lies.

Hillary Clinton, I mean my god, I mean Jesus Christ, who in their right mind chooses a guy who looks like he'd lose in a fuck-marry-kill between John du Pont and Robert Durst to run a fucking popularity contest on behalf of a notoriously unpopular war-hungry gaffe-prone wife of a serial rapist? Oh, guys, I know, great idea, what if we based our slogan off of the "I'm with Stupid" shirt? Cool? You really think I didn't want to vote for you because I was busy flirting with boys? Yeah, maybe that's what you were doing when you were young, covering up for your husband's rapes while your good friend Henry Kissinger was getting blow jobs from Gloria Steinem while she pinky-promised the CIA she'd keep her feminism reasonable, you might be, you know, mistaking your-fucking-self with me, you dense fuck. Oh, is it hard to be the most competent person in the room but not to be taken seriously because you're a woman? Is that how you feel right now, about this room? Don't be so fucking sure.

Don't be so fucking sure, Pam.

Moddie was back on the couch, looking up at the ceiling, mind ricocheting around different angry things she might say to different people. Riding the motherfucking bronco.

Fuck you, fuck you, fuck you, fuck you!

She imagined cradling David Koch in her arms like a hideous baby, gripping him by the scruff of his neck, placing her fingers firmly on both jugulars, and saying, "We like it when you sponsor *Nova,* Davey, but nobody likes the other stuff you do. You want to be a good boy, now, don't you? Yeah, you want to be a very good boy," then slapping him full force on the face a few times until his mouth bled. "Everybody thinks you're an evil, stupid man, and nobody likes you. It's clear you've never experienced love, you top-ten *Forbes* piece of shit. You look like the kind of guy whose dick makes people gossip about how gross it is, and if you didn't have money, literally no one would even acknowledge you, because you are nothing." She kept slapping him with her hands, and then she started slapping him with the weird dildo she bought online, but it wasn't enough, she knew he didn't care and that there was nothing she could do, he was untouchable, he had won a long time ago, anything she tried to do to hurt him he would either like or not even notice. He was looking off into the distance, bored, and Moddie thought about ramming the dildo down his throat and then down into his eye sockets, one and then the other, skull-fucking him to death while she screamed, bathed in his blood, and once he died, she imagined everything he had worked for and everyone who had benefited from him and helped him were blighted and suffered for all eternity, and then his corpse combusted and disappeared, but still it wasn't enough, it wasn't enough. Still, he had won!

Moddie started laughing and put her hands over her face.

"What the fuck?"

So, this is what it's like to have friends, eh? This is what it's all about, huh? This is what they're always talking about, well well well.

When Moddie was in a certain state of mind, she had a very limited view of things. It was as if she'd never left X for Chicago and Pam was all there had ever been. Little teenage slights resurfaced. Memories of Pam mocking Moddie's clothing in front of someone more popular (always, *always* mistaking popular for cool), Pam teasing Moddie in front of her crushes, Pam taking Arnie to Winter Dance, Pam acting faux startled when she learned that Moddie's verbal scores were higher than hers ("I guess it pays to be raised by an English prof"—yes, using the word "prof" like a fucking tool). Pam agreeing to meet her at the mall more than once and not showing up, even though she knew Moddie had taken the bus.

And *still* Moddie had been excited to live near Pam again, and *still* Moddie held Pam's company in high regard. "And all my life I've lived and let live," said Moddie, pacing and gesturing, and then she muttered, through gritted teeth, "*Nobody values how fucking forgiving I have been.*"

She wanted to write Pam an email, detailing her grievances, and then send that email, let it disturb and derange Pam as Pam had disturbed and deranged her. Pam, I know you think you're better than I am, but when I look at your face, a simpleton is what I see. The clunky features of the serving class, the dullard eyes of a governess. You succeed only through your aptitude for conformity.

Moddie chuckled and pretended to swirl a snifter of brandy. Her shoulders were up by her ears and her jaw was clenched so tight the muscles jutted out visibly.

Well, if that's what you choose, thought Moddie. If that's what you choose, that's what we can do!

She had no idea what the fuck she was talking about. But she knew, knew above all things, she was sending some motherfucking emails tonight.

She jogged in place for a second, then did some quick arm stretches and went to her laptop and thought for a second. She got up again and did a single push-up. Then she went to her desk and composed—thinking of the email that would disturb Pam the most.

Bethany, hey!

Good to see you at the artist talk the other night, and thanks again for having me over last month. It's really cool to know people since *childhood*. I was thinking about Football Steve the other night and cracking up.

Would you want to grab lunch or coffee sometime? Would be fun to hang out. Absolutely truly, truly no presh if you're busy, I'm sure we'll see each other around. Just doing the new-girl-in-town thing.

I am absolutely 100% in a goofy mood this year (if you hadn't, uh, noticed)—half totally liberated and happy and content and optimistic, and then half scatterbrained and turned around. Let's just say my exit from Chicago was somewhat operatic, and I'm still coming down a little.

Forgot to say I loved your piece in the *Times,* which I'm sure everyone is saying. It made me think about how we have these scientific narratives, which seem so remote and abstract, but they're just a new language for more colloquial/emotional types of languages—super cool and really great food for thought. I hope I get to read more.

Happy to be back, happy to see you, hope you're enjoying this incredible weather.

Best, etc.,
Moddie

Sounds friendly enough to me, she thought, and sent it. Let's get this motherfucker rolling.
She leaned back. Yes, good. Like a stronger dog peeing on a weaker dog's pee. Energy coursed through her, roaming around, looking for other satisfactions it might take, until it occurred to her that who she would really love to email was Jen.

The draft came quickly and automatically, and was designed to make Jen suffer and feel foolish—something along the lines of "I know you always hated me and thought I was some kind of drunken domineering bully and that your callous treatment of me was in the service of protecting your 'tender vulnerability' by relegating me to the far outskirts of our social group, but what a sham, what an absolute joke" and then details, wretched, belabored details meant to flip Jen's narrative on its repulsive head—and when she finished, she stood up and put on her jacket.
She went on a walk. The weather was still beautiful and transformative, and Moddie's hands were shaking. There were some traces of rich purple in the sky. She smelled smoke coming from a chimney and she stopped in front of a house and looked into the window. What a sweet little diorama of do-

mestic quietude! She lit a cigarette and watched the family watch TV.

She wondered if she would send the email tonight. She felt prepared to, but also felt as though she could take her time. She'd taken years so far. Her dish had been cooling. She could wait.

When she got back inside, much of the urgency had calmed, and she almost felt mellow, or, rather, vacant. She thought it might be good to do some reconnaissance. She wanted to look at a photo of Jen's face and let that be her guide. Jen was easy to find on Instagram. She clicked on the most recent photo, which depicted a sunset in nature. In the foreground was a fire, and sitting next to it was Alan in a humble Carhartt jacket. The caption of the photo was long, and the photo itself had nearly a thousand likes and hundreds of comments.

After Jen's father died that summer, Jen discovered she had a rare type of tumor, for which she was about to undergo chemotherapy and a series of invasive operations. Her chances of survival were high, she had caught it early through diligence and return trips to the doctor, and even though it was rare, survival rates were nearly 80 percent, increasing depending on how early the tumor was caught (which, again, due to Jen's diligence, was early). She had spent the past week facing her fears of death and mourning the loss of her life, which was a possibility, though likely a small one (she felt compelled to repeat this, not wanting to disturb anyone too fully with this shocking, potentially traumatizing news).

She had practiced a lot of acceptance, and she was taking the year off to work on her recovery. She was very fortunate to be able to do this, due to the money received from the death of her parent, and she wanted to acknowledge that she was grateful and humbled to be afforded this privilege while she underwent this major life event, facing down the real possibility of her own early death with, she hoped, courage, curiosity, and humor. She made a reference to her signature "sarcasm."

She also wanted to let everyone know that she and Alan had decided to elope in their beloved Door County, and from the pictures, everyone could see they were already there, one last trip before the chemo. Yes, they were married! What happy news!

Once she had completed her recovery, there would be a huge celebration with all of their friends and everyone who had touched their lives. Moddie raised her eyebrows. Planning this wedding party would be part of Jen's strength and joy over the next year. She mentioned something about how she had learned "radical acceptance and forgiveness" from Alan, which seemed like a non sequitur.

Furthermore, with this year, she was excited to do some things she had always wanted to do. She was going to resume her drawing journal and teach herself the history of European cinema. She had already bought herself a projector and made an organized schedule of the movies she needed to watch. She would write about the movies and disseminate these essays on a Substack. She repeated the understanding that she was privileged to be able to take the time for recovery and self-exploration, and that this privilege was afforded to her due to the death of a parent, her father. So many people, especially and ironically those in the caring professions such as hospital workers and nurses, would not be afforded the same abundance (her word), and she hoped she could make the most of this opportunity and share her journey and her joys with her community.

Moddie's expression shifted when she read the words "journey" and "joys."

The comments were predictable. Oh, Jen, what a sweetheart, what a jewel! Don't *die*!

Moddie thought about a comment she could leave, and then she slipped into soft, numb laughter.

She flipped through the pictures on the post, more sunset, more fire, a couple's selfie, a picture of their ugly dog Peepers, a laptop on a wooden table in the quaint kitchen of what was likely an Airbnb.

Oh, touché, thought Moddie, touché.

A bubble popped up on Moddie's laptop, informing her that Bethany had responded to her email.

> Yes, we must get together—solo hang soon. Why don't you come to game night at my place on Thursday. I'll loop you in on the thread. Nina is welcome too, but I know she likes her evenings to herself.

Pam would be on the thread of course, and would feel annoyed that Moddie had been included.

Good.

Across town, Bethany felt happy about her idea to swap out Kimberly for Moddie.

Seven

There was a sports bar at the back of a strip mall near a laundromat, where Craig and some of his friends had decided to start going after work once a week to drink. They were all gathered at a table in the back, sharing a pitcher.

Craig couldn't stop thinking about having sex with Petra, his Bulgarian intern. He wanted to solemnly pull the neck of her sweater down below her boobs, then ask her to take off her pants.

"Yeah, for sure," he said. He laughed loudly, and then said, "Oh no, for sure," and then returned to silence. His friends were talking about something, whatever. He thought about the lab.

The lights were always dim. His best students came in three days a week to do things with microscopes and bacteria, for which, as interns, they received extra credit and work experience. Over the summer, his only intern had been Petra, and this fall, she had signed up again to be his intern along with Caroline and Paul, but between Craig and Petra there seemed to be an invisible cord that tugged at them both from the inside and that brought them, speechlessly, any time they were in the same room together, within an inch of each other, standing side by side, not speaking, looking into microscopes. Craig could feel the heat of Petra's arm, even through a sweater. He looked at the microbes, but they lost all meaning. He stared at them stupidly and felt his body melting toward hers. The willpower it took to resist reaching his right arm over to her, running his hand up the inside of her thigh, moving her underwear to the side, and gently grazing her butt crack with his knuckles was in itself erotic and made him feel high.

Sometimes, after the others left, Petra would stare at him without blinking and slowly lift her hand up and slowly brush her soft hair behind her ear and then slowly run the tips of her fingers down her neck, which made Craig imagine that he could slowly unzip his pants and slowly begin to jerk off, which would lead to his slowly turning her around and slowly fucking her until he came, slowly, all over the microscope, which would be right next to her hand as she braced herself on the counter during this exchange.

Craig's hot wings arrived and he said, "Oh fuck yeah."

He felt a muscle somewhere beneath his navel unclench, a muscle he hadn't even known had been clenched or for how long. He laughed at another joke he'd only half heard.

He acknowledged that he was no longer in love with Pam, and that he would like to break up with her, fuck his intern, and then take a job somewhere else, maybe in Spain.

Craig pictured himself free. There at the sticky table, surrounded by affable men, bringing a hot wing to his lips, he felt at home and anonymous, as if he'd finally found something that could help him transcend the self he'd spent so much time creating without even knowing it. He bit into the wing. He took that old self out into the field of his heart and shot it in the face like a dog, and he looked that dog in the eyes while he did it, because he was glad to do it. He wasn't grief-stricken. There was nothing he would miss about that old dog. Their eyes locked, understanding passed between them, *goodbye!*, he pulled the trigger, and this new Craig soared higher than he knew possible, free from the constant racking guilt and boredom of his current situation, which simply could not go on much longer.

Pam was always stinging him with her stinging comments, she always wanted to bring him down, snip at him, make him feel low and stupid, because she was low and stupid. Pam had a limited mind. She paraded as if she were some kind of intellectual, but she wasn't. She was just average. Some people are better and more interesting than others. That was just how Craig felt.

He laughed at another joke he'd only half heard and said, "Fuck, man, that's funny," because it probably *had* been funny.

Yes, he was going to do it, he was going to do it. He finished his beer, poured another, and laughed at everything everyone said.

He was going to set himself free.

He had already set himself free.

"Peter," he said. "Get a hot wing out of this basket, my good man."

Peter thought, Jesus, Craig is drunk, and realized he'd have to walk him all the way home.

Craig wove around, grabbing onto lampposts and twirling like *Singin' in the Rain*. He stumbled into the gutter, then straightened up to walk arm against arm with Peter. He raised his finger and began talking about how Pam was always ragging on him for maybe engaging in a little light flirtation with his intern.

"It's not like she's stupid, she's very very smart, she seems fucking smarter than Pam, Pam just sits around watching TV and frowning all day, oh boo hoo, Pam, *boo hoo*—try to have an intellectual discussion with Pam, she just rolls her eyes at you. Does that make me a fucking creep or some kind of a pedo? So be it, Jesus. A man wants to look like a man, that's all."

Craig stopped and put his face against the bus stop pole and looked out into traffic, glassy-eyed.

"I meant to say feel like a man."

Peter nodded and said, "Sure sure, I get you, Craig. It's hard being with someone for so long. It wears on you. I don't think you want to lean into the pedophile thing, though."

Craig blew air out of his mouth and started laughing uncontrollably. He put his hands to his face and hyperventilated.

"I have feelings, too, you know. Nobody thinks about my feelings. I have feelings, too, you know." And then he screamed, shrill, "What about my feelings???"

"Okay, that's enough, man, let's pull it together." He hoisted Craig up and walked arm in arm with him. "You've got to calm all of this way, way down, man."

"Oh, I don't know, whatever," muttered Craig.

"What's that, buddy?"

"I really ought to marry Pam," said Craig.

Craig looked insane as he tried to explain to Peter that Petra made him feel like a man. "It's not fake, it's all real. I have one thought, one thought in my whole entire mind, and it's just to get there, to get to Petra, take off her pants, and get my dick in there, and if I don't do that I really feel like my life is going to be over. Did you know that this was a real thing that really happens, and that people actually feel this way?"

Peter looked around to see if other people could hear or see them. "Okay, dude, but really, just a couple notches lower."

"There comes a time in every man's life where he has to decide whether or not to leave his wife," said Craig. "Where he must choose between dull certainty and the ecstasy of the void."

Peter nodded. He knew about it, of course. Craig showed Peter some pictures of Petra. "Sure," said Peter, who had always been fond of Pam.

"This is who I'm going to get my dick up in," said Craig, and then he shouted "*FUCK!*" and called himself a pervert.

"You're a good person," said Craig, putting his hand on Peter's chest.

"Thanks," said Peter.

"You know I know you had your shit, which seemed rough," said Craig, in reference to Peter's recent major breakup.

"Thanks, yeah, I'm okay," said Peter.

"What the fuck is wrong with me?" said Craig. "I ought to hook you up. I'm going to show you my girl Moddie. She just got a divorce. I tried to hook her up with Ben Stevens but . . ." Craig made the *comme ci, comme ça* hand gesture. He scrolled through his pictures. He'd taken a few of Moddie and Pam from afar. In each of them Moddie seemed surprised. "She's got crazy eyes," said Craig. "Like a little fuckin' psycho, but she's my bro."

"Okay, man," said Peter.

Eventually, Peter dropped Craig off at his front door.

"You got it from here?" he asked.

"Yeah, sure," said Craig.

Peter hadn't been as thrilled about the "boys' night" as he'd been letting on. In fact it was a little humiliating. A girls' night, but for boys.

It had been a while since he'd gotten laid.

Peter walked home and contemplated his life. He hadn't wanted to move to Texas with Carol (he was only half in, the whole thing was a bluff call, she was *quite* angry), and since the split, all of her friends had made themselves incredibly off-limits, even for a humble hand job. Oh well, such is life. Maybe Craig would get caught having sex with his intern, and then Peter could have sex with Pam.

Peter's apartment was minimally decorated. He didn't have anything on the walls. He set his bag on the couch and turned on a few lamps. Maybe he should get a dog and buy a small house. Women loved dogs and houses.

He didn't think of himself as someone who did very well on weed, but he'd gotten some from his lesbian sister, something called Face Wreck. He didn't know what the percentages meant and didn't really care. He was depressed, so oh well. He took a healthy hit, paused, took another.

Maybe he'd started to get a little pissy on dates. He'd been out twice with a friend of Bethany's. On the second date she talked for a billable hour about home renovations, even though she did not yet own a home, and showed him her Pinterest board for open-plan kitchen shelving, and he was pretty sure that when he said, "Yeah, you can just call those *shelves*," he got moved from the maybe pile to the no pile. Another thing women loved, sorting things into piles.

Peter liked his couch. To him, it looked very modern.

He didn't really want to be set up with Craig and Pam's friend, but he didn't think it was a real offer, either.

The reason he'd said the thing about shelves in the first place was that he'd been on so many dates recently—or semi-dates, or whatever, "hangouts"—where the women were an intense mix of tedious and aggressive, like children holding court and explaining how cool their best friend was and which toys they liked best and whether or not they were popular, and if Peter said anything other than what he was supposed to say ("Wow, your best friend sounds beautiful and cool, and you seem like someone who has really gone through a lot of complex thinking about the world and how it should work"), they would begin to slowly, but with increasing malice, weave in general insults toward men, and as the frequency of these comments and insults increased, so did their specificity, until these women were making comments about his own appearance, attitudes, and things they just assumed about him—how he treated his exes and his family and coworkers—and if they'd been drinking, the conversation sometimes turned to speeches that were indiscernible from just being fucking berated by someone who hated you, even though on these dates Peter and these women had usually just met hours or at most weeks ago, so how on fucking earth, if what they said about hate being the opposite of love was true, could they already hate each other? Peter certainly didn't love any of these women. At most they inspired mild curiosity.

One drunk woman with whom he'd had no chemistry, and who kept checking her phone throughout the date, asked if she could "see his apartment." They went to his place and had a lackluster forty minutes of kissing on his modern couch, and right after she left, as Peter was scrolling mindlessly through his phone, he saw that she had tweeted "vertical slat blinds = run for the hills." He didn't even know what those words meant, but he saw that she apparently got what she came for because the likes and comments rolled on in and everyone—even some men!—agreed that whatever kinds of window treatments he had made him a sexual predator or something, a perpetual child, a slob, a middle-aged fool looking to entrap a woman into what, coming into his apartment and painting the living room and getting him some drapes?

"No, that's not what I want, that's what *you* want!" he said out loud, starting an imaginary exchange with the phantom of a woman he knew he'd never see again. That was not usually what he had in mind when he thought about women, usually it had a slightly more, you know, sexual tilt.

Everyone he'd been seeing was either perpetually single (gee) or recently divorced, and he tried to be understanding, breakups are rough, but he was also just starting to slowly hate women. Sometimes he regretted not going to Texas with Carol.

He set the bowl down and texted his sister to ask, "Should I get drapes?"

She texted back and said, "I don't think they'd match the rest of your decor."

Things with Carol, what a mess. Of course she hated him, what could he do? He'd stopped sending her emails trying to convince her not to hate him. His sister pointed out what he was doing. According to her he was being pushy and it was normal for someone who had just been dumped to be angry, and she told him, "Stop doing that, leave her alone. If you convince her you're a good guy, she's just going to want to get back together with you, and then you'll have to reject her again, and she'll hate you even more." Fair. But goddamn it, he hated to think of her telling everyone what an asshole he was, because he was not an asshole.

Peter began to feel as though he should not have smoked the weed that he had gotten as a gift from his sister.

"My lesbian sister," he whispered.

He thought fondly of his sister while he stood in the same place for anywhere between five and seventy minutes, staring at his coffee table and the large, unorganized pile of work sitting on it.

He closed his eyes and breathed. Pleasure rolled through his body and he thought of himself as a weightless essence, full of love and deeply loved, but of course this meant the weed was too strong, because he was not really any of those things. He touched his face and walked slowly to the bathroom.

The air is soft on my limbs, he thought. He turned the shower on and waited for the temperature to adjust.

His bathroom was a bright white, and in the mirror he saw that his cheeks were slightly flushed. It was easy to imagine all the women who had been in love with him looking at him like this during sex and feeling pretty good about it. The weed was making him seem very desirable.

He stepped into the shower. He knew he would have to get rid of the rest of the weed. He considered warning his sister about the weed. The love you feel when you've smoked this weed, he thought, it isn't real, and I can absolutely sympathize with you for wanting to smoke it, because I too feel an absence of love in my life, but I hate to say it, I think this weed, for just this reason, might be slightly dangerous.

He looked skeptically to the side and rested his unfocused gaze on the droplets of water collecting and trailing down the standard white tiles in the shower. Breathtaking!

Was the intervention a good idea? He couldn't tell, probably not. Probably, as with most things, better to do nothing.

There was nothing he could do to stop the impending weed crisis.

Once the dispensaries opened and everyone could go to the store and purchase this feeling of strangely erotic contentment and peace, there would be no stopping it. Once the dispensaries opened, the government and the corporations would start profiting. And once the weed crisis happened, no one would do anything or learn anything or know anything or make anything, but they would feel like they were learning and doing and thinking. They would feel confident and excited about their ideas, and when the moment of sobriety came and they tried to put these ideas into effect, saw how difficult that actually was, and felt pain and frustration, it would be difficult to convince anyone not to smoke again, not to return to the state of mind where they felt a sense of achievement and belonging.

Peter felt his mind expand, as if he were discovering at that moment, in that shower, that he was actually a genius.

He put his cheek against the shower wall and continued to let the thoughts unravel.

Already everyone seemed to have an article to point to about how weed was a cure-all, weed was moral, and you could eat it or put it up your ass if you didn't like smoking—which would be understandable, as smoking was now immoral. Somehow it was beginning to seem, in popular opinion, that the only way to truly prove you were against the unfair and unequal incarceration of Black people was to put weed up your ass, and if you happened to say something like "I'm not sure weed helps you proofread as well as you think it might" (something he had suggested to a student) it was unspoken yet fully understood that this indicated an interest in the continued extreme illegality of weed, and thereby a passive endorsement of the imprisonment of Black people, which was not Peter's position in the slightest, and he found it eerie that when he googled "negative effects of marijuana" he found that there were *no* negative effects of marijuana, which only furthered his suspicion that there was something conspiratorial going on, some strings were being pulled to improve public opinion of weed so that money could be made off of it by both the government (in the form of taxes) and corporations. At the health food store, by the checkout, he'd seen an infographic-style picture book for adults about how to smoke weed every day like a beautiful, healthy, well-rested, competent, fearsome adult woman, and something in the back of his mind had felt the flickers of a new type of fear.

A few people in Peter's life had thought of him as a prude, but he didn't really think that was accurate.

The words left Peter, his head went silent, and some emotion descended on him, descended again, descended again. He braced himself on the shower wall and wept and felt his head slipping beneath the emotion as if he were drowning in it. His thoughts were helpless and winding. He flailed without being able to put a name or words to what went through him. He cried like this for a while and then thought maybe he felt this way, like a man underwater, because of the shower. Yeah, it was probably the shower. He took a breath and stopped crying, turned off the faucet. Everything shut off in an instant. He stood there, bewildered and dripping.

He dried himself and put on a sweat suit and did a routine of stretches in his living room and thought maybe a dog wasn't such a bad idea, a little companionship, a little diversion. Maybe he could name it Chum-Chum.

When he was done stretching, he turned to lie on his back

and looked at the ceiling and thought, Well, I know this is no good, being this high, and I agree with everything I've just thought about the government. But now, since I'm already high, I should enjoy it. He reached up to the coffee table and took another hit, one more, one last one, and waited.

It was imperative that he tell his students about the fascist origins of Freytag's dramatic triangle. He was midway through fantasizing about his lecture, which he imagined—unironically at this moment—might end with his students cheering and lifting him on a chair and carrying him out onto the quad, like the poster for *Dead Poets Society*.

He wondered if the term "mimesis" could be used for predatory animals as well, or if it was only a defensive term—or if it probably just meant "mimicry." He wanted to tell them about the fake fireflies, and how creepy it is when you look out at a field of fireflies at night, most of them are looking for a mate, but some of them are looking for a meal. It's difficult to tell which is which. We're not above the animal kingdom, thought Peter, and this felt like an interesting allegory for art-making at a time when arts funding was almost nonexistent and the cost of living was slowly mounting, a time in which ideas about meritocracy and triumph and ambition were seen as a moral keystone—eerie, eerie!—and a time when creating "moral keystones" was seen as a worthy artistic aim (because nobody could afford to be an artist unless they were paid to do so by corporations that had their own interests in mind, and what TV show didn't include something about making money and procreating?), and a time in which narrative art forms were becoming increasingly homogenized by Freytag's fascist pyramid, the Hero's Republican Journey, Syd Field's Paradigm of Gibbering Mindlessness, the golden age of television, the golden age of the idiotic, regressive belief in the intellectual and artistic validity of superheroes—superheroes, Übermenschen, flawless piety, perfect conformity, flaws only there to illustrate that the flaws could be overcome, and if not that they must be obliterated or somehow assimilated and inverted and transformed into new virtues. Of course, if it comes down to all or nothing, you will always get nothing. These stupid black-and-white, us-and-them notions. They were designed to make you feel that yes you are a special hero, and everyone else is your enemy, and peace and tranquility will only come once you have ascended to the height of your "potential"—a thing of course you will never do, so you will never be happy, and you will spend your life in hellish pitiful suffering, thought Peter, and then his head spun for a moment and then he started laughing.

Oh, if only he had somebody to talk to, somebody who would understand what he was saying! But who was she? Where was she? And when would they meet?

He wanted his students to know that reward and punishment were the same thing and that maybe it was possible to step away from them both and to step toward something more complex and enriching, but this was difficult to explain, and it was difficult to explain especially without being too candid, which he always tried to avoid, because he believed it might get him fired.

Yes, much more likely he would be fired than carried out of the building on a chair by screaming and adoring students.

Of course she was furious. Of course they had talked about the future, and of course in Carol's fantasy they made this move together, and Peter joined her in her ambitions, which were definitely hers and not his. Difficult to know if he felt emasculated, as Carol had suggested, but either way, the answer was no.

A crack ran along his ceiling. His lamp cast shadows of the plant it sat beneath. Cold air came in from under his front door. Tomorrow he would be sober and tomorrow he would work on his lecture. He would try to help his students, he would try to retain his sex appeal, and one day he would meet his wife.

Eight

Kimberly was lying in bed watching videos on her laptop. Frozen abandoned pets brought back to life, best of 2017. You won't believe this beautiful dog, rejected and abandoned. Crippled dog fostering situation. Your heart will break for the recovery of this dog, who never knew the love of a gentle human touch. Abused dog clings to new foster mama.

She had been watching for hours. Each time she finished a video and began the next, she thought, This one will be the last, but with each video, a little bit of insatiable despair gained ground. She struggled to resist "Matted Starving Dog on Brink of Death" but was weak and kept watching.

"I'm her mother. After the rescue, where she was left frozen and abandoned, I nursed her back to health, and now all she wants is me. I guess you could say I'm the absolute center of her world." The foster parent of the dog spoke with firm clarity, like someone who had complete reign over her territory and who really believed she would not be fucked with easily.

One dog had been left chained to the side of the road for months with little food but had managed to rip free and was found limping in the back of a McDonald's parking lot. The video, taken from a car, zoomed in slowly, and the camerawoman said, "Ohhh, god, look, that's so sad."

The music was saccharine, generic, and triumphant.

Kimberly wanted to see it all. She liked the way it felt to watch the dog limping around, and to know it would be saved.

The title for the McDonald's dog was "Heartbreaking Transformation."

A blonde woman with tattoos came to get the dog. This was her YouTube channel. She used it to promote her cause/business of animal rescue. She got the dog into the backseat of her SUV by luring it with ripped-up hamburger. The camera zoomed in on the dog's face, its eyes rolling from side to side in terror. The close-up of the dog lingered longer than was usual for this kind of video, and right before the cut, the volume of the triumphant garage band preset music got louder, gradually. After the cut, the dog was in the back of a vet's office trying to hide in a corner while three women removed the collar from its matted neck, then gently washed its body with mange and flea shampoo.

Bobby came into the bedroom and saw Kim lying on the bed with the laptop on her stomach. She was wearing underwear that was supposed to look like a man's underwear, except the way it was cut went up between her butt cheeks, so the round fat bottom part of her butt hung out, which he couldn't see, but which he knew and remembered well. Something about this made him feel sad, and like he wanted to try to repair things between them. He could feel the walls he'd put up start to lower, and he started to relax and feel straightforward attraction and desire for her, remembering a time when he loved that she was his wife, his love, and his companion. He took a step forward and put his hands around Kim's feet and pressed his thumbs into the arches, then massaged the heels.

Kimberly complained about her friends constantly. It had long since become a mind-numbing wall of sound to Bobby, but he did notice that she seemed passionate and serious about it, so during sex one night about a year ago he called Bethany a cunt, sort of jokingly, but Kimberly responded well, or so it seemed, and it was arousing to Bobby to feel like all of the women Kimberly knew were jealously clamoring for his dick, and he even liked to imagine all of their husbands dancing around in a little circle, maybe around a fire, like a tribal thing, cowering and dancing and trying in vain to cover their tiny dicks while Bobby was on some kind of dais (a tall one, like a big column) lit by the fire, fucking Kimberly while everyone watched, and maybe there was another dais around another fire, two hundred yards away, and his manager at the insurance company was also fucking some woman up there, and they would turn and make eye contact and both start screaming at the top of their lungs and his manager would start screaming *I'm going to give you a promotion, you're getting a promotion* and Bobby would scream *Oh fuck yes* while the fires burned higher and higher as he climaxed.

Kim paused the video and withdrew her feet.

"What are you watching?" he asked.

"Oh, nothing. Just some stupid YouTube videos."

"Cool."

"I was just trying to de-stress because HR informed me that our adjuncts are starting to file for unemployment and that's just not how it works, but I'm not really allowed to let them know that I know they're filing, and I'm not really allowed to do anything that could be construed as retaliation, so I'm just in a hard place, and I'm just exhausted."

"I'm sorry, baby," said Bobby.

"Thanks," said Kimberly.

She did look exhausted in a way that made her look peaceful and gentle and approachable. Bobby thought maybe he could be a good husband in this moment.

"Do you want to snuggle?" he asked. He was starting to get an idea of suggesting that, after they snuggled, he could draw her a bubble bath, and while she was in the bath, he could order Grubhub, light some candles, and put on a movie, and during the movie he could give her a shoulder massage, and then maybe she would relax, and if she relaxed, maybe they could reconnect physically.

"No, I'm not really in the mood to snuggle," said Kimberly.

"Do you want me to draw you a bath, help you relax?"

"No, I just can't stop thinking about this one instructor who emailed me today. Just the language in her email was really presumptuous and offensive."

"I'm sorry. Maybe if we ordered some food and watched a movie, it would help you relax and take your mind off of things."

"Yeah, actually, if you could stop trying to force me to relax, that would be great, I'm dealing with this on my own, thanks," said Kimberly.

Bobby left the room.

In the days leading up to game night at Bethany's, Moddie cleaned and unpacked a little more, and when she went to the coffee shop or to Quality Dairy, she experimented with being relaxed and friendly, which went well enough that she was twice called "hun" and once, walking by an auto body shop, she was even called "mommy," which, she learned later on Google, didn't mean what she thought it did, but in a way that was a welcome surprise, and made her feel as though perhaps she was beginning to exude an approachable friendliness, which she did think would help her in the long run as she found her new position in life, whatever that might be. She meditated and stretched, and when certain feelings became too unbearable—loneliness, isolation, thoughts of the past tiptoeing ever closer, the walls of her current situation closing in—she would call her parents or do drugs and watch a movie and try to sleep as much as possible.

She called her parents that morning, learned what they were up to, asked the appropriate questions, and then, when it was her turn to speak, she gave a long and winding lecture, during which she only cried once, about her thoughts on art and community, modern anti-intellectualism, Pam's transformation, her difficulties in getting Nina to hang out in person, and her continued efforts to break free of her own limitations and ascend to some higher plane, to find some kind of escape from what now seemed to be a nonstop, Waco-like barrage of mind-numbing experiences.

"Jeez," said her mom.

Moddie laughed.

Later that night, as she parked her car, she tried to check herself and her inner comments about Bethany's large house, the Doric columns, the floodlights, hoping that she would not feel sarcastic and aggressive and thereby doom herself to a life of bitter isolation, because on game night, Moddie felt hopeful and genteel.

She rang the doorbell and waited, as if for the beginning of her new life.

When Bethany opened the door, she embraced Moddie in a way that seemed to indicate that they were already deeply connected and, while holding her, said, "I'm so glad you're here." Bethany released Moddie from the hug. "Drink?"

"Yes, please," said Moddie.

Moddie followed Bethany into the joy room and took a seat on the floor next to Chrissy and Pam, who had stopped their conversation. Moddie said hi to Pam, and then reached her hand across to Chrissy and said, "Hi, I'm Moddie, I think we've met."

"Oh, yes," said Chrissy with a strange affect, sighing, smiling, then quickly dropping the smile as she briefly shook Moddie's hand.

Pam swept her hair behind her ear and continued to Chrissy, "So, yes, I was really surprised by how easy it was to talk to David. He's really down-to-earth and we have a pretty good rapport. You know, you think of these eccentric art types and you picture someone who's particularly difficult to get along with, especially if they haven't had that much recognition—I feel like that can kind of fester—but David's really humble about his career, and he's very, very work focused. Everything is a creative problem for him. His art comes first."

Bethany returned from the kitchen with a bottle of wine and a large wineglass, which she filled over halfway before handing it to Moddie, who took a sip and said, "Jesus, this is good wine."

Bethany laughed and made an expression that seemed to indicate something like *You caught me red-handed!* Out of the corner of her eye, Moddie noticed Pam checking her phone.

"This is making me feel like I've never even had wine before," said Moddie.

Bethany clapped once and smiled, and then slid Moddie a plate of some unnervingly good local goat cheese.

Pam leaned back against the couch and took a sip of wine, looking bored, and then she asked, "Where's Kimberly tonight? She never misses these."

Bethany smiled slowly and said, "You know, I think she just couldn't come."

Pam raised her eyebrows and said, "I see. Oh, speaking of people who never come out, Nina brought Tony by the office the other day. It was so sweet, I hadn't seen him in ages."

Moddie ate more goat cheese. Focused on the unique flavor.

"She drops by the office a couple times a week," Pam added. "I told her she should bring him more often. I'm just so happy she's got someone good in her life now."

"One of these days we'll get her out here, but still no boyfriends please," said Bethany, picking up the dice and rolling. She sighed, moved two spaces, and said, "Oh, well."

"Ah, you're playing Sorry," said Moddie. She knew the game from childhood.

"We already started," said Chrissy, "but you take my place. I need a drink. I'm green. It's my turn."

"You seem to be losing," said Moddie.

"Oh, really?" said Chrissy.

"It's just a warm-up game," said Bethany.

Moddie took a second to look over the board, and then she rolled the dice. Six. She moved the green piece six squares until it landed where a yellow piece sat. She used the base of her piece to flick the yellow piece over and then said "Sorry" in a British accent.

"It's fine," said Pam.

There was a conspicuous lull in the conversation. Nobody

seemed to be stepping up, so Moddie lifted her wineglass and said, "Have you recently lost interest in the things that used to bring you pleasure?"

"Yes," said Chrissy. "Who wants to know?"

Moddie took a drink and then asked, "Over the past two weeks, have you been sleeping significantly more or less than usual?"

"Mmmm-hmmm," said Chrissy.

Pam raised her eyebrows and widened her eyes at the wall.

"Over the past two weeks, have you noticed an increased difficulty in concentrating on simple things, like reading the paper?" asked Moddie.

"Yes I have, I hate my child, so ha-ha-ha, yes I'm depressed," said Chrissy in a strong, high-pitched voice.

Moddie glanced over at Chrissy and couldn't tell if Chrissy was doing a bit, or if she meant what she'd said, and Chrissy, as she struggled to relax the grin that had become plastered on her face, couldn't tell either.

"He's a tyrant and he's ruining my life," Chrissy added, saying "ha-ha-ha" again at the end, but was it true? She didn't want to pretend this wasn't the case. In an abusive relationship, the first thing the victim does is downplay and hide the abuse, and she didn't really feel as though Adler were abusing her, so she thought she should say it, admit to his tyranny, so that everyone would know that things with her son were actually very healthy. She pictured him squatting down, screaming, shitting himself, then standing up and crying. Chrissy kind of dead-eye zoned out for a second, replaying this sequence on a loop, then abruptly picked up the cheese knife and said, "Listen, I just want to have a good time."

Moddie laughed loudly, despite herself, and said, "Hear, hear." Pam raised her glass, kind of vacantly looking at the wall, and took a long sip. Bethany lifted her phone up above the Sorry board, took a picture, cropped it, captioned it, and posted it to Instagram.

By the time the night wrapped up, no one was really smiling or looking at one another. The conversation had moved haltingly from topic to topic, as if game night had been a mandatory social hour for coworkers, which, Moddie realized a little too late, it had been.

Bethany gave Pam a meaningful hug that included a luxurious amount of back stroking. "I'll see you tomorrow," she said, and then as she was saying good night to Chrissy, Bethany looked over at Moddie and mouthed "stay" right before miming a cigarette.

Moddie nodded.

While Chrissy buttoned her coat, Bethany said, "Give Adler a kiss for me if he's still up."

Out on the semi-enclosed back porch, Moddie waited while Bethany went upstairs to let her husband know they still had a guest. It was dark on the porch. Moddie wasn't sure what she and Bethany would talk about, and she felt agitated, like she was waiting for a job interview.

Bethany returned and said, "Thank you for waiting," then lit a large scented candle and shook loose two cigarettes from a nearly full pack of Camel Blues.

She settled into her chair and said, "So I want to hear more about *you*. I was so glad when you reached out."

Moddie laughed a little and said, "Ah, well."

"Don't be coy," said Bethany seriously. "I've known you since you were thirteen. I get off on bringing people into the fold, and you're my next project. Catch me up."

In accordance with Nina's recent suggestion that she might

be able to paint herself as a more sane, approachable, and sympathetic figure, Moddie explained that, after high school, she'd gone to the Art Institute and for the past six years had worked as a grant writer and sometimes as a silk-screen instructor at a notable nonprofit for kids in shitty school districts. She had a semicollaborative art practice with her ex, was primarily interested in drawing and printmaking, went to a lot of art openings and shows in Chicago, did a few group shows from time to time, but her breakup had been ugly, complicated, and now she wanted to take time to learn who she was outside of Nick, and outside of her college clique. She hoped she'd be able to reconnect with her art practice, among other things, but at this moment, she was still in the middle of adjusting to all of these fundamental, major life changes. Very soon, she was going to look for work, but she had a little cash from her retirement fund, which she hated to use, but she had really, desperately needed to regroup.

"I was sad to leave that nonprofit gig," she lied, "and there's a lot I miss about Chicago," she lied again, "but I don't know, it was just time," she said, performing the version of herself she thought most likely to elicit sympathy.

Moddie put out her cigarette.

"That's all very impressive," said Bethany. "I had no idea that's where you worked. I've been following them for years. What a strange coincidence." As Bethany continued to respond warmly to Moddie's speech, Moddie grew depressed and lonely. It felt cheap. Another relationship founded on a total misrepresentation of events.

Bethany poured Moddie another drink and asked, "You doing okay?"

Moddie jerked awake as if from sleep. "Oh, yeah, totally."

"I was thinking," said Bethany, "that I might be able to help you."

"Oh, okay," said Moddie.

"With work stuff, of course, but also, if you need to talk," said Bethany. "I would imagine that if I were you, I'd have a lot of strong feelings. I'm sure you've got Pam and Nina and tons of other people to talk to, but if there's anything else you'd like to talk about, I'm here for you. In your email, you said your exit from Chicago was operatic." Bethany said the last word with a subtle inviting upswing.

"Well," said Moddie.

She wasn't sure if she should say it all. Something held her back, the hand of caution and formality, this was too much too soon, but the wine, the cigarettes, the candlelight, and Bethany's familiarity goaded her, so she took the risk and filled Bethany in on the complete story of her time in Chicago, what Alan had done, how Nick had reacted, her anger toward Jen, her explosive outbursts, her guilt, regret, and her confusion—why was she still so upset when she had wanted out, did Alan really not know, had it really been so bad, was she overreacting, was she sick, did she deserve relief?—and while she spoke, she lost track of her surroundings, clicking in and out of emotions, memories, and present sensory input, and by the time she finished, she wasn't sure how long she'd been talking.

"I'm not sure if this sounds stupid to you," she said. She laughed and drank more wine to keep from screaming.

Moddie was expecting Bethany to shrug her shoulders and counter with an example from her own life, which is what people tended to do—was what Pam and a few others had done—when she mentioned her experiences with Alan, so she was surprised when Bethany said, "Oh no, I wouldn't use the word 'stupid.' I'm really sorry that happened to you. It's terrible."

Moddie shrugged. "Thanks."

"Hmm," said Bethany. "Have you talked about this with any of your other Chicago friends? These outbursts you describe happened mostly in connection with Alan, so it seems to me like every time you had to socialize you were having a response to unprocessed trauma, and you most likely have complex PTSD."

It was strange to hear someone say it so bluntly.

"No," said Moddie. "I'm afraid they would just pretend to care, but then secretly resent me for disrupting their narrative."

"I see," said Bethany. Her voice was soothing and rich. She lit another cigarette and the orange glow illuminated her face, briefly, before it faded back into darkness.

Bethany breathed in sharply and asked, "Has it ever crossed your mind to tell Jen?"

"Naturally, but I'm afraid I can't," said Moddie.

"Why not?"

"She was just diagnosed with cancer." As Moddie said this, she felt like she might burst out laughing.

"Oh, yeah, I see," said Bethany.

"She and Alan just did some kind of camping trip elopement thing. I saw it on Instagram. Everyone is being very supportive, so, of course, if I tell her now," said Moddie.

"It might seem villainous."

"Yeah."

Bethany laughed quickly and quietly out of her nose, and paused. Her eyes lingered out into the backyard, which was lit by the moon and the windows upstairs, where her husband sat working into the night. Every time Moddie spoke, she felt anxious anticipation—braced for the slap of mockery and disinterest, but it never came.

"I do have an idea, if you don't mind," said Bethany, after a solid minute had passed.

"No, I don't mind," said Moddie.

"What might it be like if you emailed Alan? He wouldn't tell anyone, of course, so you wouldn't have to worry about adding to your villainous reputation. If she has horrible health problems, and he's taking care of her, I'd imagine that's exhausting. And a camping trip with someone who thinks they might be dying." She laughed, shook her head. "Camping on its own is hard enough. He's probably emotionally and physically drained right now. He might even be on the verge of snapping."

Moddie was listening.

"If you think about it, this would probably be a terrible time for him to get the impression that you were about to go public about the assault. Of course if you confronted him about this, his mind would naturally go there. It might even make him feel a little nauseated all day, every day, while he drives his uptight, ailing new wife to and from chemo for the next however many months, wondering when the other shoe might drop, wondering if she would leave him if she knew, wondering if the support he'd been given over the past ten years would disappear if people really knew the truth about his character—which, of course, if she left him, she would say why. Who could resist the added sympathy and certitude? Imagine the things you might be able to make him imagine with just a simple email."

Bethany's three-wick Voluspa candle lit her from beneath. The light from the flames danced across her chin, cheeks, and forehead, glinted off the center of her pupils, and created a strange distortion of her face, which looked more angular than it did in normal light.

"I know you're worried about whether or not he actually knows what he did, but believe me, he knows exactly what he did. Who knows why he did it. I'm sure he thought he deserved to have you, and now he believes he deserves to never think about you again. But what if you could," said Bethany, and as she began to describe a situation in which Moddie was like a ghost, trailing him and haunting him, but with little to no disturbance to Moddie's daily routine, with in fact quite likely a return of energy into Moddie's life as she transferred the burden back over to Alan, Moddie felt herself relax deeply, and began to imagine the things that Bethany said, to imagine herself in Alan's living room, where she had been once or twice before, and suddenly, she could see him lying shirtless on the couch, clear as day. She turned her head and saw that Jen was in the other room, baking some kind of grain-free meal-replacement power ball. Moddie approached him on the couch and slowly extended her arm. She could picture everything so clearly, she even felt herself move. It wouldn't be so much that Moddie herself was haunting Alan, but that what Alan had done would sever itself from Moddie and return to Alan, where it belonged. Moddie raised her finger and brought it nearer to Alan's torso, closer and closer, until she could feel the hair and then the flesh covering his guts. She pressed deeper, deeper, right into where his liver was, until he sat up slightly and flinched.

"This way, you could finally move on from this painful period in your life," said Bethany. "And once you're feeling better, maybe we can talk about putting your teaching and grant-writing experience to use."

Moddie was rapidly reviewing the conversation back at home. She couldn't believe the things she'd said, and she couldn't believe Bethany's response—not just sympathy but strategy.

The conversation had taken many turns—light discussion of the political atmosphere, high school reminiscences, David Winterbottom, and Bethany's hopes for the future of the Visiting Artist Program—after which Moddie mentioned that, despite not wanting to in any way step on Pam's toes, Pam who she loved like a sister and respected like one of the old masters, she did know a lot of incredibly talented female artists whose names she'd love to add into the running, but if and only if it wasn't in any way intrusive or presumptuous. Moddie started laughing.

Bethany had seemed incredibly receptive to the idea of being sent a list of these names, and mentioned wanting to foster a collaborative environment in the art department, a department which she did hope one day Moddie might join. Bethany had been afforded many opportunities as a result of restructuring at the university, which had been necessary after the sex scandals. She had hiring power, budgetary power, and had been charged with slowly redesigning the department, and she had in fact, quite coincidentally, if you can even believe it, been looking for both a new Printmaking I instructor and a grant writer.

Which meant, quite likely, one day soon, Moddie would work in the same department as Pam.

She smiled.

Moddie turned up the heat in her apartment. Suddenly she felt incredibly cold. She turned the shower on and stepped in and thought about her future.

This all seemed good, very good.

She got out of the shower, got into a sweat suit, dried her hair, and opened her laptop to look at Zillow. Of course, if she had a job, she would need a house. She found an interesting turn-of-the-century farmhouse a few towns over. It needed massive repair but was only ninety thousand dollars—and if there was one thing Moddie craved, it was massive repair. She felt positive in a way that surprised and delighted her. To look into the future and see contentment was not something she had expected, at all, and she found the experience incredibly moving. It didn't even matter if it worked out, but to have some sense of footing and general direction, what a relief.

And all because I told the truth.

She made a list of fifteen early and midcareer female artists whose work she admired and who she had met in passing, or had emailed with during her lonely pen pal phase, and included their websites, links to interviews, and short paragraphs about why she thought they would each work well in the program and sent this all to Bethany.

> Hey—here's what I'm thinking. I'm sure a lot of these people are on Pam's list, too, and again I don't want to step on her toes. This is just to let you know who is on my mind.
>
> Thanks for having me over and thanks for the *deep talk*. One of these days I'll get it together to return the favor.

Beth responded quickly to say, "Already liking all of this—we will make sure not to step on Pam's toes! Let's talk next week about a potential printmaking class for you this winter. Standing offer. It'll still be on the table if you need more time. See you soon <3."

Then she took a breath and decided to write to David, whose email was listed on the university website.

> Yo, it's Moddie. Fun running into you the other day. We're both new here, even though I grew up here, so if you're bored, do you want to drink some beers and play air hockey sometime? No presh if you don't want to. I'm emailing literally everyone I have been in a room with over the past four months.

She knew it sounded aggressive and weird, but she wanted the "yo" and the "no presh" to indicate that she really did not care, and that this was in no way meant to be romantic, but she worried her shadow self was showing, the shadow self that did want to engage in physical congress with him, and she was surprised when he wrote back almost immediately.

> Uh, thanks for the overwhelmingly hospitable offer. Sure, I'm free and bored Weds–Fridays.

She wanted to write something about how she might be having a nervous breakdown but couldn't tell if it sounded flirtatious, so she just said, "Haha, sorry. How about this Weds any time after 5?" to which he replied, "Cool, 6:30?"

I am a normal person. It is normal for people to contact other people with whom they share interests and common acquaintances. It is normal and it is healthy to make connections with people in your immediate physical surroundings. I am relaxed. People are not secretly plotting to humiliate and harm me. This is what I wanted, to return to the bosom of my youth and gently lay down roots so that I might flourish. Yea, verily.

Moddie got out a beer from her refrigerator and looked at her list again and, feeling confident about her appeal as an acquaintance, decided to write to Kara, who she had hung out with four times, and who she had invited to do a workshop at the place for underserved children in Chicago, and with whom she'd had a kind of telephone and email friendship for several years. She'd also bought three of Moddie's drawings, eighteen-by-twenty-four-inch grotesque pencil drawings of people from Chicago, which could still be seen in some of her Instagram photos on the wall in her dining room, looming large and lookin' good. They had fallen out of touch. Moddie saw that Kara had won an award recently.

> Kara, hey, what's up? Much has changed with me since we last talked—I was just recommending your work to a friend of mine and saw about the award. This made me smile. Congratulations and much deserved! Very proud of you. I would love an update, whenever you feel bored and inclined to write.
>
> I am no longer in Chicago. Nick and I broke up, which I think is for the best in the long term, but of course it's rough at the moment (it was my idea, so I get the anguish but not the outward sympathy—poor me!). I decided to move back to my hometown, where I have friends. It's a college town. I drive everywhere, and can go to Target whenever I want.

I tell myself I will spend one year doing whatever—read, make work or not, etc. etc., which is freeing and nice in a way. I have vague project ideas.

Do you know/have you met David Winterbottom? He's a visiting artist here. Can't get a read on him, can't tell if he's cool and funny or somewhat of an asshole. We're playing air hockey next week.

I think I'm going to come to NY soon, too, on sort of a recharging museums and theater trip. I can amuse myself, but if you're around and up for it, I'd love to buy you a beer.

Congrats again, hope all's well,
Moddie

As soon as she sent it, she felt surprised that she'd said she was going to New York, a thing that she could obviously do but that had not occurred to her to do. There was no reason, in fact, that she could not spend the next two months in France, but she put that out of her mind as too frivolous.

Suddenly, the thought crossed her mind that her email had been way too forward. It seemed as though she was assuming friendship with a total stranger who had just become successful, which in some ways made Moddie's interest in Kara suspect. That wasn't why she was interested in Kara, but it felt like it was, which made Moddie feel a great disdain for herself.

Talking with Bethany had made her bold, and, in the past, boldness had spelled danger, but maybe there was some way in which her friendships in Chicago had really warped her understanding of what was and wasn't appropriate behavior, and the only way to get over that was to confront those things head-on, with an email to Alan, as Bethany had suggested.

Just as suddenly as she'd questioned her email to Kara, she felt certain that emailing Alan was the correct thing to do. She drank a little more beer and began a message.

It took her two hours and two beers to write the email.

She included a detailed and high-octane account of the assault, a series of questions about his frame of mind at the time, requests that he admit that he knew what he had done, and a lengthy and brutal critique of his recent body of work.

Afterward, she felt slightly stunned and disoriented, and wandered around her apartment, doing god knows what, pacing, returning to the laptop to reread the draft, googling random people from her past, drinking, peeing, stepping out onto the porch, slipping into momentary fugue states, flitting erratically from one piece of furniture to another, until slowly she came back to herself and ate some bread in front of the TV.

She looked at Alan and Jen's accounts on Instagram. She was pretty drunk.

She read through the captions and comments on their posts, and immediately began to doubt the idea that Alan would be rejected by his community if they learned what he had done to her. They all looked so happy—why would they give that up? They went camping together and had cookouts. They showed at one another's apartment galleries. They dressed the same and had similar tattoos. They had inside jokes.

Rejection, sadness, the fabric of our lives.

She reread the cancer post and felt like she'd been scooped. They were already suffering.

The next morning, Moddie had a headache from all the booze.

She lay in bed for a while, aching and feeling embarrassed for telling Bethany so much last night, for emailing Kara, and for thinking there was anything she could do to make Alan suffer. She thought about Nick, and thought that he was right, she was too dramatic about it, and then she whipped around through many different feelings about Nick, Alan, and everyone back in Chicago until she curled into a little ball and screamed into her blanket like a person serving an eternal sentence in solitary confinement who'd just learned that the afterlife was real, and there would never truly be an end.

She didn't want to care about any of this anymore. She wanted to be done, but she couldn't be done until she had some clarity. She felt she would do anything for clarity. She had never been religious, nor had her parents, but in that moment, she clasped her hands in front of her face and said, "I will do anything that you want me to do, I will do anything that you say, I'm yours, I will do anything, just get me out of here, get me out of this hell, I can't stand it any longer, just get me out, not another single day, just point me in the right direction and I'll do anything you say, anything anything anything. Just show me what I'm supposed to think and I'll never turn back, just get me out of here."

For some reason, saying this provided relief, even if she normally would have found it melodramatic.

She unclasped her hands and looked at the ceiling, feeling purged.

She got up, stretched, and made herself some coffee.

Looking out the window, it seemed like it would be another nice day out.

She checked her email.

Her inbox was fuller than normal.

Bethany invited her to a movie, Nina sent her a screen grab. Her mom sent a few poems and a few pictures of their dog Quilty and said, "A thought: Why don't you come and stay with us for a week? We would love to see you. Take the Amtrak, make us dinner, walk away feeling you've done your filial duty. I imagine that's good for endorphins or serotonin or whichever. (Is this manipulative? Quilty misses you.)"

Kara wrote back to say thank you and that she wanted more details about the breakup, she would love to see Moddie in New York ("Move here, please, we have Target!"), and that she knew David's ex-girlfriend and that the breakup was "not pretty, no, not pretty at all—he might very well be an asshole, do what you will with this information."

A little art-related and political junk mail, and then an email from Alan. Moddie's stomach turned.

> I am so sorry that you have carried around so much anger for so many years. Looking back, I can recognize that my behavior was aggressive and inappropriate. I completely apologize for my actions. You and I have always had a strange friendship. What I remember most is all of the years of close and constant friendship and how many times we hung out over the past years.
>
> If you would like to talk on the phone about this so that I can give you closure, I am available for that.

Moddie walked into her kitchen.

The next few hours were a blur. She had not meant to send Alan the email she'd written—rather, it had been one of those "write the letter you need to write, and send a saner version later" kinds of things, but what was done was done, and after standing in her kitchen for a few minutes, she burst out laughing.

She tried to take a sip of coffee, but then she laughed again, until she was drooling coffee down her chin and onto her old pajama shirt, and even that seemed incredibly amusing.

She laughed again, this time quickly, wiped herself off with a kitchen towel, then smiled and thought, Fuck. She felt as though she'd given herself an incredible treat, and all she could do was whisper "thank you."

All of the light in her apartment seemed golden.

She got onto Gchat and told Nina what had happened, and then got in touch with Bethany to do the same, and they all three decided to meet on the park bench outside Jensen at twelve-fifteen.

Moddie got some fruit together and then went through a few boxes in the closet to find an old lunch box from the Container Store.

When Moddie got to the quad, she saw Nina walking out of a building. They both waved.

"What the fuck, dude," said Moddie when they hugged.

"Yeah, you tell me what the fuck," said Nina. "You're looking radiant, by the way."

Moddie filled her in and then handed Nina her phone so that she could read both emails.

Bethany came out of another building and walked toward them, waving.

"Heeeey!!!"

"Hey!" said Moddie. "I feel insane."

Nina finished reading and handed Moddie's phone to Bethany.

"Holy shit," said Nina.

They sat quietly while Bethany finished reading both emails, and when she finished, she handed Moddie her phone and said, "That was so articulate."

"You don't think the stuff about his sculptures is too much?" asked Moddie. "It's not, like, excessive and incoherent?"

"No, are you kidding? It's beautiful, you should be an art critic," said Nina.

"Yes, an art critic, there's a thought," said Bethany.

Moddie felt strange, like she was upset, but she couldn't stop smiling. "I guess I've just wanted him to acknowledge it and to apologize for so many years, but now that I have this apology, it feels anticlimactic, like oh, actually, maybe that wasn't the problem or something," said Moddie, her mouth contracted in a weird smirk. "Like I'm overplaying my hand, and the email I sent him barely even registered. Like it's the same thing as getting late fines, and the librarian writes you some kind of out-there email about the value of the institution, and you're just like, *Okay, lady,* but then you go on with your day."

"No," said Nina, in a drawn-out, skeptical way. "I don't think so. First of all, his email isn't an apology. He can see how his behavior was 'inappropriate'? Fuck off. He's trying to round it down to like 'Yeah, I guess I was a little pushy, but boys will be boys, haha' rather than copping to a legitimate violent sex crime that could, let's be real, get him barred from living near elementary schools, and then he has the fucking gall to shift responsibility to you for 'carrying around anger all these years,' as if anger is not the appropriate emotional response to all of this? No. He doesn't need to apologize for your anger, he needs to apologize for his actions. Your 'years of friendship'? Uh, okay. Get the fuck out. What a weasel. He does not want to talk to you on the fucking phone, that's a sham, he just doesn't want stupid fucking Jen to find this in his email. You know he deleted this message and then emptied out his trash. It's so insincere and self-serving. I'm losing my mind right now. I hate this guy, and I guarantee he's running scared."

"You really think so?" asked Moddie.

"Yes," said Nina sharply.

Moddie opened up her lunch box and took out some grapes. "I really appreciate all of this," she said, but she still couldn't get the weird grin off her face.

"For what it's worth," said Bethany, "since I know you've been gaslit about this over the years, I just want to tell you plainly that I don't think this is a real apology, it definitely seems strategic and placating, and in a way, that should make you feel good. It harmonizes with the rest of your experience. And now you're free. You don't have to repress anything anymore if you don't want to. You can tell whoever you want whatever you want whenever you want about what he did to you." She smiled and gave Moddie a jovial arm squeeze and then patted her shoulder.

"Exactly," said Nina. "Now you're living back in reality."

"Also, don't worry about Jen," said Bethany. "I know you feel rejected by her and you have a lot of anger there, but let me tell you, she did not win. Look at who she just married."

"Yeah, plus she has *cancer*," said Nina.

Moddie laughed. "Yeah, but it's curable."

A nice breeze traveled across the quad and rustled the remaining leaves. Nina reached for some grapes.

"In that case," said Bethany, "you still have options. We can be as strategic as you want about this. Let's say her cancer gets cured and she and Alan stay married. People who get married usually want to have kids. Most women who want to have kids don't want to have kids with a sex criminal. So, if Jen does get pregnant, you'll know that Alan didn't tell her. Don't contact him again. Let him stew. You're done dealing with him directly. Let a few years go by, and he'll probably think he's in the clear. That's good. That'll work for you. You can monitor her social media to see if you think she's changed her ways and become worthy of your forgiveness, and if not, we can do some research on the most fragile developmental stage for a child, for instance, at what age would an increase in fighting and a divorce have the strongest and most negative impact on a child's lifelong bond with their parents. Maybe something around eight or nine, when the child is starting to test more boundaries and gain more independence. Let's try to find the age at which the child is most likely to say 'I hate you' and mean it. Just bide your time and tell her then, and tell her without sparing any physical or emotional detail. You can even remind her of the times when she rejected you or hurt you, and in light of this new information, this should make her feel shame and should disrupt a healthy amount of her narrative identity. 'Good Jen' will get a nice hard club to the face. Probably around that time, when the child is eight, they won't be in love or having sex anymore anyway, and she'll be grateful for an excuse to leave him and to publicly humiliate him in exchange for moral support, but it won't come without a price—nothing like this ever does. She'll get her freedom and she'll get the attention, but in exchange, she'll be haunted by the images of you—sexy, young—being pinned down by her husband. We know she doesn't like you, so this will play an interesting combination of emotions in her—an orchestra of jealousy, hatred, sorrow, and repulsion—and she'll have to lie about how she actually feels in order to get the sympathy and attention she craves. She won't be able to ever say a single unflattering word about you again. Isn't that beautiful? If she does, it will disrupt the delicate balance of what people will need in order to be able to support her, but even if she does this perfectly, everyone will slowly turn away. That's just how people are. In this new order, you are the primary victim, she and the child are the secondary victims, perhaps in many ways more tragic, but only in ways that include a little disgusted fascination—*How could she not have known?* Oh, it's not her fault, of course, no one will think that exactly, but she will be tainted, and she will have to walk a fine line when she explains her situation. Her animosity toward Alan will blossom in ways that now would seem to her unthinkable, and she will experience new and varied passions of hatred. Time will tell what these may be, but one thing's for sure, that every time she looks at her child's face as it utters 'I hate you' with all of the passion and conviction of innocent youth, she will see Alan's face, Alan's face tainting her face, and she will think, I hate you too, and in this child, for years and years, until it dies, will be these two people who hate each other, stuck together, trapped, screaming, both outside and in, 'I hate you,' and every waking day for Jen will be as if lived on the other side of a wretched curse, and some days she will pray for death, the dreamless sleep, and even on days when she thinks she has moved on from this, moved on from you, there will always be the lurking notion that these memories and understandings will come back and take the wheel of her thoughts again," said

Bethany, looking off into the distance. Then she shrugged. "Or, if you do decide to forgive her, you can always think of yourself as a sort of fairy godmother for the child."

Nina put some grapes in her mouth, nodded, and pointed at Bethany. "Now, that's what I'm fucking talking about."

Pam left her office and began the walk across the quad to the small restaurant where she was meeting David. It was just outside the range of where people from school had lunch, so it was private, which she took as a sign that they both had something going on in the back of their minds about what they were actually doing. They'd been meeting more and more often, and their conversations had become more intimate. She could feel herself drawn to him, magnetized, and the energy between them kept her up at night and occupied her mind throughout the day.

Halfway across the quad, she saw Bethany, Nina, and Moddie on a bench under a large tree, Bethany's arm around Moddie, and all three of them cackling and eating grapes. Ice ran through her heart.

She turned abruptly, not wanting to be seen, and walked in the other direction.

On Moddie's walk home she decided to call her mom to tell her the news—that she was no longer a liar, a reject, or a fuckup, and had finally been accepted into the bosom of sisterhood.

"Hey, Ma."

"Hey, honey, how are you?"

"Feeling excellent," she said.

"That's good to hear."

"Yeah. So, you know how I told you Pam was running this Visiting Artist Program thing?"

"Yeah, with the guy who seemed like an asshole?"

"Haha, yeah, that one. She got that gig from this woman Bethany, do you remember her? I've been hanging out with her a little bit, and she's actually pretty cool and giving me advice, she had something in *The New York Times,* you know, and she's interested in having me maybe try out a printmaking workshop over winter semester. I mean, when she found out I had teaching and grant-writing experience, she seemed pretty interested, I would even say she seemed impressed. I think that could be really good. Just, like, get a little cash, dip my toes back into working. I was thinking I could do that, and then on top of that, I could go do some open figure-drawing classes at the community college. I looked it up, it's super cheap, and maybe I can even teach over the summer, too, I don't know. This could be revolutionary for me, if you think about it, time to work, creative engagement, a supportive community. That's the mystery of life, you know, all things leading to other things in an impenetrable chain reaction."

Moddie kept chattering excitedly, twice as fast as normal. She'd been circling the block where she used to live, walking around and around and around her old house, stopping every once in a while to stand beneath her favorite tree, as if she still lived there.

Her mom said, "This all sounds good. And of course, as you know, this is a really great time to take things as slowly as you'd like, there's really no rush, but I'm so happy you're finding—"

"Yeah, I'm feeling really hesitantly positive. I mean, I just feel like it's been so crucial to get some time to myself to process things, and I really feel like I'm calling you from reality," said Moddie, staring into her old living room window.

"Okay, that's great, greetings," said her mom, slowly.

"Haha, yeah. Oh! Also, I got your email about visiting, and yes, I would love to do that, I mean, that's a fantastic idea. I can bring my great new mood to town," said Moddie, and then she laughed wildly, her eyes roaming up to a tree branch, where a squirrel looked down at her, not perceiving her well-laid plans as anything more than an incoherent series of irregular noises.

I'm just as good as she is, thought Kimberly, rereading Bethany's op-ed in *The New York Times*. I could easily do this.

The administrative offices were twenty minutes from closing, and Kimberly thought she would go straight home and start taking notes for a lyrical essay she was going to write about how it felt to be an underappreciated woman—something she thought there would be a lot of traction surrounding, because of all of the awful realities that had been made public recently.

She would channel all of her life's thoughts and feelings into this essay. It would be a distillation of her selfhood, and then once she got through that, she would get back into a regular production schedule, and maybe she would even be able to secure a column for herself. It wouldn't have to be at *The New York Times*. She was thinking that in two years, she would have a solid portfolio and would be able to launch her career as an essayist and finally leave her job, which had lately become a series of thankless frustrations.

She googled herself and thought, Well, first of all, I'm more attractive than Bethany, not to be a huge bitch, but people would be able to project their fantasies onto me more easily than they would be able to project their fantasies onto her. Plus, Bethany did not seem to be working on her essays. She seemed to be focused on her administrative role at the university. Kimberly snorted and fluttered her eyelids like a malfunctioning Furby.

Kimberly thought about that movie *The Devil's Advocate* and something Al Pacino had said—"They never see me coming." That was his asset, because he was short no one took him seriously, and he ruled the world, because nobody saw him coming. Well that was the same for Kimberly, nobody saw her coming. She knew how to turn things into lemonade, so to speak.

She scrolled past the link of the radio interview she'd done where in the comments a few men had said unkind things about her and how she didn't know what she was talking about—well, she could use that in her essay. Bulletproof. They didn't know what *they* were fucking talking about.

She walked over to her intern's desk and said, "Jessie, how's your timeline looking?"

"Oh, hey. I'm almost done. I could have it done by noon tomorrow."

"Hm," said Kim. "Jessie, is the workload too much?"

"No, I don't think so. I'm really sorry. I had a paper due this morning, or I would have been able to work on it last night."

Kimberly pulled up an office chair next to Jessie in the cubicle. She laced her fingers together and leaned forward and smiled and asked, "Can we talk for a second?"

"Sure," said Jessie.

"Do you have passion for this role? Because, I guess, when I look at you, I see a young person who is coming in and going through the motions. Is there something you're more passionate about? I'd really love for you to be able to succeed, and I like you, but I'm just not sure if this is where your passion lies. When I was your age, I had a very strong passion for the work that I did, and I just don't see that reflected in you, so I was just wondering what your passion is. Maybe if this is not your passion, it's time for you to go out and find that thing that really drives you, so if you need to leave in search of that, you should let me know."

Kimberly got into her car and drove. She had decided to mute Bethany on all social media, instead of unfollowing or blocking, which she was not ready to do (too strong of a message), but muting seemed like a healthy response after she saw the post of the Sorry game board on Instagram with the caption "game night with some strong-ass ladies" and saw that she had been replaced by Moddie, who seemed to have no social media (hoity-toity!) but whose name was listed nonetheless.

Fuck them. Didn't anybody else give a shit about entitlement? The post was a direct message to Kimberly that her concerns had been read and dismissed, and she was being replaced, flagrantly, with a privileged interloping bitch who was being handed Kim's spot in game night, just like she'd been handed everything else. Well, Kimberly was going to go visit her brother in L.A., and his girlfriend worked in television, so fuck you and your stupid fucking game night. Her brother had a guest room and they had lots of friends who worked in the industry and Kimberly was going to take advantage of the open invitation to visit and she was not going to bring Bobby, because it was healthy to foster self-independence from within the bounds of a committed monogamous relationship. She'd always felt she'd practice ethical nonmonogamy, which was something she'd told Bobby at the beginning of their relationship, but when she thought about doing something like that with Bobby it nauseated her, because she didn't trust him to do it maturely. His sexual identity was very juvenile. She wondered if her brother and Angie were ethically nonmonogamous. All of their friends were (seemed, from the internet) very attractive and happy. She could imagine them all having group sex.

Kimberly pulled up to their house and parked outside, since they didn't have a garage. The car bounced when she jerked up the parking brake. She wanted a different house. This one was so small and all of their neighbors were renters. She and Bobby had talked about moving, but it was just another stalled conversation, like the conversation around having children and the conversation around getting a dog and the conversation around Bobby taking up a few more of the financial responsibilities for one year—just one year—while Kimberly gave herself a sabbatical to complete some kind of personal project before they had children, which she knew seemed gendered and old-fashioned, the man as the breadwinner, but if you thought about it a different way, it actually seemed progressive for Bobby to make space for Kimberly to shine her light—all of this Kimberly was thinking at a very loud volume inside her head as she walked into her house, threw on some lights, opened her laptop, and started taking furious notes.

> Any man who doesn't respect Woman's power and Dignity deserves strict and unequivocal correction.
>
> Love my body. Fear my body. For you shall never know My Mind.

Men have been sent to their rooms for the time being, while Woman takes the time to fix the problems they have created.

Men are interchangeable.

Men are fools and it is time they are put back in their place, as slaves.

Power brings pleasure. It is time for Woman to reclaim Her Pleasure.

He will no longer Control She.

A well Behaved woman has never Made History—now is the time for certainty and reclamation. She shall Rise and Rise.

Burst My bubble and be showered with the filmy suds of my furious discontent.

It took her fifteen minutes to bang this out.

Kimberly reread what she had written and thought it sounded pretty good, very powerful, and then she thought about that adjunct, who likely thought she deserved her spot because of her "talent" rather than her experience, but literally anybody could write short stories, it was easy. All you had to do was think about yourself and your emotions and type it out in an artsy way. Kimberly had always thought she could write a novel about her experiences. It would be a great hero's journey, and would show the adversity she had faced at the hands of men and other authority figures of privilege.

She began to type again, this time a story upon which she might base a mass-marketable novel.

After twenty-five minutes of pure typing, she sat there breathing heavily, thinking, I can be artsy, too, you stupid fucks. This will work. This is already fucking working. I'm already harnessing my passion into creativity. Already harnessing my divine fury, my righteous vengeance. She made a pact with herself that this was who she was now. She would apply herself and let herself shine. She would tell her story, and then she would be undeniably successful, and then everybody would want, most of all, to come to *her* party.

That's right. *My* party.

She laughed quietly like she was over it, and then made an executive decision, opened a compose window in Gmail, added all of her friends and acquaintances, and sent them this email.

> Going to be in L.A. for a while to beat the gloomy weather and see family between Christmas and New Year, but when I'm back, let's have a party! Our place. January 12th. 8pm until whenever. Hot toddies. Maybe dancing. I know it's super early notice, but just wanted to get everyone on the calendar. Miss you guys!!!

Nine

In the mornings, David felt relatively fine, sane, "normal," but at night he felt like a psycho.

He was sitting on the couch drinking his third beer with a cigarette in his mouth, unlit.

It was one-thirty in the morning.

He lit his cigarette. He felt horrible. Everything was worse at night. When he looked out into time he saw nothing. He saw his body living here forever and he felt himself dead forever. No one loved him. He'd done and said evil and selfish things and he would never be forgiven.

He couldn't stop having flashbacks. Aurelie rigid on the couch while he kept explaining to her why it was so hard and unpleasant to spend time with her. It was like talking to a wall. He kept feeling so furious with her, wondering why she wouldn't just engage, but any time she pushed back, or if she ever called him an asshole, he would just think I fucking hate you so much

I could die. That was something he'd said, too, and whenever it left his mouth, he thought he might literally explode.

But she got mad too, she'd been fucking insane too, and she was always fucking crying, Jesus Christ, it was endless. He dipped back into the past and saw her on the couch muttering to herself, I'm telling you I can't take much more of this I'm telling you I'm warning you *I'm warning you* I can't take much more of this why do you always look at me like that what did I do I hate you too what are you doing what did I do how did this happen what did I do?

Just so dramatic, always implying that he was some kind of a monster, which he wasn't. If you thought about it, she was the monster. What kind of a monster dumps their boyfriend of fifteen years the first time they get even the smallest amount of recognition? She was in Berlin, and he was in hell. He should be in Berlin with her, because he was the one who had made the investment in her and had nurtured her. Who was she without him, and who was she with instead of him? He pictured mocking candlelit smiles in a warehouse and rolled into the fetal position facing the back of the couch and punched the cushions, screaming. He remembered her crying and saying I'm sorry I'm sorry I'm sorry please please please and he felt like he was going to vomit. He tried not to remember telling her that he wasn't attracted to her anymore, and that the only reason he stayed was that he thought she might try to kill herself if he left because in all the years he'd known her, she hadn't exactly seemed emotionally competent. Everything in his body wanted to stop what was happening. He wanted his life back, god, his life his life his life that bitch. Now he couldn't even watch movies where people cried, had relationships, or said nice things to each other without his palms going cold and sweaty and feeling like he might throw up or start sobbing, she was sorry? No she wasn't.

Before he became the visiting artist in this land of dowdy idiots, back when he was still in the city in the apartment where she'd dumped him, the week Pam reached out to him, he overheard their neighbors talking about him. Laughing at him. They were calling him crybaby.

Oh god, fix it fix it fix it please god fix it.

He sat up and lit another cigarette. He was a fucking piece of shit. He was such a fucking shallow piece of shit. Is this what you wanted?

He kept going back and forth between guilty and furious. He couldn't be on one ground for more than a minute before it tilted and slid him back to the other thought. He felt like he was a fucking hostage on a pirate ship.

David had done monstrous things. Monstrous feelings had come through him and compelled him to act. Jealousy, pride, entitlement, anger. Sometimes he'd hated her and it had made him ecstatic. He could see her crying through a crack in the door, and he just walked by, bored and almost happy. Everything inside of him ripped open and blossomed out and he wept.

She was a fucking bitch. He'd made sacrifices for her. He'd sacrificed fifteen years. Think of what he could have done if he hadn't been chained to her, taking care of her, staying in that same fucking minor city because that's where her job was.

In the third year of their relationship they'd had an opportunity to break up but hadn't. "I don't want to go to Amsterdam, you're all I want. I can't be away from you for a year, you're all I want." Well, that had been fucking dumb of him. When the tables turned!

Pam was fucking Victorian, and on top of it, she was his boss, which made him feel like a whore, what a blow, yet another, to his fucking masculinity—a kept boy in a shitty town, and not even getting laid out of it, either, Jesus fucking Christ. For a few days in the beginning he'd felt like he could make something out of this shattering, demoralizing Midwestern experience, but it all evaporated, oozed out into the lands of impossibility, and he'd been eating at Panera, even at times enjoying Panera, he hated Aurelie so fucking much for doing this to him, she could have dumped him at any other time, why not when he had that extra 50K and that gallerist in Atlanta was trying to sleep with him, that would have been a much more convenient time for him, but instead he'd gone on vacation to North Carolina with her parents—the absolute opposite of what could have been in Atlanta. He'd be out of here soon, just a few more stupid fucking months and he'd be out of here with some money saved. He hadn't been able to make any work to show for this stupid fucking exile. The other day, he'd been so fucking furious at his inability to work that when he opened up the program on his computer, he just sat there staring at it, hating it, picked up the pen mug and threw it against the wall, and then put his face in his hands and started crying. He could have been nicer to her, he didn't really know what love was, he'd been ruined early, ruined by his mother, who both spoiled him and hated him, and so he subtly coerced the women in his life to do the same, to baby him but also to resent him, and when he noticed them resenting him, he would always unleash, ranting at them and blaming them for his failures, he did this most with Aurelie, but also with his two college girlfriends and Mindy from high school, he couldn't be changed, he'd loved her so much, he'd thought they'd be together forever, he'd been planning on it, some kind of cottage. They'd get some kind of cottage together with a rose garden just like Darwin's and this would be after his big artistic breakthrough, after he'd completed what he expected to be his life's work, the work that finally made people understand what he'd been trying to articulate, artistically, since he was twenty, and they would finally just be able to read and lie in a hammock, maybe there would be some children there, some cats, and long leisurely days filled with beauty and love and they'd love each other so much, they would be the same person, a joint organism created by love, that was all he wanted, was it too much to ask, such a simple beautiful dream?

It had never occurred to him that he could skip the prideful artistic validation part of this fantasy and go straight to the hammock—they'd had the money to buy a small place where they could have had this garden. She broke up with him, or so she said, because she loved him so much that it shredded—that was her word, an awkward word, perhaps—*shredded* her to have him treat her so coldly, and to see that he was incapable of true kindness and incapable of seeing the ways in which he projected his own artistic insecurities onto her, and that he was always undermining her progress and then guilt-tripping her for being ground down by his relentless hostile negativity, but could that have been true? It hadn't felt true, no no no no, that couldn't have been what it was, how it was, he was often so good and so kind, how could she forget, the garden, he'd had that in his heart, the garden had been in his heart, so how could it be that he was so awful, so bad, such a monster?

Craig reread the email about the party at Kimberly and Bobby's, still incredulous.

"This is fucking early notice," he said. "It's not even Thanksgiving." Then he sort of yelled, "This is like two and a half months' notice!"

"Yeah, well," said Pam. "That's Kimberly for you."

"It's kind of weird, don't you think?"

"She's probably mad about something. She's probably telling us this far in advance to make it awkward if no one shows up. Now we can't pretend we had something else on the calendar, and if we don't show up, she can send us one of her famous emails."

"Hm. Well, I'm definitely going to their party," said Craig. "Bobby is my new bestie."

Pam said, "Yeah, well, that's nice."

Pam was on her laptop at the kitchen table and Craig was standing by the fridge, leaning on it casually.

"This is *weird*," he said again. "Do you think she's doing it consciously, or do you think it's unconscious?"

"I think most things with Kimberly are unconscious."

Craig said "Hm" again and reread the email.

"Should we order dinner? You want to watch a movie?" he asked.

"Yeah, we could order. You watch something, I'm trying to put in a little extra work tonight," said Pam.

"You want Thai food?"

"Yeah, sure."

"You want the usual? Kee mao?"

"Yeah, that's good."

"I think I'm just going to play a game or something," said Craig.

"Sounds good," said Pam.

"Okay, well, I'll order the food then."

"Cool."

While waiting for the food to show up and playing a game in his office, Craig got too curious and texted Bobby, "What's with this party?"

"Fuck you gotta get me the fuck out of here please"

"lol what happened"

The food arrived. Craig and Pam went into their separate rooms. Pam could only eat a few pieces of the kee mao. She felt queasy sitting at the kitchen table alone, hunched over her laptop.

After their latest lunch, she had walked David back to campus and their arms had touched. There had been an entire block where they had walked with their arms pressed together, and when they crossed the main road and entered the campus, they had both instinctively pulled away. This meant something. She knew this meant something. They hadn't just touched accidentally, they had walked pressed together, and when they were back in view of everyone, they'd pulled away.

Now there were so many things she needed to think about, and suddenly so many things that needed to be taken care of. She couldn't eat the kee mao. Each bite felt like dried rubber cement.

When she'd seen David outside the restaurant, she'd known for certain she wanted something to happen between them. While he finished his cigarette, they talked about his classes. Some of his students kept asking him questions about making money. He had no idea how to respond. Pam had said, "You need to tell them about grants and fellowships. The parents want ROI."

She remembered the face he'd made, which was alluring and sexy and crushingly mean, and which Pam could not fully interpret but which she wished to submit to completely.

She said something about how it was stupid, but it would get them off his back. "I've written a few grants. Why don't I come in and talk to them about it?"

He shrugged and said, "Sure," while maintaining his esoteric expression and leading her inside the restaurant.

She replayed this interaction in her mind, sitting at her kitchen table, avoiding dinner. She had replayed it so many times, it had likely altered somehow, but she couldn't be sure how.

In the restaurant, the conversation drifted and became personal, as it always did. It started off businesslike, but then it was like he guided the conversation toward intimacy with his eyes. Pam's chest felt uneasy, and then she heard herself saying, "I love that I'm able to bring someone like you here to connect with the students, and I'm incredibly grateful for my position, but the students do have their limitations. There are limitations in the administration, too. I often fantasize about moving." This last part she hadn't meant to say, and it was a thought she hadn't been fully aware of until she sat there with him in the back of that dim restaurant, eating a mediocre salad.

He looked at her, and that same unease returned. He said something vague about moving, and Pam offered up that she didn't think Craig would come with her if she moved. His eyes flashed into hers again. She smiled and her stomach dropped, but at the same time her chest felt buoyant, and then all of her attention moved down to her ankle, which was so close to David's she could feel it, feel the heat. He said something vague again about moving and then he said, "It's important to be with someone who won't limit your potential," and then he leaned forward to lift his coffee cup, and in doing so, shifted his body slightly so that their legs touched beneath the table, and later they walked for several blocks with their arms pressed together.

She opened her eyes and was suddenly back at her kitchen table. She thought about throwing some of the kee mao away, underneath a few paper towels, so Craig wouldn't ask her why she hadn't eaten. She put a wide noodle in her mouth and regretted it.

She googled David and looked at his picture, then googled David's ex-girlfriend and watched a video of her doing some kind of spasmodic ballerina shit in Rome.

Craig walked into the kitchen still chewing a spring roll and said, "Check this out. I was just texting with Bobby, and he didn't even know about the party. Isn't that fucking crazy? She's gone totally crazy! Apparently she was upstairs and he was downstairs when she wrote the email, and she didn't ask him or even tell him about it, she just sent the email. He was just watching TV and got invited to a party at his own house," said Craig. "That's fucking wild."

"Yeah, that's crazy," said Pam.

Craig shook his head, laughed, and walked back to his office while typing something on his phone. "I'll keep you updated," he shouted.

She sat there numb and then opened her cover letter, knowing it was time to make life changes.

Right after lunch, Pam had written to Bethany to say, "I'd like to do a one-day crash course in grant writing and fellowship applications in David's class." She'd thought the "I" was pronounced enough, but Bethany wrote back immediately and said it sounded great, and that she would kick it to Moddie. "We've been bouncing around ideas for things she could do, this could be perfect."

This was not something Pam had meant to "kick" to Moddie, and it wasn't fair, Moddie had no business in a classroom. She had no experience. She didn't have a terminal degree. She was demonstrably unhinged. This seemed insane to Pam, but Moddie always got what she wanted, ever since high school. Pam could always feel a malicious glee radiating off of Moddie when she sauntered into a situation, asserted her superiority, got what she wanted, got bored, then left—and she always left. She left her job and her boyfriend, her art community, her art practice, and her beautiful apartment in Chicago. She hadn't just had a breakup, it was like she was on the lam.

Pam liked Moddie's parents, and she wondered if they were disappointed, they must be, and honestly she felt sorry for them. Moddie had slowly grown into a shiftless loser, definitely a bigger loser than Pam, all that wasted promise and support, and it made Pam laugh to think that what she'd probably needed growing up, rather than permission to skip math class senior year to participate in nude figure drawing, was much more discipline. She'd probably needed to be yelled at more often. There wasn't anything special about Moddie, all she knew how to do was draw dicks. Anybody could draw dicks. Pam felt herself get very angry about this, and she picked up a pen and drew a small dick in the margin of her notebook and then scribbled it out.

Her heart was beating more than it needed to, because her body thought she was engaged in physical combat. All she had to do was assert herself more, visualize, follow through, and she would beat Moddie in the end.

She laughed.

Her anger was clarifying.

She opened up a Google Doc and typed.

I do not ever want to have sex with Craig again. I do not want to marry him, and I do not want to have his children. I do not want to live in my hometown with my childhood friends doing thankless administrative tasks for a bunch of students who don't even care. I want to move to a different city, not New York or LA, because performative wealth makes me uncomfortable, but something like Austin, Portland, or Atlanta. I would like to run my own artist residency.

In that moment, for just a moment, she felt as if she had already arrived.

She put her face in her hands and her mind entered into blackness.

Tired, so tired. She would need to make a spreadsheet for jobs, a spreadsheet for her budget, a five-year plan, rewrite her CV and cover letter, set job alerts, write to people to let them know she was looking, and all of this while she was so tired.

She priced out apartments in town, and what she could afford without Craig was bleak. No washing machine, no hardwood floors, no yard, no peaceful neighborhood streets—everything available to her was like a tiny little prison. She doubled her utilities budget, and subtracted that from what she thought she could afford on rent, and the results got worse.

That was enough for tonight.

She added a tenth of a serving of kee mao to her calorie tracker and saw that Craig, her only friend on the app, had spent sixty minutes doing cardio this afternoon while also meeting his calorie goals, and something about this touched her and made her feel sad and small and afraid, and she didn't want to have to do all of this stuff, she just wanted to go to bed. She folded her arms in front of her on the table and put her head on her arms and let herself hang for a minute in the space between not crying and crying.

She put the kee mao in the fridge, brushed her teeth, put on pajamas, and then knocked on the door of Craig's office.

"Yaaaeeeuuusss," he said. "Come in."

She opened the door a little, leaned her head against the doorjamb, and said, "Can I have a hug?"

"Sure thing, baby," said Craig.

He got up quickly from his chair and walked over to the door and gave her a hug, rubbed her on the back, and rocked her a little.

Pam started to cry.

"Everything okay, my sweetie?" he asked.

Crying made it hard to think, and because she couldn't think, she couldn't figure out how to stop crying.

"I'm just so tired," she said.

"You want to cuddle?" he asked.

Pam nodded, sobbed, and said, "Yes."

They got into bed and Craig held her and stroked her hair. "You're going to be oooookaaayyy," he said. "I'm really impressed by all of the work you've been doing. It really makes sense that you're so tired. But you're doing a really great job. You're killing it. I'm sorry you have to work so late, too. They should lighten your load a little—but I bet it'll be easier next semester. All of this work carries over, and it gets easier each year. In a few years, it'll be smooth sailing." He kept scratching her scalp, in the exact way she liked. "Maybe for the next few weeks, we should both lighten up a little. You shouldn't be working so late. Maybe next weekend we should rent a cabin and walk in the woods and try to unwind. I think that sounds really nice, don't you?"

Pam nodded.

"Doesn't that sound nice, my Pammy Lamby?" He took her hair and flipped it over her face so it looked like two floppy ears. "My little Pammy Lamby got all tuckered out?"

Craig hit her softly on the forehead with her ears and sang the Pammy Lamby song. She laughed and smiled and felt completely relieved. She closed her eyes.

"I'm going to make you some tea, I'm going to bring the laptop in, we're going to watch *Prime Suspect,* and I'm going to give you a shoulder rub," he said.

Craig got up and went to the kitchen. Pam felt cocooned in all of her things, her lamps, the paintings and posters on the walls, her plant, the rug, the antique dresser she'd had since high school. Every object had a warm glow.

She could hear Craig making tea. It was deeply comforting. He opened the fridge to get out the milk, because he knew she liked to have peppermint tea with milk and honey. Her pillow was so soft, and the sheets were nice and clean. She was looking forward to watching *Prime Suspect*. Helen Mirren was certainly about to prove herself. Certainly about to catch the rapist. All will be well, she thought.

From the kitchen she could hear Craig say, "Pa-am! No wonder you're exhausted, you didn't eat any of your kee mao," which felt like a dark smear over her relief.

The night that Moddie and David were going to play air hockey, Nina agreed to go on a walk because the arcade was near her apartment in the small neighborhood where many of their high school crushes had lived.

"Are you going to make love to him?" asked Nina.

"No," said Moddie sweetly, bashfully.

They walked through the park where they'd had a terrible fight at seventeen, past the seesaw, toward Caleb's old house. Moddie had mostly been attracted to Caleb because he wore a large sweatshirt.

It had been getting darker earlier each week. The sky was a rich royal blue that deepened as you looked up from the horizon. A few stars were becoming visible, and the streets, as always, had that artificial quality, like a film set, the streetlamps catching the undersides of the leaves, which were now brown, yellow, and orange. The air smelled like cool dirt.

Moddie still felt alive with possibility and she wanted to keep talking about the email she'd sent to Alan, the freedom of being single, and the intensity of the truth. It had only been a few days, but it felt like telling the truth had coincided with a generalized stimulation of the flow of energy in her life, like her true self was beginning to take root again.

"I just feel like I was spending so much energy and so much time trying to live in two separate realities, so much of my energy was going into repressing this Alan shit, and not wanting to face what that meant about my relationship with Nick, and now that I've said it out loud, I'm able to move on and think about more stuff—I just really feel like I'm about to be myself again, finally."

Nina got her hat out of her bag and shook some lint off of it.

"Well, anyway, how are you doing?" asked Moddie.

"I'm pretty good," said Nina.

"How's Tony?"

"Yeah, he's pretty good."

Moddie looked at Nina and then looked over at a cat that was rolling around in a driveway.

"You guys should come over for dinner sometime. It's crazy we haven't hung out yet."

"Yeah, for sure," said Nina. "I'll have to check with his schedule."

"Great."

They walked and walked and kept talking. Moddie kept saying things about how "the truth shall set you free" and Nina kept bowing and saying "Yea, verily" with her hands in prayer pose. Eventually they parted ways, Moddie to the arcade and Nina back home.

Moddie's palms were clammy. It wasn't a date, she was sure of that. For something to be a date you had to say "Would you like to go on a date with me?" so the other person, if they weren't romantically interested in you, could have the opportunity to say "I'm flattered, but I just got out of a long relationship/I'm seeing someone else/I'm not dating right now/I see us more as friends," or whatever gentle no they could think of, so she was in the clear, it was not a date, and she could hide her attraction in the jovial banter of a platonic, bro-to-bro friendship, and also, she had heard he was an asshole, so it didn't matter if he rejected her, she wasn't interested anyway.

She approached the hot-pink, run-down arcade, the site of much exhilarating youthful anguish, pushed open the glass door, and descended into the dim, cacophonous basement. She texted David that she was there, no rush, and he replied he was a block away. She ordered a foamy beer in a plastic cup and staked out an air hockey table. When he arrived, she regretted this whole idea, he was too tall, too intriguingly grouchy.

"Ay, what's up?" she said.

"Hey, Moddie," he said.

"You can get a beer if you want to loosen up for the game," she said, nodding to the kiosk where a forty-year-old man with gauged ears leaned on the counter, looking into nothing.

He raised his eyebrows, laughed slightly, and said, "All right."

The walls were painted a rich hot pink, the floors were black, and the smallish arcade was crammed tightly with machines—pool tables, video games, pinball machines, and DDR around the perimeter, darts in the back near the parking lot exit.

Moddie felt strongly that he didn't quite know what he was in for.

In addition to swimming, which Moddie did with the zeal and strength of a genuine psychotic, air hockey had been her great athletic triumph. She and the puck were one. The only person she ever lost to was Nina, and even that was rare.

In the beginning, she let David come close, just so he wouldn't quit playing. He pulled ahead around point four, Moddie always trailing him by a point, but when he got to six, she put two in within seconds.

"*Lucky* break," he said.

"Oh, I *knooow*," she replied, laughing on the inside and sinking the final point.

She let him win the next round, which seemed to satisfy him, but from then on, it was a massacre, during which she toyed with him and occasionally let him score, kept him engaged, but then would humiliate him with a streak of simple shots. David's air hockey form was polite, bordering on prudish, and involved pool-like banking, something coming from a math brain, but he hit too slow. Moddie's style was ugly and rapid, David said "barbaric," at which Moddie laughed, and then later he said it was like playing Mortal Kombat with a girl who kept winning by slamming all of the buttons on the controllers without learning any of the actual moves. "Basically like not even playing a real game."

"Oh yeah?"

She did an impersonation of his style by holding the paddle with the tips of her fingers, lifting her pinky, banking it, and saying "I'm David" which distracted him so much the puck slid into his goal on the outer left edge.

"The worst are filled with passionate intensity," he said, finishing his second beer.

"I grew up on these courts. We're going to play until I see your knuckles bleed."

He rolled his eyes.

They played round after round and David didn't get any better and Moddie did not slow down, she moved her arm chaotically, guided by instinct, making contact with the puck again and again and again and it felt like it meant something, something she did not understand, and David seemed to grow tired and bored with losing, and when he suggested they play something else, Moddie shook her head and said, "I knew a kid in high school who got high on PCP and ripped one of those machines out of the wall," nodding toward a pinball machine.

"How's that for local color."

He scored. She smiled. She passed the puck back to him slowly and he scored again. She placed the puck on the table and it floated like mercury while she tapped it around from side to side.

"Well, this is getting boring," said David, even though this was the first time anyone had asked him to hang out in a non-work-related setting in over a year.

Moddie was thinking about what Kara had said about David being an asshole, and in that moment, it seemed clear to her that he was. She watched the puck and felt it tap the paddle and saw it hover slowly, which was how she felt standing there, as if she were hovering slightly.

"You remind me of a professor I had in undergrad," she said.

"He was a very nice and intelligent person, I suppose," said David.

"Well, at first, I thought he was a loser," said Moddie. "On the first day of class, he seemed unprepared and overly interested in convincing us that he was a cool and relaxed kind of guy, the kind of thirty-six-year-old we twenty-two-year-olds might want to be friends with. I mocked him to my friends and parents. But I was vain and weak and secretly ambitious. When he began to compliment my work, I was flattered. I started to think he wasn't so bad. When he started to send me emails, suggesting artists whose work I might respond to, then I started to look forward to his class. I had never done well in school, and as I said, I was weak and vain and it was easy to win my affection. I thought this might be the beginning of my life, my new life as an artist, and that finally someone had seen what I could offer and was interested in guiding me to the next phase. I put in days of extra work to prepare for his class, so that I wouldn't miss this opportunity to be chosen as someone who might be able to follow my bliss as a member of an artistic community. The work of his that I saw online, which at first I'd thought was lame and corny, now felt rich and connected to a long history of thought—his whole class helped to position this opinion, and by the middle of the semester, I thought of him not as an incoherent dweeb, but as a representative of the eternal, the ineffable, and possibly a genius. As my opinion of him changed, I imagined so too did everyone else's, and in those weeks, I felt as though the faces of the entire world were turned to look at him, and by bringing myself closer to him, the faces of the world might look upon me, too. I told him I liked the artists he'd been mentioning and had been to the Video Data Bank to watch recordings of their performances. He said, 'I love to think of you in the dark, looking at all of this.' The line kept getting pushed and pushed. Of course, one night I went to a gallery opening he'd suggested I might like, and afterward, we got drunk in an alley and made out, then walked along the street together, but we couldn't make out in the street, he said, in case any of his students happened to walk by. He looked back and forth, like someone crossing the street, and then we would hide in an alley, make out. He said he was too drunk to drive me home and gave me twenty dollars for a cab, then he said, 'You should give this back to me in class, haha, put it in my shirt pocket or something,' and I said, 'Haha, yeah.'

"He was part of a cabal of Satanists who worked at the school. They all made flicker films. The week after we made out, he moved into my apartment for the rest of the semester. When he was left alone in my apartment, he made drawings and hid them in books and other places so that I might find them later and think of him. And later, I did find them—for months and months, pictures of my own gravestone, drawings of me sleeping, random shapes, I found them everywhere, constant reminders. While he lived with me, and even after he left, he continued to recommend things, including books by Crowley and a few books on astral projection, which I thought I might be able to use to spend time with him while he refused to answer my calls. He was very spotty about answering my calls after I submitted my course evaluation on the last day of class, which was the day he moved out, unceremoniously, while I was in Etching II. These books emphasized that I ought to eat and sleep less and also that I ought to write down any time I felt some kind of strange magical or mystical presence, which I did, dutifully, happy for once in my life to be considered a good student and not wanting to disappoint. He was, in those days, my only thought. Sometimes I would sit on my floor and meditate, imagining that I was entering his mind and compelling him to text me. Sometimes this would work, and when it did, I felt drunk with power. He disappeared for a while. During this time, I could often feel the presence of some long lean figure entering my bedroom at night, standing in the corner of my room and watching me sleep. I never felt disturbed by this, rather I felt curious and excited.

"Eventually, my meditations stopped working, and I could not get him to reach out to me. Texting him or calling him never worked. I had to reach him on the astral plane. It had been nine days since I heard from him, which was lucky, because if you added three and six, his age, it was nine. I walked as if asleep into my bathroom and chanted over my flip phone, random sounds and words, whatever came out of me, got undressed, and bathed my body in the saliva that fell copiously from my open mouth. I dressed myself again, put on a shell necklace, several of my luckiest ribbons, and left my apartment with my cell phone in my hand. I walked, not knowing where, but following impulse, until I was in a field in a park beneath a large tree, underneath a full moon. I got down on my knees and dug a small hole, placed my cell phone in the hole, buried it, and continued my walk. Along the way an elderly drunk man gave me a single red rose. Back in my bathroom, I rubbed the rose petals all over my nude body, dressed again, and returned to the park, where I dug up my phone to find a text message from him, asking me if I'd ever seen the film *Congo* starring Tim Curry. I went home to practice my astral projection meditations and was visited again by the long, sexless figure, who seemed to me to be some kind of an angel.

"Months went by without my seeing him, and then I ran into a classmate at a party. She had just finished an affair with my teacher. She was furious and drunk as she described the stupid details of their dalliance, and I listened, unbelieving at first, as he had promised, many times in person and over the phone, in exchange for my patience and loyalty, if only I would wait another year, two years, however long until the time was right, to marry *me,* promised that we would elope, and that we would get a futon on our honeymoon in Japan. How I now loathe futons. My classmate talked to me as if it were all gossip. He had told her that I was insane and that she should not talk to me. He told her I was obsessed with him, some type of maniac who had tried to kiss him at a concert, but we'd never even been to a concert, and in fact he'd said that in me he had found some kind of double, his own life reflected in a young woman. I left the party and walked three miles to his neighborhood, in mourning. I didn't know his address, but I did know his block, for he had mentioned it to me many times. He often talked solely of himself. I walked for hours around his block, bargaining, praying for him to meet me on the street and to make this all untrue—to make everything this classmate had said a lie, and to take me back and give me the love he'd promised. I walked for hours, but I did not find him. I found the house I believed to be his and I squatted down, drunk, and peed in his gutter, looking into a window I thought might be his.

"When I got home, I was furious, and I knew for certain he was a coward. I opened a book to distract myself and one of his drawings fell to the floor and I began to laugh—he should not have left his drawings here. I texted him and set the phone on my large wooden table and sat in a chair motionless until he responded. 'Why didn't you tell me Darlene was your girlfriend?' 'I don't have girlfriends, I just have people who I date.'

"Of course, this was insufficient.

"I laughed again and gathered all of the drawings and every item of his I had, a copy of *The Crying of Lot 49,* two pens, a sock, and the DVD of *Congo* I'd purchased to give to him, and which I had watched several times in a dizzied mania. I tied these items together with my lucky green ribbon, placed my cell phone on top of the bundle, placed my hands on top of it all, closed my eyes, and meditated for hours, channeling all of my anger at his cowardice and his lies into the bundle, and vanquishing any remaining longing and sympathy in my heart. I stopped when it was time to stop, and I got into bed and lay awake while I felt the figure enter my room again. This time I allowed it to come closer. This time I understood that this was the thing that had been within him that had compelled the thing that was within me, and now I had no more need for him, because I had this thing for myself. It approached the foot of my bed. It placed one hand, then the other, one knee, then the other onto my mattress and slowly crawled to me like a liquid, and when it hovered over me, black and inviting, I knew that my heart and my spirit were connected to something larger, and when it bent its face, which had no features, like its body, which had no definition, close to my ear—so that

I could no longer see it, but feel it—it asked me without words what it was that I wanted, and I told it without words what it was that I wanted, which was for this man to suffer, and then it brought its fingers up to my face, stroked my cheek, and told me that I would have whatever it was that I wanted. I fell asleep and did not dream, but when I woke it was as if to a dream.

"The next day, I saw the machinery of the universe, and I was floating in a sacred channel. Animals stopped to look at me when I passed, and twice a flower bud opened its first bloom as I approached. All I had to do was glance at a person, and I would get what I wanted. People moved away from me on the subway, gave me retail discounts for seemingly no reason at all, and I was able to talk myself out of failing a class with an ease I had never felt before. The song of everything sang for me. At night I would sit down in front of my bundle, and without speaking my wish with words, I would place my hands above it and the channel would open, and things would flow through me—anger without love.

"After three weeks of this state, I broke. I couldn't do it anymore. I contacted friends, family, I broke, I cried, I ate, I slept, I drank, and slowly I reentered the world of the living and clumsily began piecing things back together, because during this time I had isolated myself completely and my life was a wreckage. I was punished. Terrible things happened. As I came back to life, I began to experience terrible headaches. For a little over two months, I had all of the symptoms of brain cancer. Aphasia, disorientation, splitting pain, nausea. The smells of toast, oranges, and eggs haunted me. And then just as quickly as it started, it stopped. My life moved on, but it always held the faint imprint of this experience.

"Time passed. Years later, when I was twenty-nine, I received an email from my professor asking if I could speak with him on the phone. On the phone, he wanted to tell me he was dying of brain cancer. He also wanted to let me know that he had always wanted to be with me, and that he was glad I was doing well—laughable, as I was not doing well, and had only told him I was doing well because he had brain cancer. He said, 'I did a lot of things I'm not proud of, and I feel like I'm being punished somehow.' Of course, I told him I didn't think it was his fault that he had brain cancer, and that I was so sorry. I tried to ask him about what he had said to Darlene about our time together, which made him very angry. I dropped the subject and I never heard from him again.

"The day he died, I felt as though he visited me, just for a moment. His presence was simple, plain, just the feeling of being in the room with an average man. I nodded goodbye to him. When he left, I felt a strange movement of emotions—neutral sadness, exhaustion, relief, and then, oddly, satisfaction. A smile moved across my face. I was at my grandma's house when this all happened, pretending to listen to her talk about pediatric diabetes. But I really wasn't listening."

All this time, Moddie had been gently scoring on David. He was sure it was well past time to leave.

Moddie walked all the way home from the arcade, through the neighborhoods, across the two main drags, passing the strip mall, all the way to her apartment, on the way purchasing a six-pack of Red Stripe and a pack of American Spirits. She hadn't felt this way, this unapologetically good, in a long time, maybe not since childhood. She felt like she was some kind of thing flying through the night. She thought about high school, how awful the teachers were, how overwhelmingly boring and time-consuming and Sisyphean the homework had been, and how the homework had been designed secretly by the government to force her into menial labor, rather than to allow her to engage in critical thinking, but it hadn't worked.

The Red Lobster sign was ablaze. She turned down her street.

She neared her apartment and thought, Oh fuck it, who cares? She remembered David's face, he wouldn't even look at her, just looked down and said, "I think I'm going to head out," and it should have been embarrassing, but it wasn't, because nothing was going to be embarrassing ever again.

"This is my vow," she whispered. She was going to be her unhindered self, "and no man" she whispered again, sliding the key into the lock.

When she got inside, she chose a date to visit her parents, bought plane tickets to visit Kara, booked an Airbnb in Brooklyn, bought theater tickets, made a list of twenty books she had always wanted to read but that she had not yet read, and ordered these books to be shipped to her apartment, and once she was done she felt stunned that this was what she could do now with all of this freed-up energy—live her life to the unapologetic fullest.

She took a moment to remember what Bethany and Nina had said about how all of this was positive, telling the truth was positive. She thought again about David and the way he'd looked at her, and then she felt ashamed, as if an error had been made, and this made her feel frustrated and impatient. She couldn't escape, no matter what she did. She'd done what she was supposed to do, she had severed ties with the things that made her stomach churn and made the little whispering voice in the back of her mind (nobody likes you, you could always die, pathetic, worthless, foolish, talentless, humiliating, evil, stupid) grind on and on, the cruel jolly rhythms of her internal torturer—she'd cut ties with those things, like everybody told her she should, like the world said she should, but it did nothing and she felt infuriated and stomped her feet there in her living room, jumping up and down and muttering, "Stupid, stupid, stupid."

It was probably stupid of her to have broken up with Nick. She felt the draw of this kind of thinking, alluring like hard drugs. She'd been stupid—at each turn of her life, she'd been stupid, and when she parted with David, he wouldn't even look her in the eye.

"Stupid," she said again into the empty apartment.

Would you even want to get dinner with Alan and Jen? No. Of course not. I'm too stupid for that.

"I don't want to get dinner with anybody," she said. "Why the fuck would I want to do that?" Only makes me feel like shit.

If she walked into a room filled with everybody from the last fifteen years of her life—and what other life had she had but that?—she would feel awful, awkward. None of them cared about her. They didn't even notice she was gone, and if they did, it was probably like noticing your neighbor's leaf blower had finally stopped, subliminal relief from a minor annoyance.

She lay down on the couch and cried for a while, like a baby, somebody help me!

I don't want to make friends, I don't *want to*.

After she finished crying, she felt calm, and started to think about things rationally.

She had a right to be angry, and she had a right to express why. She had done her best with the situation, she'd been empathetic and caring and she'd considered the other side, she'd tried to let bygones be bygones, but they wouldn't let her, always rolling their eyes at her, pretending like they didn't understand. Alan had said he wanted her to find closure. Maybe she should take him at his word.

Closure. She rolled her eyes.

Alan was insane if he thought he could provide her closure through some kind of stupid phone call, as if all she wanted was to hear him say "I'm sorry," as if it weren't well past too late for all of that, and as if she even wanted closure, anyway—maybe she would one day, but that night, as she pressed her body deeper into the cushions of her terrible sofa, the only thing she wanted was revenge. She was not the only one who should have to suffer. It wasn't fair that Jen, her torturer who hated and exiled her, with all of her prissy little facial expressions, and all of her little insinuations that Moddie was defective, and all of her plausibly deniable backstabbing, got to be off in Door County, happily married and heroically beating cancer, while Moddie had to be all alone with her horrible endless thoughts in this wretched apartment.

She began to draft an email in her head.

It included phrases like "forced his way into my apartment" and "pervasive, continuous sense of alienation."

Moddie drank another Red Stripe, lit another cigarette, and thought it over. She knew it would forever shut and seal the door to friendship with Nick or any of those old people. If she told Jen, she could never go back. That felt fine. It felt clear. Final. The word "final" blazed inside of her.

She opened up her laptop and began to draft another email to Jen. She imagined that she was a character, the type of woman who could have gotten sympathy from Nick. She was gentle, apologetic, confused, calm, reasonable, and within this framework, she wove the poison details.

A smile twitched at the corner of her mouth. She allowed herself to believe that this might actually cause them both some suffering—if she could get the email just right. The smile flicked again and was followed by an airy, vacant laugh.

Will I send it, yes or no?

She looked at Jen's Instagram. It was still unclear how bad her cancer would be. The prognosis was still undecided. Another twitching smile. Another mild laugh, and then the heavy laugh. The endless laugh. Moddie covered her face with her hands. She leaned back and kept laughing, laughing and giving everybody cancer.

Ten

Actually, the more she thought about it, the more her entire situation was no longer acceptable, and the behavior of others was no longer excusable.

The gray days had begun. It was a gray Tuesday, a hateful Tuesday. She didn't want to go home, not at all.

Kimberly walked down Mayfield Street, where students had small fires burning on the front lawns of their large, dilapidated houses. It was dark out. She'd been walking for hours. The flames lit the coeds demonically from the bottom. Laugh it up, she thought. Kimberly became less aware of her own self and body as she glided over the pavement, circling the block over and over and thinking of what she could do, what she should do.

The students certainly weren't thinking of what they could or should do. They stood around stupid to danger, laughing. Kimberly drank in their energy and thought with a mirthless pleasure that they would soon be punished by life and that their happiness was a transient sham.

She smiled. Her eyes widened.

Bethany should have given me that position, not Pam, and *The New York Times* should have published my work, not Bethany's, but it won't be long until everybody knows who the true genius of this town is, no, it won't be long, by this time next year, everyone will know.

The episode of the local radio broadcast she'd appeared on and downloaded ended, and Kimberly reached into her pocket, brought out her phone, and began it from the top. The music played. The journalist introduced her.

Maple trees. Dying grass. Flat horizon. She walked back to her car. Soon she'd be in Los Angeles. Then everyone would know. She could see an infinity pool looking out over the hills. Tropical plants. Exotic people. Kimberly touched the cuff of her wool coat and imagined instead it was silk. This was where she was going. Convertibles. Easy days. Fresh juice.

At home, she opened up a Word document and wrote a cover letter the likes of which had never been seen. She heard Bobby walk around downstairs, and even from upstairs she could hear him urinate. She could not wait for her life to be different.

She rewrote the About Me section: An artist and writer navigating the world with wit and intelligence. What was untrue about that? Who would tell her that this was not true?

Weeks passed and Craig noticed a kind of mellowing in Pam. She didn't criticize him as much and they didn't fight, but she seemed forlorn, and in the evenings when she came home, he was trying to do better. He made dinner and did chores and asked her about her day. She said a few cryptic things about how she wasn't so sure where things were heading.

"We can go anywhere you want. We can do anything you want," he said. He could hear a slight desperation in his voice when he said these things, and then he would laugh. "Truly. We're still so young, and if you want to go somewhere else or move or get another job, I'm in full support of that, and I just really want to support you."

She was quiet when he said these things, and this made Craig want to ask again, How was your day, what are your dreams, what would you like for dinner, would you like to get lunch some day this week? We're both on campus, why don't we ever do that?

He'd gotten much too cavalier about his crush on Petra and he feared she'd heard something about this, about one of his drunken rants. He was an open book, really. The word to describe how he felt with Pam these days was "desperate." This didn't feel good, it felt bad. Was this what it was like to be dumped? Was there anything he could do to stop what seemed to be happening?

"Is there something you'd like to talk about? Anything?" he asked, what else was he to do, but she always said, "No, I'm just tired." He would kiss her and she would kiss back for a second and then pull away and leave the room without saying anything, and normally he would have started an argument, but this time it was different and Craig was on his best behavior.

Somebody must have told her something. Each night they spent together in their cold, dark apartment, which was now mostly silent, twisted something inside of him and made him nuts with insecurity, but he couldn't get her to talk to him, so someone must have said something.

One day, he planned to meet a friend for lunch off campus and as he was walking through the quad, he saw Pam walking with David and he almost called out but something stopped him. They'd lived together for six years and had talked about starting a family, but something held him back. This isn't right, he thought, something is very wrong. He hid behind a tree. He put his palms flat against it and peeked his head out from behind it and watched.

Oh, you devious bastards, he thought. Oh, you sanctimonious bitch.

David was standing much too close to Pam with his hands in his pockets, probably playing with his dick, he should be arrested, a pervert, a pedophile, tilting his crotch toward Pam and staring at her intensely, Pam pouting, smiling, and stroking her hair and neck like in an old porno. Craig watched them and followed them and then felt disgusted with himself, but not for watching, disgusted that he hadn't figured it out sooner.

He never told her he'd seen her with David, but he did follow them two more times, just to be sure. The second time, he saw their arms brush together and their fingers entwine briefly, once, so quickly he thought even they could deny it had happened— Officer, no, we just lost our footing for a second and bumped into each other.

After that, all of his feelings toward Pam cooled. Even his anger.

He waited for her to say something. He watched her. He was learning what everything meant, what her behavior meant, and while learning, he dipped back into memories and wondered if she'd been unfaithful to him periodically throughout their seven years together.

Judging by her behavior now, it would seem as though she had been.

Craig and Bobby started to spend more time together in the evenings when Pam was off flirting with her lover, David Winterbottom. During these hangouts, Bobby talked seriously about his intention to divorce Kimberly.

"I mean, I'm pretty much done. She's a fucking psycho, and any time I disagree with her, she says I'm gaslighting her."

"Dude, Pam does that too."

"Her mom is a shrink, and she has all of this technical language built up in support of her idea that she's not being fucking batshit. Like this Christmas break stuff. That was weird. We all agree that was weird. I feel like someone who wasn't a crazy person would have said 'I'm going to my brother's for Christmas' instead of mass blasting all of my friends about it and then inviting them to a party—it's fucking unhinged, and if I try to say, like, hey, that was weird, she freaks out and acts like I'm like fucking Bluebeard and she's 'just not going to take it anymore.'"

"Preach it," said Craig.

Since Kimberly, who Bobby described to Craig as a screamer and a door slammer, had made such a big deal about how she was going to be in L.A. for two weeks, and had made such a big deal about how Bobby couldn't come with her, and such a big deal about asserting her independence, Bobby thought it seemed like an appropriate time to initiate the separation. While Kimberly was in L.A., Bobby would move all of his things out and into storage, and then he would stay with his brother Stan for a month while he looked for an apartment.

Craig strongly suggested Bobby contact a few divorce lawyers. "You should have everything squared away before you talk to her. She'll probably go ballistic."

"Yeah," said Bobby, and then "Fuck, I wish we'd never gotten married."

Craig nodded solemnly, feeling glad he and Pam were not married.

Those nights, when Craig returned home to find Pam curled over her phone on the couch drinking wine in her own private world, he never once told her about Bobby contacting the divorce lawyer, or how seriously degraded Kim and Bobby's marriage had become—even though he knew Pam didn't like Kimberly and that this was just the kind of gossip she loved.

He was still waiting for her to talk to him, and to confess what she was doing behind his back with David. "He's her fucking employee," he said one night to Bobby. "How low can you get?"

Luckily, all of the students thought Moddie's speech in David's class had been a joke, a bizarre rant for their amusement structured around useful, practical information about making money as a fine artist. She said a lot of things about "the brotherhood" and about how making art was to manifest a tangible version of the soul, and that not all souls were equal. Tawdry work was the result of a tawdry soul, undeveloped work the result of an undeveloped soul, and even if you used a formula to make your art, hoping to hide behind the thoughts and gestures of the great minds who had come before you, even this laid bare your formulaic soul, your selfish feeble cowardice and fundamental lack of curiosity. Let every man be judged by what he makes real in this world. The man who plants and tends a geranium and remembers the name of his cashier at Kroger is higher in the eye of god than the charlatan who copies Cy Twombly at the coffee shop, charging thousands of dollars and thinking himself a guest at the dinner party of eternity. Woe to he who makes this error, and woe to he who mistakes accolades for artistic clarity.

When the speech ended, and she'd given them all of the

valuable links for grants, residencies, and fellowships, she bowed and made a beeline for the door. When she passed David, they locked eyes for a second, then he looked down and said, "Okaaay."

Her erotic feelings toward him disappeared completely after air hockey, and now she thought of him as a loser. She confirmed this on the phone with Kara, who she'd been getting closer to over the past month, as Kara was also single and didn't have a desk job, either, so they had their coffee together over speakerphone in the mornings. It was Kara's opinion that David's work had taken a dive. Things had gotten around about what a shitty boyfriend he'd been. Nobody really wanted to support him anymore.

Whenever Moddie ran into David, or rather when she saw him eating lunch at the Noodles & Company downtown, bending awkwardly over the bowl and hoovering, she thought there was no reason for him to be so smug. He looked frail. She had no more illusions about him. Her mind was becoming clearer by the day, the whole future seemingly laid out before her, each next step rising out of the abyss of her mind, fully formed and obvious. Bethany was giving her a job. She was a professor now, and everybody liked her.

Kimberly worked most nights on the website for her lyrical essays, which she wanted to have ready by the time she went to Los Angeles as a proof of concept for herself as a writer. She had a spreadsheet going of ideas for posts she could make on social media, and she started to read the news and to make herself information-retention flash cards so that no matter what conversation came up, she would be ready with the correct and most dazzling opinions.

Her diet was working. The fluctuations in her blood sugar

made her feelings about Bobby even more acute and clear. She felt very certain she was about to shed this life like a skin.

Bethany had scheduled a "blowout winter party!" to coincide with Kimberly's vacation, the exact dates of which Bethany got from Bobby, the traitor.

Nina went home every day after work.

In this town, once the weather cooled, the clouds came in and stayed until spring. There were no subtle, beautiful variations in the gray. The sky was just an oppressive, uniform dome.

The week before Bethany's party, and two nights before Kimberly's flight to L.A., Bobby told her everything.

"I told her I was moving out while she was in L.A., I told her I didn't love her anymore, I told her the relationship was over, I told her I'd been to a divorce lawyer and that I wanted to handle this maturely through mediation. I told her she'd been treating me terribly for almost two years, and that any time I tried to talk to her about it she refused, and because of this I'd lost all trust in her, the damage was done, and my decision was final."

"Fuck," said Craig. "How did she react?"

"She hit me a bunch of times and called me a fag," said Bobby.

Was it possible to make contact with the unseen world? Were rocks really the storybook of Earth? And if so, why wasn't everybody freaking out about it all the time? How do you know if something is real? When you have a sensation of something that's hard to describe but feels like it explains everything, how do you know that that's not the real thing and all of this easy-to-explain stuff is the fake thing? Can you just make stuff real, like Tinker Bell, clap clap clap? These were the thoughts in Danielle's mind as she swept behind the counter at

Panera. A guy in a gray overcoat tried to open the door, but it was locked. He looked down at the handle and then pulled it again and again, like if he busted it open, maybe Danielle would give him an Asiago bagel instead of calling the cops.

"We're closed," she said.

He pulled on the door and then banged on the glass with his palm, while saying something she couldn't hear.

She held her hands up and said, "Sorry, dude, closed."

I can feel the disease spreading. I still have hope, but day by day I grow weaker and reflect on the joys of our world and the tenderness of love. My heart is broken apart with sweet happiness and love for all of my friends and the joyful simple sounds of a crackling fire as we return to our favorite #doorcounty #airbnb

The last of the geese were leaving. The clouds were settling in. The winter drinking was beginning in earnest.

Eleven

David was admiring himself in the mirror again. The tiles on the wall behind him were green and there was a dark beige linen shower curtain, a wooden bath mat, and a framed poster for the 1997 local jazz festival above the toilet.

It was so fucking cold. He couldn't go outside without physical pain. When he went outside, his eyelashes and nose hairs froze, and some days he even thought he felt the blood at the very outer layer of his face turn crunchy, like a Slurpee. Last week, he'd seen a colleague of his, a woman, walking down the street in a full snowsuit with the hood up, toddling along in rhythm with the blind-accessible crosswalk—beep boop beep boop beep boop. He couldn't stop thinking about her. With every beep and every boop she took a step toward him, waddling out of his unconscious like a cartoon demon. His eyes were glazed over, but his face was still pointed at the mirror. He hated everyone's winter gear. Some people even wore ski goggles.

His dick looked both longer and wider in the off-white waffle-knit long johns he'd bought at the tractor supply store. His hands traveled over his torso. He began his customary silent rant about Pam's Victorian sexuality—what a bust. Her fetish seemed to be not fucking him. What a pervert. How annoying.

He looked at his crazy skin in the mirror and thought about how much it sucked to be dying. Forty-two!

All he wanted was the last twenty years of his life back. He should have broken up with Aurelie ages ago. Fuck, he did not want to go to this party, but Pam was his boss, and Bethany was her boss, so he certainly did not feel he had a choice. He looked at his phone and reread the email, hoping for some secret code that would allow him to stay home.

David,

Welcome to our humble flyover country! Pam has spoken so warmly of you, I thought I ought to extend an invitation. I have a tendency to throw these little monthly get-togethers, and I thought—given the well-known bleakness of our winters—I would invite you round.

[date, time, location]

Let me know as you find time!

;)
Bethany

Jesus fucking Christ.

"*Wuwink!*" said David, grinning and making jazz hands at himself in the mirror.

Bethany had decorated her house to resemble a co-op party. She put up multicolored fairy lights, black-light lamps, black-light posters, spinning disco lights, lava lamps, and had rented a smoke machine. She had bowls of Doritos and pretzels and kegs, and made a playlist on her laptop. She was hoping this would encourage people to get drunk, unburden themselves, and do some innocent things that could fuel the gossip mill for the rest of the winter, and then she would be known as someone whose parties were not to be missed, and then maybe more and more people would be drawn into her orbit, and she would have a more intricate social machine to maneuver. There was something in the air that night. She thought it was going to be a good one. She locked the door to the basement, so that everyone would have to commingle.

David approached the door. Bethany's house seemed enormous to him, and he didn't understand why it had all of these Doric columns on it. He could hear music blasting from inside. He pushed open the door and entered into a crowded, narrow hallway.

"Of course it wasn't actually mutual, but I felt like it was mutual. I was just very unhappy, and unable to make myself happy within the relationship, because he wouldn't make space for my growth and healing."

"Wow. I think it's great that so many women are making that choice for themselves these days."

"As we get more money, and become increasingly better educated, and culturally as men become more, well I'm sorry to say this, but, um, *lesser*," said Ellen.

"No, you can say that."

"Because I know you're still with Arthur, so I don't mean to," said Ellen, pressing her fingers to her chest and laying her other hand on Belinda's forearm.

"Arthur's personally great, but I do know what you mean, I've seen it in others," said Belinda, transforming her eyebrows into a compassionate and serious expression.

"As we become more self-sufficient, you will find that more of us will make this choice to live on our own, and by speaking out against the micro-oppressions we have experienced in our relationships, we strive to remove the mantle of stigma associated with being a divorcée." Ellen stroked the ends of her shiny hair with one hand.

"Personally, I love to see a woman empowered, and I'm really proud of you. I feel like if it were me, I don't think I'd be taking it as well."

"Oh, sure, sometimes it's hard, but in life, you have to do what you think is right—otherwise, what's the point?"

"Of living?"

"Mmm-hmm, yeah."

"Sorry, excuse me," said David, angling past the women into the party.

It wasn't that you knew when it was over, or about to be over, but there were little moments you wanted to cling to as everything was falling away. Please, don't go. The last time on the couch watching a movie. The last time the body was familiar. The last time the life you were living was yours, before you were pushed out into cold confusion. Even when David hadn't liked Aurelie, he had needed her, because she was so thoroughly familiar, and so thoroughly his, he sometimes forgot he didn't look, feel, and smell exactly like her, and being able to look at her and see himself helped him feel alive.

Pam knew, instinctively, that Petra and Craig hadn't crossed the line into something physical yet. She knew what would happen if they did, he'd go insane, he'd flood with the trifecta, dopamine, serotonin, oxytocin, and he'd mistake lust for valor and he'd ask Pam to leave. Imagining Craig imagining himself as courageous and strong was embarrassing, but Pam acknowledged that she felt bloated with this, too, every time she was alone with David, the impending trifecta, the seductive doom, and the clearheaded understanding that if David only asked, she would leave Craig and start a new life, but he hadn't asked, and when she reflected on this, she didn't know if what she felt was relief or despair.

Sometimes she was disgusted and angry with David. He walked around with a cynical withholding depressive air, a knowing look in his eyes, bedraggled, dark circles, alone, both ugly and enthralling, and there Pam was, clean, fair, innocent, basically married. Wasn't he supposed to seduce her and manipulate her into breaking her vows? He made himself come off like some dangerous lothario. Sometimes she wanted to go up to him and scream "Get that hankie out of your fucking pocket" like that scene in *Cruising*.

David was depressed. Some days he didn't feel depressed, but he was lonely, and he missed Aurelie, and he missed taking care of her. Hadn't he taken care of her? She made it seem like everything he'd done was bad. He felt better when he thought of her as a bitch. Off to her glorious life in Berlin without him. He couldn't stop thinking about her. He was obsessed. He couldn't work. He went through the motions of these stupid classes dazed like he was waiting for the electric chair and all sense of reality had left him long ago. Every day was more absurd than the last. When he saw people laughing and smiling, he wanted to go up to them and say *Don't you know what happened?* Take a look around you, it's only going to get worse.

Something had to move in one direction or the other but she thought if she tried to break it off with Craig, it wouldn't take, and that there was something evil, maybe evil, keeping them together, in the same way you found yourself over and over at the same desk every morning doing something boring, or having the same tedious conversation over and over, or how like in life you could have an idea of what you wanted but no way to will it into being, and something wicked kept you where you were.

The music was loud and Bethany's house was packed. David was drinking Oberon from a red Solo cup, nodding, cornered.

He saw Pam across the living room.

"I know it's kind of silly, but I thought I'd decorate it like a co-op party," said Bethany. "Everyone is always talking about wanting to go back in time and change things, so I thought—why *can't* we go back in time?"

"Yeah, it's intense," said David, having no clue what a co-op party was.

Bethany laughed and nodded. "Yes. The boys aren't even allowed in the basement."

She was being conspiratorial, but it was like talking to an absolute foreigner, with no interest in the native customs, only a passing interest in sleeping with some of the locals and taking some of the money. He'd end up doing some kind of Gauguin shit with his experience here, he thought, returning to civilization with an artistic account of the tribal customs. So much for being friendly. He was only friendly when it benefited him.

Pam, what an unsexy name. *Pam.* She was wearing a gray wool sweater with a hole on the elbow over a white button-up and jeans. She looked like she hadn't showered in a few days, but she'd put on cat eyeliner ("That's interesting" –Craig), the rest of her face colorless except for the dark circles under her eyes. She hadn't been sleeping. David was vulnerable to the appeal of visible distress, like any intellectual man, but he still didn't think anything was going to happen.

Bethany kept talking, explaining things to David that he didn't even have the energy to feign interest in.

It looked like Pam was trying to laugh about something. She laughed, then her face twitched and returned to a hollow stare.

The women in this town were for the most part a disaster. Everything they wore was athletic or orthopedic or practical in some way, and all of their denim was stretch denim, which puckered awkwardly at the knees and ass. Denim was French, actually—*de Nîmes,* from the town of Nîmes, though there was nothing French going on here. They had all taken to wearing those extreme topknots in their hair. It was a kind of suffragette Kate Chopin look, but greasy.

When Aurelie went around in her lazy, comfortable clothing, she wore leotards and cashmere sweaters, because she was a dancer. She'd also spent hours and hours looking over pictures of artists from Black Mountain College, where her grandmother had been a ceramicist, so she knew that what you were supposed to do was buy one (*one*) pair of jeans and wear those in, get paint on them, patch them when they wore out, and after ten years, you would have something uniquely yours—it was an aesthetic choice, and like all aesthetic choices it did communicate something that was not necessarily so superficial. It communicated a slow, developing, and consistent commitment to something that only had the value it was given. Aurelie gave her pants value. One look, and you knew who she was.

The fashions of this town communicated a kind of dull, cheerful heartiness. Very buxom, that would be the word, very, yes, incredibly Germanic. What was communicated by these fashions was a zest for bargains. David had barely known what T.J.Maxx was before he came out here, but now he seemed to be living in it, steeped in it, his mind slowly becoming a T.J.Maxx, the maximum consumption for the minimum expense. He taught his classes with a recycled syllabus and he lived for free and spent his money on Noodles & Company and Panera and frozen pizza, just lying on the couch, eating Jack's, waiting to die.

Pam hadn't been able to eat very well lately because the fighting and the looming decision—would it be Craig, or would it be David—were bearing down on her so intensely it all seemed to sort of flatten out her stomach, making food impossible, and all she could eat was toast, bananas, oatmeal, and an occasional power bar. She'd lost nearly ten pounds this way, and she felt weak all the time and couldn't sleep and all she could do was smile and laugh. No nuanced emotional delivery was possible, no real communication was possible, all that was possible was some version of "Haha, cool." She'd gotten dressed in a haze, almost sleepwalking each leg into her pants, but because she thought she would see David, she'd put on makeup.

In the winters, Moddie liked to dress for warmth and comfort, and in general, she liked to have as little of her body showing as possible. The look she was employing that night involved an oversized beige wool sweater, long johns, black jeans, two pairs of socks, and uncombed hair.

Nina, who was standing next to Moddie in the kitchen, feeling free and rounding the corner of her third jungle juice, wore red tights, a purple turtleneck, a leopard-print caftan, dangling eyeball earrings, braids, and enthusiastically applied makeup that included red glitter. Together, they looked vaguely like Mummers in a play involving a goblin and a sheep.

Everybody had become much fonder of Moddie once they learned through the grapevine that something slightly awful and scandalous of a sexual nature had happened to her in Chicago, and that she was not in fact an unemployed woman of gross privilege but an ally of Black nine-year-old painters working as a freelance grant writer, and she had just been hired by Bethany as a professor. Gooble gobble.

Out of the corner of her eye she saw David lurking around looking for someone to talk to. She took a drink and leaned in toward Nina and said, "The problem with your work, Sharon, is that it isn't very good, now, is it?"

"A little obtuse, now, wouldn't you say?" replied Nina in a pompous voice. "It's difficult for us, as the audience, to really, ah, to really understand what it is you mean by these images, which seem quite frankly randomly chosen and entirely derivative of things no person in their right mind is even thinking of anymore."

"Sharon, Sharon, we mean no harm, now, really, but it just isn't very good and so all we're wondering, Sharon, is why on earth would you want anybody to see these things you've made?"

"The lord," said Nina abruptly in a Foghorn Leghorn voice, "will not speak to you through Twittah. If you want communion with the lord, you're gonna have to turn to your scriptchas."

"Interesting, very very interesting," said Moddie, nodding and holding her chin like a prime-time reporter.

"He will come down from the mountaintop and he will

rain upon you his divine and clarifying wisdom, and in that moment, Sharon, shall you truly realize that your work is not, uh, not I say, not very good, now, is it?" said Nina.

"Well, uuuuh, the thing about me which you might not know is that I didn't do quite so well in high school," said Moddie, shifting the bit and wiping at her face as if she were nervously answering questions in a high-stakes Barbara Walters interview. "I know you think, Oh you're so smart, oh you're so successful, oh you're so beautiful, didn't you get all A's in high school, but no, the fascinating thing about me is that no I did not, in fact."

"Homework was simply too middle*brow* for you, darling," said Nina, giving Moddie's face a little slap.

They were both amusing themselves intensely—in the sense of "Oh, I see we're amusing ourselves," meaning, in the sense of behaving in a way that would be received scornfully by people who had forgotten how to have fun, or had never had it in the first place.

"Tonight," said Moddie, "I love everybody."

Peter had been eavesdropping on Moddie while he talked to Craig and some other guys. One of the guys was talking about what it was like to be a business owner.

"We're mostly in PEIs and acquisitions. I'm in talks with two smaller businesses, thinking about buying them out and folding them into our main infrastructure for outreach."

Craig wasn't listening. "Oh, hey, there's Moddie," he said, then looked at Peter and pointed. "Did you want to meet her or not?"

The entrepreneur kept talking, seamlessly turning to face the fourth guy in their circle.

Peter was still a little overdosed on Craig since walking him home from boys' night.

"Come on, what the fuck?" said Craig.

They went over.

Moddie and Nina were holding on to each other's hair and Moddie was saying, "If you work hard you *will* triumph!"

"This is my friend Peter," said Craig.

"Hey," said Moddie. "How's it going?"

"Oh, I'm fine," said Peter.

"Well, that's great," said Moddie.

"Oh, I know you," said Nina.

In the other room, Pam thought there was no reason why it should be weird for her to talk to David, but she'd been avoiding him. There was no reason she should feel it in her gut when she walked up to him, but she did.

"Hey," she said.

He raised his eyebrows and said, "Hey."

"Did you see the smoke machine?" she asked.

"Yeah, I did."

"Wild," said Pam.

"Yeah," said David.

"Hey, do you want to have a cigarette?" she asked.

"Ummm, sure," said David.

They went out into the backyard, even though it was freezing, and David said, "Fuck, it's freezing."

They stood there silently for a while.

"I'm going to be honest, I'm not sure what you want from me," said David.

Pam didn't say anything.

"I mention it because I keep getting all of these signals from you that you're interested in me, but we never do anything about it. You're the one with a boyfriend, so if you want something from me, you should make the first move. I'm just being honest here."

His voice was unwelcoming and he kept raising his eyebrows.

"Fuck it's cold," he said again.

Pam was having difficulty speaking. She looked over at a snow-covered gazing ball wedged into the ground near the outdoor AC unit.

It wasn't supposed to be this way. When they finally talked about this, it was supposed to be romantic, but he was making her feel like that was childish and stupid, and that everything she'd dreamed for herself and her future was stupid, too.

She knew. She knew he didn't want to be there. It wasn't permanent. He could have used his time better. He'd never wanted to stay here and fall in love with her and travel the world with her as artists and equals. She knew. She knew her romantic notions were stupid.

"*Hello,*" said David, waving.

Pam turned her head to look into the kitchen window and saw Moddie smiling and talking to Peter and Nina. The whole kitchen was lit with candles. Peter laughed loudly and crossed his arms so tightly it looked like he was giving himself a hug. His eyes were on Moddie, sparkling.

Oh, god. Well it made a little bit of sense. Aside from Craig, Pam and Moddie did seem to have the same taste in men. Angry, opinionated, needy. Pam had hooked up with several of Moddie's most intense teen crushes. Of course Pam knew that Moddie was interested in David. Moddie had no poker face. And of course that had been part of the appeal. Peter was a nice guy, and Pam always thought he'd been slightly attracted to her. One night several years ago, she'd even thought they might hook up at a party, but she was still in love with Craig back then, so she hadn't let it happen.

Peter was likely dragging the bottom of the barrel after

Carol had told everyone he was an abusive asshole and a bully. Well, she wished him luck. She imagined Moddie wasn't an easy girlfriend.

Moddie and Nina were really making Peter laugh. Peter reached up and scratched his head, then bent over slightly, gestured animatedly, and said something that made Moddie laugh. Pam watched Moddie's face—amused skepticism shifted into sincere pleasure and back.

"Did you want to fuck me when you invited me here, or what is going on?" asked David.

The next-door neighbor's cold, greenish motion-sensor light clicked on.

"I just wanted to run a visiting artist program," said Pam.

"Okay, but, like, how did you even hear about me? Nobody has reached out to me to do a talk or a show in like eight years. There's been no press about me, I've had trouble finishing projects, I've mostly just been teaching at a school no one has heard of. It doesn't make any sense."

The truth was, Pam had heard about David from Moddie over a decade ago, after David did his talk at the Renaissance Society. Moddie and her friends had, that month, seemed convinced that David was making the most interesting work of all, and that what he was doing was the natural next step in art history. They'd all been very drunkenly, vehemently convincing about it, and this had made an impression on Pam—she had believed them for over ten years, bided her time, and when the chance came, she thought she would be the one to seal his fate in the canon. Every time she hung out with Moddie, she felt extremely anxious that Moddie would recall this drunken evening and recall that it was Moddie, in fact, who had found David, and then Moddie would gloat and somehow slip in and steal Pam's glory.

Pam looked in through the window again and rested her eyes on those glowing, happy faces. She felt stony and destructive.

"You didn't do anything with Moddie, did you?" she asked.

"You have got to be fucking insane," said David. "Do you mean sexually? No man in his right mind would do anything with Moddie. She is a legitimate psychopath. I am not that fucking desperate. She is fucking crazy."

David was very upset. He'd been here for four god-awful months, hadn't gotten laid once, hadn't gotten any work done, and now he found that he was just some kind of pawn between these two unremarkable women. What the fuck. He looked down at his cigarette.

"I don't even want this," he said. He flicked it into the yard. "Coming here has been one of the biggest regrets of my life."

Peter felt very grateful that he'd never tried to make a pass at Nina, even though she was attractive. Moddie was finishing an interesting story about having a blackout panic attack while trying to tell some freshman art undergrads about grant applications, but accidentally going on a winding incoherent rant instead.

"But even then, I got rave reviews—such is the genius of my intuition."

She bowed.

By now, he was trying very hard to impress her.

"I got too high once and came up with an idea for a lecture on the fascist origins of mainstream screenwriting."

"Freytag?" asked Moddie.

"Yes!" said Peter. "You know about this?"

"*Debit and Credit,* baby. Yeah, I've got Google."

"I'm teaching early modernist literature, and my students have all of these very bizarre moral reads on the books, which I believe comes from their native narrative intake, which is mostly all of these stupid fucking comic book movies."

"Whoa, whoa, whoa, buddy," said Moddie. "If you didn't see *Wonder Woman,* I'm pretty sure you're a rapist."

"Well, exactly!" said Peter. "Exactly. Well, film, but probably actually TV, has quite obviously replaced literature as the dominant narrative form. That's not controversial, it's just true. So now people are learning how to create narrative identity out of their own experiences using this model we see in film where good triumphs over evil. We see ourselves in the characters as good, and we internalize that to mean that we are good heroes and anything that upsets us or gets in the way of our heroic and constant ascent is evil. We don't understand anything about the dark parts of our own nature. All of those parts are repressed, so of course, when we see those parts of ourselves expressed in another person, we attack. We vanquish the evil in ourselves by exerting control over others, through shaming, shunning, accusation, boycott. And this is the cultural norm right now, for some obvious and relatable reasons."

"Sure."

"In criticizing oversimplification and scapegoating, I'm not trying to oversimplify and create a new scapegoat. Some people and some actions should be condemned. Some things are objectively bad. But it's gone too far, and when I see the Marvel Universe mind confronting the complexity of James—it's wild. They get angry. So, I wanted to try to trace this narrative lineage back from *Wonder Woman,* for example, through Syd Field's screenwriting books, Joseph Campbell—who was a Republican who fucked his students, if the author's identity is important to you," said Peter, raising and shaking his finger, "back in time to Freytag's Pyramid, *Debit and Credit,* and this whole idea of the objectively perfect narrative form or structure, and how this entire notion, which has created the 'new paradigm,'" Peter made a face, "of storytelling, is based on an intense philosophy of racial purity, is essentially propaganda, and is incredibly spiritually limiting, and the best thing we could do would be to become aware of exactly what it is we are consuming before we let it dictate our inner moral and aesthetic compasses."

Peter was very excited.

"So, you wanted to do a lecture about how all of your students are fascists but don't know it?" asked Moddie.

Peter shrugged. "I was high."

"How did you imagine it would go?" asked Moddie.

"*Dead Poets Society.*"

Bethany had wanted to spice it up by inviting some students, and she'd invited some of Petra's friends, who were in the corner subtly bullying Craig. He'd left Peter and Moddie and Nina to try to find Bobby, and these girls had found him by the keg.

They were really laying into him.

"Are you by any chance a science teacher?" one of them asked.

"Uh, yeah, that's me."

"You're like working in a lab?" asked another.

"Yes, I do work in a lab."

"So, you've got a lot of, like, really good interns probably."

"Of course, yeah, I always have good interns," said Craig. A little bit of him knew where this was going. All three of them grinned at him.

"Your research in the lab must be very *intense,*" said one of the girls.

"I've actually heard so much about your internships," said another one. "You know, I've heard that your students can really lean on you for support."

Craig made an awkward coach face, like *Come on now, girls,* but he didn't have much room for authority, since last week in the lab, Petra backed up against him and he pressed his boner against her butt and then put his forehead on her shoulder and exhaled and moaned. The moan was humiliating and echoed through his mind on a loop. Oh, oh, ooohhh. Jesus Christ. What the fuck.

One of the girls looked at Craig's dick, then back up to his face. She thought it was very funny that this was Petra's guy, and she almost started laughing.

"Yeah, I've heard that you give very firm but gentle guidance," she said.

"Okey dokey," said Craig.

Craig took a survey of who was within earshot.

"Yeah, I've heard you really stand behind your students," said the third girl.

"All right," said Craig.

His emotions were bashing around inside him. He couldn't believe Petra had told them. He was so fucking stupid. He hadn't even tried to do any damage control. How many people had they told? Didn't they know he could lose his job and his girlfriend and his whole fucking life?

Stupid. Girls this age were so fucking stupid and careless. He had been so fucking monumentally stupid. Pam was going to find out. He was going to have to move. The thought of going back into the lab next week was humiliating. Oh, fuck, he was going to have to talk to her about this. She had to stop telling people *immediately*. He was enraged at Petra. All of the sweet things he'd thought about her were erased. He'd been completely convinced they could fall in love, didn't she know that? She was probably punishing him for pulling back his affections while he tried to sort things out with Pam, and that was not the kind of behavior he thought Petra capable of.

Whose fucking idea had it been to invite students to the party? Craig looked around, feeling ill. There were certain parties that you knew would be mixed, but parties here were always adults only. What the fuck was Bethany thinking? Just get a bunch of students and university employees together at a kegger and see what happens? Was she insane?

Craig saw Bobby across the room. He looked happy and carefree. He was doing shots with two twenty-year-old guys. He was a wholesome man. He was a good man. Craig wanted to be a good man, too, like Bobby. He wanted to run straight over to him to start doing shots with those boys. Craig knew what a healthy intergenerational relationship looked like. Craig had been a mentor, too, at one time. Oh god, just let me go back.

The girls wouldn't stop teasing him. Didn't they know what they were doing?

No, Craig, they don't know what they're doing, and that's why you're not supposed to fuck them! said a small, high-pitched voice at the back of his mind—but, I didn't fuck them! Anybody could approach at any moment, anyone could come up and ask "Hey, Craig, want to introduce me to your friends here?" and from that point anything could happen, and this truly had to stop, god, why won't they stop *mocking me,* he had to do something, so he said, "Okay, that's enough," in the tone of voice his dad used to use and that used to sear Craig so deeply when he was little—the voice that said *You thought I loved you, but I don't.* He couldn't help it. It just came out.

Pam's toes were numb with cold.

"I just don't understand why you're being so harsh with me, I didn't do anything wrong, I was just trying to help you out and give you an opportunity, and I'm sorry if my emotions got in the way, and I'm sorry we've had a miscommunication, and I just wish we could . . ." said Pam, but she didn't know what to say next.

David just shrugged cartoonishly and said, "Well, I hope this doesn't negatively affect our professional relationship, Pam."

The party rearranged again. Moddie leaned against Bethany's fridge telling a story to Chrissy.

"After Lincoln died, Mary Todd went completely insane. She'd already been pretty nuts. She had prophetic dreams, saw ghosts, and was completely convinced that her dead son Willie stood at the foot of her bed every night, but when Lincoln died, she went deeper, and she was probably manic, because she started obsessively buying stuff. She bought like two thousand pairs of gloves in a month or something, so her son decided to have her committed so she wouldn't spend the family fortune. And when she was in Bellevue, she used to have this recurring nightmare that a Native American man snuck into her window every night and sat on her chest and removed a single bone from her face and put it on a necklace, and once the necklace was complete, something very terrible would happen," said Moddie.

"Get the fuck out of here," said Chrissy.

"Something terrible," said Moddie. "Something dreadful." She widened her eyes and lifted her fingers. "And if you dream of a Native American Indian, sneaking into your window at night, beware," she continued in a ghost-story voice. "Beware that he doesn't finish his *neeeeecckklaace.*"

"You are making this up, you are a liar, this never happened."

Moddie laughed and said, "Honestly, at this point I can't remember if I'm making it up or if I read it somewhere."

Peter hadn't wanted to be clingy, so he left Moddie and Nina a while ago, and was nowhere to be seen. Nina was in the corner talking to Craig. Everywhere Moddie looked, people seemed agitated and energized and definitely drunk.

"Fuck, I want to dance," said Moddie. "Should we get this shit started? I want to listen to the Bee Gees."

"Fuck it, I'll dance," said Chrissy.

Moddie walked confidently into the living room and took control of the laptop, and once the Bee Gees came on, she started dancing in a wild gyrating way. Her good cheer was contagious. Several other women joined her, dancing, some of them awkwardly raising the roof. She looked over at Nina and beckoned her to join, and Nina nodded and raised a finger and mouthed "One sec."

Moddie danced and watched. Craig looked like he was about to start crying. Nina was holding him by the shoulder and talking and nodding. Nina started rubbing Craig's back. It looked like she was saying, "Hey, it's okay, it's okay, really."

Craig gestured and seemed to be explaining something heated. Nina shook her head slowly and patted him on the shoulder again. Moddie moved her hips and felt the alcohol swim around in her mind. She felt so free and so light and so good. Bethany's husband, from his armchair by the fireplace, hit the fog machine and a billowing white cloud rose up from the ground, while all of the multicolored lights moved across Moddie's arms and across the faces of all of her new friends.

Slowly, she writhed out of her enormous wool sweater and tossed it onto the couch. She put her hands on the bottom of her thermal and began to lift it slowly, while winding her body to the tune of the Bee Gees. She locked eyes with Chrissy and removed her thermal, beneath which was a leotard. "How many shirts are you *wearing*?" asked Chrissy, and Moddie said, "So, so many," and then she held her arms out, underside up, and watched the lights move over them, then she laughed, thrusted, and turned around. She saw Pam coming in from the back porch, looking ill.

"Uh-oh," said Moddie. "I think trouble's a-brewin'."

"What?" shouted Chrissy.

"Don't you smell the trouble in the air?" asked Moddie, looking into Chrissy's eyes.

"No, I'm having so much fun!" shouted Chrissy.

"Hell yes!" said Moddie. "Dance, dance, dance!"

"Dance, dance!" shouted Bobby from the kitchen. "Who the fuck is playing my song, and who dares to disturb my slumber?"

"It is I!" shouted Moddie.

Bobby ran at her and they began to dance together.

"I heard you dumped your bitchy girlfriend," shouted Moddie.

"Fuck yes I did," said Bobby.

"Me too, my boyfriend was such a bitch," said Moddie. "I dumped all those fuckers."

"Fuck yes!!!"

They high-fived and started dancing more and more wildly. Petra's friends stood at the edge of the living room, and one of them asked to be put to death if she ever danced like that "in my forties." They all burst out laughing. Bethany couldn't believe her luck. She couldn't have asked for anything more perfect. Her husband hit the fog again. Bethany removed her phone from her pocket and aimed it at Moddie and Bobby, and when Bobby dipped Moddie, she took the picture and put it on Instagram.

> taken at the exact moment moddie shouted new friends @bobbylobby #danceparty #moddieyance

Things cooled down. Craig and Pam left. The remaining guests were mostly undergrads.

"I'm so sweaty," said Moddie.

"You made my night," said Bethany. "I could not have pictured or hoped for a more dazzling, a more—"

"I am very drunk," said Moddie. "And I have to go home."

"Call me tomorrow, we should have brunch."

"Yeah, cool," said Moddie.

She walked from the kitchen to the foyer to look for her shoes. Nina was there, texting, waiting to give her a ride.

"What was up with Craig?" asked Moddie.

"Oh, Jesus. I'll tell you in the car. I'm going to go call Tony. Meet me out there?"

"Yah."

Moddie sat on the stairs and put on her boots.

Peter came over.

"Hey, are you taking off?"

"Uh-huh," said Moddie.

"That was really fun," he said.

"Yes," said Moddie.

"Do you want to hang out or see a movie sometime?"

"Sure," said Moddie.

"Like a date," said Peter. "Unless you're not into it, and then just a hang." He had his hand on the wall and he was leaning down slightly. He was drunk. "Just trying to be straightforward."

Moddie laughed and said, "Um, sure."

"Can I give you my number?"

"Oh, you know," said Moddie, refocusing her eyes onto his face, "my phone has been dead all day. Have Craig get my number from Pam." She stood up and felt lightheaded and then said, "Whoo doggies."

Peter looked slightly embarrassed and said, "Oh, okay, cool."

Moddie took a few steps toward him, slowly, put her hands on his shoulders, looked him in the eye, and said, "I want you to contact me," and then she reached down, grabbed his hand, and brought it up to her lips for a kiss, curtsied, and left.

She ran down the steps of Bethany's big, floodlit house toward Nina's car. The cold air hit her face. The air smelled familiar in a way that opened up Moddie's sense of self, hitting her right in the amygdala.

When she got into the car, she started laughing.

"I kissed Peter's hand and then curtsied and left. We're going to go on a date."

Nina called her a slut, and then she said, "I really like him. He's cool."

On the drive home, Nina filled her in on Craig and Pam's situation, which Moddie found hilarious, and then she started to open up more about Tony.

Moddie was getting the spins.

"Since Brad, I realize I've been really emotionally unavailable. I think all of this stuff with my jealousy or whatever is just me throwing up obstacles—that was something Tony said, that when I get jealous, it's just because I'm afraid of more intimacy with him. And in a lot of ways he's the best boyfriend I've ever had. He's kind and he's really funny. You know I'm not crazy about shrinks, but I think we're going to go into couples therapy to work on our intimacy issues. He's started bringing up kids and marriage, which, as you know, I'm not interested in, but I want to really take some time to explore it some more, and maybe Tony's right and I'm just afraid of something that might be really good for me. And like, I know, I get it, I'm not always super available," said Nina.

Each streetlight was like a fresh slap in the face. Moddie's cheek was pressed to the cold glass window and her eyes were roving around. She focused on the quickly passing blacktop beneath her and it seemed to be a dark sea over which she was flying, and then she looked up and worlds of red neon strip mall signs flew by and seemed completely alien to her and much more beautiful than she had ever noticed, and she thought a thought without language about how she could really truly be happy with only the simplest things on earth, while Nina kept talking about different things Tony thought, and some other shit Moddie couldn't quite string together. She looked at the red light coming from the late-night Red Lobster sign. She was drunk in that wild, dreamlike way. Nothing existed but the feeling of a car carrying her forward. The sensation of cool glass. Oh sweet, sweet simplicity. Oh, sweet, sweet freedom.

"And Tony is just really helping me work through some of these issues." Nina pulled onto Moddie's street and stopped in front of her apartment. "And he's kind of the most important person in my life."

Moddie's head spun and she said, "Yeah, well, never met him," and then laughed.

She slammed the door and walked in a curve to her house, and somewhere in Door County, Jen sat in the corner of an

Airbnb in a comfortable chair, face pale and gaunt, talking about the mysteries of love, and what their wedding reception would be like once she got better, and how once she was strong again she wanted to use her body to make a baby with him.

Alan thought there was no fucking way Moddie would tell Jen. She would have done it by now if she was going to do it. He didn't think about it all the time anymore, but that email had fucked with his head. Why wouldn't it? She was completely factually false about the event, and some small part of her had to know this, or why else would she have been friends with him all those years? Some part of her had to understand that this was a false accusation, or she would have told more people, she would have told Jen by now, for sure. Part of her had to know that what she'd done, threatening him in this way, was really shitty and selfish. She'd always been jealous of his relationship with Jen, and she was just taking all of that out on him now. She had to know that. That's why she dropped it.

"I want to use my body to make a baby," said Jen, again, from the chair, and Alan didn't know why she was phrasing it that way, something about it was a little repulsive, maybe part of what was gross was her skeletal face, the dark circles under her eyes, like being asked to mate with a corpse, but he wasn't entirely against the idea. Having a baby. That might be nice.

"Okay, baby," said Alan. "Let's do it. Let's make a baby."

A baby.

"We're updating everything over to a new system. It's so intense. You would think that by now, you could just buy a new system and everything would be able to auto-transfer, but not at all. If you do that, everything is just completely messed up forever. And also one of the big problems with it is that we have a lot of people in our system who are deceased, so what I have to do is go through name by name and enter it into the new system, but before I do that, I have to look up the name, see if they're deceased, try and figure out if this is their correct address—also, if it's a couple, I have to try and figure out if they're divorced. Because, of course, if you send a gala invitation to a dead person's ex-wife, that woman is not going to give you any money ever again, and especially in this town, there are a ton of fragile egos, so you want every person you're hitting up for money to think they're being hit up for money because we as an organization know how rich and famous and important they are. We have to present the illusion that every person on the list has some clout we're after. So it's actually a really delicate thing, and requires a ton of detective work, which is, naturally, pretty fun in L.A., because this is where all of those detectives are from." Angie laughed.

Kimberly had made the mistake of looking at her Instagram an hour ago and had seen the photos from Bethany's party, and ever since, her ears had been ringing and she'd felt a little dissociated. Her brother's girlfriend, Angie, worked doing outreach for some kind of production company, maybe, or maybe it was a nonprofit that had something to do with child actors. She'd been talking about it for an hour, but Kimberly still didn't understand what was going on. They were all sitting on the couch eating hummus and carrots.

Kimberly had imagined this week going very differently. She had imagined they would be going to parties with writers and actors, but she had been informed that no one in L.A. really drinks, because of all of the driving, but that they could go to the cute bar around the corner, just the three of them, and maybe their friend Danni would join. Danni worked in a boutique.

"So, what do you do? Your brother tells me you're an academic," said Angie, after an affable shrug.

This was the moment she was supposed to say she was a writer and show her brother's girlfriend the proof-of-concept web page with her essays.

She looked around their small apartment. She needed to look for another job. When she got back, she would have to pack, hire movers. Bobby had seemed very final about this. She had asked him if he was really sure this was what he wanted. He repeated that he'd been trying to talk to her for over a year. She had no friends she could stay with in the meantime. She would likely have to stay in the empty house to save money, until she found a new job, and until they found a buyer. Her lips felt numb. She described her job.

Twelve

Moddie threw her keys on the couch, turned up the heat, undressed in the living room, and put on her Target sweat suit. She felt happy and relieved to be home.

She charged her phone and thought maybe she should watch something on Criterion before she fell asleep, and then in the morning she'd get brunch. Brunch! What a gas. Dancing, parties, dates, a good job. The sweet and simple life, everything unfolding, everything harmonious. One foot in front of the other. Life was coming so easily now, she remembered the feeling of dancing, everybody smiling at her, wanting to know her. I belong, I belong—the quiet pulse that ran from her cheeks to her fingers, the feeling that filled the room.

She sat on the couch and opened her laptop and, guided by unthinking impulse, checked her email and found only one new message, in bold, "FWD: Sale of Chestnut-Yance Farms."

Her stomach dropped, and from the middle of her guts, a

sour dread crawled outward until it reached every edge of her body. Partly, she wanted to shut her laptop and place it in the dumpster, to continue to ignore this matter, which she had successfully pushed from her mind, but here it was, whether she liked it or not. Her parents had advised her not to count on it. It was a complicated process involving many different people and there was no way to guarantee the outcome, better to be prudent, but of course, on the other hand, better not to dismiss the possibility altogether.

Moddie opened the email as slowly as she could, not wanting to know but unable to resist. She knew there was a chance she was once again about to slide from this reality to the next.

Dear Moddie,

Here she blows. The sale was finalized this afternoon. I have attached the forms, which include your dazzling post-tax total. Yowza. Let it soak in. You'll need an accountant, you probably shouldn't keep this on your debit card. If you live modestly, this will make a substantial difference in how you are able to spend your days. We'll discuss this all tomorrow. I know you're at a party tonight. Enjoy yourself.

Much love,
Keep it real,
Your Dad

Moddie opened the PDF and then leaned back on the couch. She put her hand over her mouth and said, "What the fuck?"

She stood up, no longer feeling drunk, and walked two full laps around her apartment laughing like she'd just heard a great comeback. "Hohohohohoooooohhh, daaammn."

When she sat back down, both hands over her mouth, eyes wide, she realized how empty the apartment was, how silent.

She hadn't thought about Nick in a long time. For the past month or so, when he would come into her mind, she would close her eyes and breathe until he left, but now he was there in the room with her, vividly, his face right next to hers, his legs right there on her couch. She wrapped her arms around his neck. She felt like a lemon getting squeezed, all of the sour juice rushing to her face and heart, and she felt like she could smell him, faintly, and then she started sobbing, imagining he was there to talk to, imagining she could bury her face in his neck, this man who knew her in her full context, and who would understand, more fully than anyone else, what this all might mean to her, and she felt so relieved to see him, and so tired and so happy, but then she recoiled as if she'd just discovered she was hugging a spider.

Suddenly, she remembered a brief exchange.

Nick grabbing her stomach and jiggling it and saying, "Look out, everybody, she's a member of the leisure class! When people find out about this, they're not gonna be *happpyyyy*! Better start being nicer, nobody likes a rich girl, better shape up, or they're gonna come knock knock knock knocking," rapping against her stomach, "for that noblesse oblige," saying this in a cheerful rhythm, "which might be better than if they came for your," he tapped her on the stomach, then the chest, then the shoulder, and then three times swiftly and pointedly on the top of her head, smiling and doing a little jig with his tongue hanging out. "If you think people don't like you now, just you wait! Just you wait until they find out about this!"

Moddie's head was curled almost completely in toward her stomach, and she was rocking slightly.

"Better figure out how to hide it! Better keep it stored away in your little hidey-hole!" Stop it, stop it, stop it! "Oh, come on, for Christ's sake, lighten up."

She could remember the feeling, like hot wet hands around her throat.

Outside in the cold in her stained parka, Moddie lit a cigarette and began walking around the neighborhood, aimlessly. Something's always coming from the outside, there's nothing you can do about it. You can try to be kind, you can try for revenge, but there's nothing you can do, it's always someone else's decision what happens to you, not yours, it's all an illusion. Having any kind of ambition is a joke, you should never really try to control your future, that's dumb, just do what you think is right in reaction to whatever sensory input is coming at you at any given second. Why would you think you knew the best outcome, anyway? Isn't that arrogance? You don't actually know what you want or what's good for you. There's no real narrative, nothing means anything, it's random, we assign it meaning, it's meaningless, everything is meaningless, her eyes on the sidewalk as she walked around and around, stuck in the dark pit of thoughts. It's too much, I'm alone, leave me alone, good riddance, leave me alone.

It was sometime between two and four in the morning. Almost everybody else was sleeping.

Eventually, she found herself in a clearing she had never seen before. If she hadn't been drunk and stunned, she might not have entered the clearing, sometimes the neighborhood, especially at night, could be dangerous, but there was something enticing about it—the clean white snow surrounded by bare trees and the appealing benches lined at the far edge, which seemed like empty seats in a strange theater. She could hear the snow compress with each step as she approached the bench. She sat and waited and watched. Her mind quieted. The words stopped attacking her. She looked up and saw Nick's face floating in front of her and she felt as though she were being given something. She raised her hand and tapped his forehead—*boop*—and he floated back and away, back to his life where he belonged. Finally, it was over.

She looked up at the sky, which she hadn't yet noticed. It was a dark blue-black, abnormal for this time of year, no clouds. She looked down at the untouched snow, which of course wasn't really white, but held many colors, cool gray-purple, yellow, green, red, and a few strange colors she couldn't identify, and as she realized this, she noticed that the snow seemed to be glowing. She looked up, but it felt like she was looking down into a deep pool filled with life, the sky and stars framed by the branches, which seemed like thin fingers holding something out to her. Moddie felt that eerie calm that came to her when she was very angry, but this time there was no anger, just quiet. She felt so quiet, like something was about to happen.

In the center of the sky, about a hundred yards above the snow, began a deep, red beat. A pulse. Each time the sky pulsed, the outline of a shape emerged. Three smaller shapes inside a bigger one. At first it seemed flat, but then a wave ran over the shape from the lower right corner to the upper left, and each time it passed over the shape, the red pulse dimmed and the shape took on more form, until it seemed substantial, as substantial and real as the trees and the lamppost and the ground beneath her feet. The red light dimmed, and the object itself seemed to shimmer, but it didn't seem to move, until it sank about ten yards, paused, then shot back up to its first position. It did this again and again. Down, pause. Up, pause. Again and again. Then it went to the left in a diagonal pattern, paused. Down, pause. Right, pause. Then it moved into the center of the triangle it was drawing with its movement. Over and over, shimmering. Moddie couldn't speak it, and she could barely even mouth it. "What the fuck?" This object in the sky, almost dancing, just for her.

The longer it moved, the quieter her mind grew, and Moddie knew she was looking at something else, something other. There was no doubt. She couldn't look away. In this moment, there was no separation between herself and the field and the snow and the thing. She knew it would be indecent to ever try to describe it, that this was meant for her alone, her treasure. On the bench, in the field, as the audience, alone.

Thirteen

Moddie,

I don't even know if you're getting these, but I need to write to you. It's the only way I get to talk to you.

How long did it take you to stop loving me? Was it fast? What does it feel like? Does it feel like there's something you vaguely remember from the past, like "What was the color of the Frazier's sign, was it pink? I can't remember."

Is that where I live now?

Did you want to forget me, or did it just happen?

Who taught me to be like this? I really don't know who taught me to think about myself and other people in such hateful terms. I certainly thought a lot of hateful things about you. A lot of times I behaved toward you like you were someone I hated. Why did I do that? Somebody taught me this, but probably without meaning to.

When you told me you might get a million dollars (or was it two?) it just made me hate you. That was what made it final. You didn't fuck me for years, and then you didn't even want to share your money with me. Now that's sadistic.

You're like some kind of a demon. Do you have any idea what it was like living with you? You would just sit there at the kitchen table with your arms crossed and your legs crossed, drinking and chain-smoking. The only way I could access you was to join you, though you probably have a similar, inverted, take on this. Probably you think I was the one making you drink.

You could be so, so mean. I would tell you about something, and somehow you would be able to intuit the most vulnerable spot in my heart and you would jab at it. I admit that oftentimes you were very funny when you were mean, and I did like it when it was directed at other people, but living with you was like living with a rabid talking weasel. Sometimes I was even afraid to be around you, and it only got worse when you found out you'd be getting a million dollars (or three? or, I'm sorry, was it "only" 750? surely you must have gotten the final number by now). You traipsed around like King Shit, and then you felt guilty about it, and then you started flagellating yourself again. Again! If it's not one thing, it's another. You're the only person I know who could turn good fortune into torture. Who on earth gets angry when they find out they're getting this kind of money? Well, that's you, everything good is bad. You always had a flair for drama.

No wonder I receded into my work—also, what an odd complaint. I thought you liked me because I receded into my work. You always seemed to want me to work and to suffer, and I did my best to please you, but nobody ever suffers up to your standards.

When Gracie came around, part of the appeal was how jealous it made you. I liked the attention and, mea culpa, I liked making you suffer. I knew it was over—even if I didn't know it, I knew it. When you broke up with me, I've never been angrier or more fucked up in my life. Actually, all of my angriest and worst memories come from you.

Having sex with Gracie was the single most beautiful and transcendent experience of my entire life. There were actual moments during our lovemaking in which I wanted to die, because I understood the moment wouldn't last, and I couldn't bear the thought of another moment outside of our transcendent congress. Especially thinking about going back to you and all of your terrible mood swings, the anger and bitterness churning around in our sexless pseudo-marriage. What I'm trying to emphasize is that while my body was entwined with Gracie's, I literally thought "somebody please kill me, I want to die." That's how happy it made me to have sex with her. It was my ultimate experience.

Then that reality—life with Gracie—became my base reality, and from there, I started to sort through my feelings toward you.

Obviously, I knew as soon as you became a millionaire, you would leave me. I figured it out well before you did. It was pitiful to watch you try to insist that it wasn't true, and then to watch you struggle with it. Your dawning realization that I had outlived my usefulness to you. You insisted that you always chose the ones you loved (!). I don't know why you said it so angrily and desperately. It wasn't exactly reassuring, you screaming that at me. On the days I was angry with you, it was easy to say hateful and vindictive things, because as I saw it, you had already broken up with me, so I had earned some leeway for my behavior, which, in my anger, I didn't feel like checking. I wanted to let it rip, like you did. You probably think it's different for you, and you might say something about how you couldn't help it, and that maybe your viciousness was part of your "mental illness," but being an asshole is not recognized in the DSM (we used to have fun reading that, didn't we?).

I really pursued Gracie, and I allowed her to believe all of my flights of romantic fancy about how fated and life-affirming our union was. I didn't fuck her at first, which probably only made it better, physically speaking. I waited. I wanted to see if you would make a move. I wanted to see if you would continue to insist we give it another shot, and I wanted to know what it felt like in my gut to know that you were planning to move back in. I wanted to know what it felt like when the zombie approached my door. When that moment came, all I felt was terror and anger, so I slept with Gracie, and then I felt that sweet transcendent freedom. Choose your imagery, I was a balloon cut free, a ship leaving the harbor, something like that.

I really convinced myself that I should give it my all with Gracie. I thought she was going to save me. I wanted to believe in love. Who doesn't want to believe in love? But of course, the more time I spent with her, the more I began to see her through your eyes. She wasn't as talented as you.

Her feedback on my work was uninteresting. She loved things we had long ago given up as corny. I could feel the little version of you who lived inside my head begin to take more control, and that's when I started writing you these messages.

We all want love to be real. I was willing to go through a lot to keep believing love was real, so don't tell me I didn't know how to be loving, and don't say I never put you first. I put you first for ten years. What do you imagine it looks like when people are together for ten years? What do you think life is supposed to be like? What would it take to satisfy you? When I think about what you might need in order to feel satisfied, a chill runs down my spine. I always thought you had outsized expectations.

I broke up with Gracie. I had to. Every time I looked at her, you would start whispering to me. You are alive in me, and it is very real.

When you and I got together, those were the happiest days of my life. Weren't they the happiest days of your life, too? Weren't we so innocent? I love us back then. When I picture us young and together and happy, I feel so happy. In those early days, sometimes I would look at you and think *this is it*. This is the beginning of my real life. I loved driving around with you, taking you to parties, listening to you talk. You were so good looking. Maybe when you first get to hell, it seems great for a while, but then time passes and you realize where you are, and it's all the worse because at first you thought it was exactly what you'd always wanted. I'm not saying this is how I feel now, but this is something I thought while I was sorting through my feelings. Now I know that that was all wrong.

I really love you. Think back on things. You loved me too. I made a mistake. God knows you made mistakes, too. Where did this new zero-tolerance policy come from? That's not you. That's never been you.

Who is going to speak our language with me now? All of the jokes, all of the shorthand, everything we could say to each other without talking. Sitting here alone, sometimes I feel like an endangered species. I'm alone, and I lost my mate. I'm just going to sit here, alone, without you, and I'm going to fade away. Doesn't that break your heart? That this me that you knew, and that only you could know, is going to die? I'm keeping vigil, and I'm trying to keep us both alive. If you think about all of the good times, it should really break your heart. We had something special. There's nobody like you. I don't want to die. Come be with me. Come home. I'm sorry I never wrote you a love letter when we were together. I should have done that. But I did so much to make you happy, and I can't believe you're choosing to forget that. Who are you now? Have you already died, my sweet Moddie? My sweet Margaret Anne? You are the love of my life. Don't you remember the feeling of belonging when we were together? All I want is for you to let me come home. I'm so tired and I just want to go home. I want to go out and buy a new rug together and I want to make fun of people together and I want to get a dog, or do anything you want. I was wrong about what I thought I wanted. I've learned my lesson. I'll let you make every single decision. I see you now, in front of me. I hear you now saying yes, yes, yes.

Just please, let me back into my life.

I love you, I love you.

I love you,

Nick

The next day, the blizzard came. It covered the town in thick, quiet, pure white and the sky cleared as it never did in winter, and it glowed a rich blue. Schools and businesses closed, and people felt alive, people felt free, they made elaborate breakfasts and enjoyed the simplicity of one another's company, and everyone felt they were returning to themselves, and that this return was good.

Adler had never been sledding before, and Chrissy thought it was as good a time as any, what with the picturesque winter wonderland outside, which part of her thought might never come again. She wanted him to have this memory. She put him into a snowsuit, wrapped a scarf firmly around his neck, and together they began to walk through the deep untouched banks to the long, steep hill behind the middle school.

When they got to the top of the hill, everything seemed very quiet. She bent down to him and showed him the sled and explained how it worked. "You just sit on it, and then Mommy gives you a little push, and it's like a very fun and special slide, one that only comes every once in a while. You remember when you were brave and did the slide?"

Adler's eyes moved across the field and down to the very bottom of the steep hill. Not looking at her, he asked if she was going to come with him.

Chrissy smiled and ran her mitten along the side of his hooded face.

"No, honey. Mommy's not going to come with you. And this is a good lesson for you to learn about how to be brave and self-sufficient. If you spend your life looking for external things to make you feel better, like Mommy coming with you on the sled, or Mommy telling you at every waking moment that everything is going to be okay, it's never going to be enough. You'll never be satisfied. Real life and real satisfaction come from inside," she said, tapping him on the heart through his snowsuit, "from the things you learn to do for yourself. Does that make sense to you?"

Adler nodded.

"Now, who's gonna be Mama's good boy?"

She picked him up and put his little body on the sled.

Up above, the sky was cold, blue.

Acknowledgments

I feel so lucky that Claudia Ballard introduced me to my editor, Ben Greenberg, and that he wanted to work with me on this book. Claudia and Ben are both incredible. Huge thank you to Leila Tejani, Oma Naraine, and everyone at Random House and WME.

Mojo Lorwin read *Banal Nightmare* about a million times, and his feedback and insights were completely invaluable. Rachel Glaser, John Maradik, Patrick Cottrell, Alicia Kroell, and Naomi Huffman all provided crucial feedback and/or company. My parents? The best. Thank you. All of these people are excellent, I am lucky to have them in my life, and I HEREBY ACKNOWLEDGE THEM!

Also, thank you very much to John Wesley's estate for permission to use his painting *Yelling* on the cover.

About the Author

Halle Butler's first novel, *Jillian,* was called the "feel-bad book of the year" by the *Chicago Tribune.* Her second novel, *The New Me,* was named a Best Book of the Decade by *Vox* and a Best Book of the Year by *Vanity Fair, Vulture,* the *Chicago Tribune, Mashable, Bustle,* and NPR, and *The New Yorker* called it a "definitive work of millennial literature." She was named one of *Granta*'s Best Young American Novelists and a National Book Foundation 5 Under 35 honoree.

About the Type

This book was set in Sabon, a typeface designed by the well-known German typographer Jan Tschichold (1902–74). Sabon's design is based upon the original letterforms of sixteenth-century French type designer Claude Garamond and was created specifically to be used for three sources: foundry type for hand composition, Linotype, and Monotype. Tschichold named his typeface for the famous Frankfurt typefounder Jacques Sabon (c. 1520–80).